Footsteps crunching on gravel now . . . a click, the boot lid going up a fraction and the light coming on . . . the lid lifting more. Jack just lying there, not breathing at all now.

'*Mierda!*' someone said. A hand came down to his head, hovered in front of his nose to see if he was breathing. Then the scarred driver's worried face appeared inches away from Jack's.

NOW! Jack thought, swinging his right fist round from behind his back and slamming it into El Carnicero's head with all the force he could muster.

There was a sudden scream as the blade pierced the man's cheek, another yell as he jerked back and cracked his head on the boot lid. The driver ducked forward again and Jack punched his fist into his nose, heard a crunch and felt blood spattering down on him. Then the man had both hands to his own face and was reeling away . . .

WHITE DEATH

Andrew Neilson

SPHERE BOOKS LIMITED

SPHERE BOOKS LTD

Published by the Penguin Group
27 Wrights Lane, London w8 5TZ, England
Viking Penguin Inc., 40 West 23rd Street, New York, New York 10010, USA
Penguin Books Australia Ltd, Ringwood, Victoria, Australia
Penguin Books Canada Ltd, 2801 John Street, Markham, Ontario, Canada L3R 1B4
Penguin Books (NZ) Ltd, 182–190 Wairau Road, Auckland 10, New Zealand

Penguin Books Ltd, Registered Offices: Harmondsworth, Middlesex, England

First published in Great Britain by Sphere Books Ltd, 1989
1 3 5 7 9 10 8 6 4 2

Printed and bound in Great Britain by
Richard Clay Ltd, Bungay, Suffolk

CHAPTER ONE

RED!

Jack Ryder depressed the clutch and notched the tiny gear-lever into first. In less than ten seconds green lights would start the Monaco Grand Prix. He squeezed the accelerator until the engine was raging like some monster trapped in a cage. If the lights didn't change soon the racing clutch would burn out and the beast would break free anyway.

. . . eight, seven . . .

Jack was third in a line of twelve single-seaters, with a parallel line of twelve to their left, all roaring too, covering the grid in a stinking haze of exhaust fumes. Formula One cars had exposed wheels which were frequently ripped off at the start. It crossed Jack's mind that at forty he shouldn't be doing this any more.

. . . four, three, GREEN!

Twenty-four brightly coloured missiles shot forward as though from a multiple-launcher. Within three seconds they were doing the ton. Three more and they would have to sort themselves into single file for a tight right-hander called Sainte Dévote. The trouble was everyone wanted to go first.

This was probably the most dangerous moment in the Grand Prix season. The principality's narrow street circuit was an anachronism which survived only because its unique setting made great television. So did the inevitable shunts.

Ignoring an opening on his left, Jack clung to the inside line through the first corner. If you moved even slightly away from it someone would dive for the opening. Monaco

1

encouraged suicidal tactics because overtaking there was almost impossible. And exactly that had just happened behind him. He felt a thump in his back, fed on opposite lock, then looked in one side-mirror and glimpsed a car launching itself over another's rear tyres. Jack concentrated on powering through Sainte Dévote, then checked his mirrors again and saw blurred mayhem behind him. Maybe the track was blocked. He'd worry about that if he saw red flags. The great thing was a gap had opened up behind him, although the leading pair had broken clear in front.

Jack mentally changed gear and concentrated on precision driving as he charged uphill towards the *belle époque* casino. He took the ideal line through the S bend in front of it, carefully avoiding the wheel-breaking kerbs. The track dipped towards another right-hander called Mirabeau, then took in a couple of hairpins before reaching the tunnel.

One moment he was in glaring sunshine, the next in comparative darkness curving right at 160 . . . 170 . . . 180 miles an hour, eyes adjusting to the artificial lighting when just as suddenly he was out in the blinding May sun again. A tricky chicane led on to the Mediterranean harbourfront, lined by packed grandstands and yachts. Another hairpin followed, then the Gazomètres right-hander, and Jack blasted past the pits. No red flags. Sweating, swearing marshals had just managed to clear the wreckage from Sainte Dévote in time. Jack raced through it beginning the second of seventy-eight laps.

In fourteen Grand Prix here, how many laps had he already totalled, he wondered. Thousands if you included qualifying laps. They'd taught him the tricks needed to survive this unique event. Above all you had to concentrate hard all the time, Jack reminded himself. He was finding that difficult now, especially since the leading pair were almost out of sight, and the first corner shunt had given him a cushion to lean back on.

Third place. Could he convert that to first? So far this

had been a season of miracles. Before it, team-owners had thought of him as an experienced driver who'd never won the World Championship and wasn't going to now. They'd signed up rising stars instead. Then one of Frank Brady's drivers had been killed tyre-testing, and Jack had been offered his place on a race-by-race basis. That was a typical Brady hard-touch, the idea being that he could drop Jack if someone more fashionable became available.

A string of scoring finishes, including two second places, had stunned everyone though. Brady's engines weren't the best that year, but his chassis possibly was. That suited Jack's smooth technique perfectly, especially at Monaco, and so far he'd made the most of it. A win here would put him on top of the Championship. Incredible.

Impossible if you go on day-dreaming, Jack told himself. So what was he going to do about it? He couldn't catch the leaders with their all-conquering Japanese engines yet. But time and time again this season they'd burnt each other out of races in one way or another. At the pace they were setting they'd eat up their tyres by half-distance. Great! A plan began to form in Jack's mind. He did a quick calculation, then backed off slightly. For the moment he was going to drive as *slowly* as possible to maintain third place.

Each time Jack passed the pits now, his signal board told the story: the leaders were breaking away at a second a lap, and the pack was catching up with him. Frank Brady took to leaning over the barriers and waving furiously. Jack ignored him. Only when one pursuer reached a position to overtake him did he put in a single scorching lap to open the gap and demoralise his rival at the same time.

It sounded easy but by half-distance Jack's four layers of fireproof clothing were soaked in sweat. He was changing gear thirty-five times a lap, and the palm of his right hand was badly blistered. His helmet-heavy head was constantly punched backwards, forwards or sideways by the tremendous acceleration, deceleration and cornering forces. He was struggling to keep upright, but each moment that he succeeded gave him strength to fight on.

After forty laps the man in second place stopped for new tyres. Jack first knew about it when he took the Courbe des Gazomètres and saw him come charging out of the pit lane. That was exactly why Jack had let the gap open between them – so he'd be right behind him now with a chance to spoil his fresh rubber. Instantly, Jack began to attack, worrying him every inch of the way by darting from side to side, forcing him off the ideal line in the corners to defend his place.

And when they reached Gazomètres next time round, Jack saw the leader coming out of the pits, having just changed tyres too. Perfect. Now Jack was close behind both of them. He braked ridiculously late for the corners, locking up his tyres in clouds of rubber smoke and forcing his opponents to do the same. Jack could feel his slicks going off – losing grip and vibrating. He'd have to change them soon or at this pace he'd crash. But it was the second-placed man who blew it, slamming the door in Jack's face at Mirabeau, then losing control and spinning into the barriers.

Second place! But Jack had to change tyres now. He shot into the pits for four new slicks and rejoined the race thirty seconds down on the leader, a young Frenchman called Alain Deneuve. Thirty-five laps left.

Settle for second.

The temptation flashed through Jack's mind as he weighed up the position. With new tyres and fuel in hand it would be easy to hold off his pursuers.

Sod it, he thought, *I'm sick of being runner-up!* And at that moment all the disappointments of his long career seemed to fuse into inspiration.

Deneuve had a reputation for being fast but erratic under pressure. Jack intended to pressure him all right. He began to drive with a controlled fury that was awesome to watch, blasting past back-markers without a moment's

4

hesitation, carving perfect lines through the corners and sliding to within an inch of the kerbs. But all the time he was guarding the advantage his fresher slicks gave him, feeling for the slightest sign that he was pushing too hard.

Jack was catching up with Deneuve at just under a second a lap, but was that enough? And then with ten laps to go the leader came into sight, and Jack redoubled his efforts. The Frenchman's car was understeering on corners, its front tyres near the end of their short life. With two laps left to go, Jack was just a few yards behind. But now the mainly French crowd was on its feet, yelling its hero's name until it was hoarse. Deneuve seemed to respond. Getting past him would take some doing.

Worry him to death. Racing into Sainte Dévote, Jack was still too far back for a real shot at overtaking, but went for the inside line anyway. Instantly the Frenchman covered him.

By the time they reached the casino, though, Jack was right on his tail and in a position to have a go. He jinked from side to side, then started to overtake on the inside as they plunged down to Mirabeau. Deneuve steered towards him and interlocked wheels.

'Bastard,' Jack muttered as he backed off, but he'd expected it. The leader wasn't going to wave him past now.

Jack dived for the inside again at Station Hairpin and was gratified to see spurts of smoke shoot out from the Frenchman's tyres. He'd got him going. Darting about, lunging for the inside line, worrying him every inch of the way, Jack charged after his opponent as they rounded the harbour for the penultimate time. But where could he overtake him? What would Deneuve least expect?

An attack in the tunnel.

Jack took the inside line into every corner now, then made a fist-shaking pretence that the door-slamming retaliation was unfair. Until the pair of hairpins before the tunnel. There he started yet another inside lunge which sent Deneuve across the track in defence. But suddenly

5

Jack switched back on to the ideal line, ignored his opponent, and put everything into a perfect exit from Station Hairpin.

He came out of it fast, while the Frenchman scrabbled for grip and slid wide. In an instant Jack was alongside, pinning him off the line into the following bend. And now the gaping mouth of the tunnel was ahead of them, Deneuve's car skittering towards the outside of the track as Jack fed in every last ounce of power and began to overtake.

Got him, he thought as they plunged into shadows side by side at 150 miles an hour.

A glancing blow. Jack looked left, his eyes not yet accustomed to the change in light. The Frenchman had banged wheels in a last desperate attempt to stop him passing, but Jack was on the inside line, curving right and pulling clear. And then the madman tried to interlock wheels again.

Jack just had time to fear what could happen should their tyres touch – then they did. His rear left climbed Deneuve's front right, flicking Jack's car into a horrific series of somersaults. It whirled through the tunnel like an out-of-control missile, smashed into one wall which ripped off the nose, bounced across the track in a storm of sparks, and finally screeched to a stop against the opposite side. Deneuve's spinning car cannoned into the wreckage, but the Frenchman struggled out of it.

Still strapped in his seat, Jack was only half-conscious now. He felt terrible pain in his left leg, as though his foot had been torn off too. Then, mercifully, he was falling into a big black hole. And his last thought was: *What do I have to do to win?*

CHAPTER TWO

Medellín, Colombia's second city, is set five thousand feet up in the central range of the Andes. Apart from the spectacular scenery, its two million inhabitants have the added advantage of an exceptionally healthy climate. But Medellín is also the cocaine and murder capital of the world, with the highest per capita homicide rate of any city anywhere – seven and three-quarters a day. That number is no mere statistic either – often only parts of bodies are found.

Julio César Mosquera was one of the men who had helped make Medellín what it was now. Tall, in his early fifties, with silvery hair, a long face and a patrician nose, he liked to play the aristocrat and almost looked the part. The illusion was spoiled only by his deadly dark, hooded eyes.

On this particular morning in early June he was to be found at his thousand-hectare *finca* in the foothills overlooking the city. Built in the Spanish colonial style, the main house was a spacious two-storey building surrounded on both levels by open verandahs. Julio César was seated behind his mahogany desk in his white-walled, wood-beamed study, while opposite him sat his *consejero*, Aurelio Canafisto. Both of them were examining a small silver dish full of whitish flakes in the middle of the desk.

'Try some,' Julio César said in his gravelly voice.

Canafisto was about the same age as his *capo*, but shorter and fatter. Now his plump face took on the critical look of a connoisseur. He licked the tip of a forefinger, touched it to the first dish, then massaged a few flakes into the gum behind his upper lip.

'Well?' Julio César demanded.

'It's . . . ummm . . .'

'This is no time for courtesy. Be frank.'

'All right. It's terrible, the worst I've ever tasted. What on earth are we making it with now?'

'Anything we can lay our hands on, since the government's cut off supplies of processing chemicals. They're seizing half our output, too, and what does reach the States fetches less and less.'

Canafisto sighed and shook his head. 'We should never have hit the Minister of Justice.'

'He was planning our extradition to the States. We had no choice.'

'But look at the result: our precious government working hand in hand with the gringos to cripple Colombia's main export.'

Julio César made a dismissive gesture. 'Let's not go over that again. What's done is done. Now we've a surplus of coca-leaf paste, restrictions on processing chemicals, and our prime market is saturated. What are we going to do about it?'

'I thought you asked me here to talk about Spain.'

'Exactly. Go ahead.'

'Well . . . it's a promising market of course. There's the common language and numerous transport links, and we've an excellent contact in our Madrid embassy. He's helped us set up a distribution network of expatriate Colombians.'

'And General Franco?'

'What about him? He's dead.'

'Exactly! Since his death there's been all that progressive legislation, like decriminalising the possession of *any* drug for personal use. That has really opened up Spain for us, and now that they've joined the E E C it's a gateway to the rest of Europe.'

'Agreed, agreed.'

'Then why did we export less than a tonne there last year?'

8

Canafisto checked the figures in a file. 'In fact we exported just over a tonne, but Spanish police seized the difference.

'By using dogs to sniff traces of processing chemicals, right? So why don't we send the coca-leaf paste itself to Spain, which doesn't smell so strongly and costs us far less, even if they do manage to find it? We can process it there, because, unless I'm mistaken, there aren't any restrictions on the chemicals we need.'

'Well, that's true,' Canafisto said thoughtfully. 'But there's still a snag: Spain has very strict currency export restrictions, so we'd have to launder the proceeds there too – although Spanish property might be an interesting proposition, right now, as values are catching up fast with the rest of Europe.'

Julio César frowned. 'I seem to remember our first "investment" there hasn't turned out too well.'

'That was rather unfortunate. We were promised planning consent for apartment blocks on some beach land near Marbella.'

'Which never materialised?'

'No. But our land agent contacted me recently to say someone wanted to take an option on it.' The adviser referred to a telex in the file. 'A Lebanese called Sami Nassar.'

'I don't trust that agent – he sold us a pup in the first place. And I don't like Arabs. Anyway, I'm sending Angel over to set up the processing, so maybe he can deal with this Arab at the same time.'

Canafisto coughed nervously at the mention of Julio César's surviving son. Angel's elder brother, his father's favourite, had been gunned down two years ago in a feud with a rival drug baron. The adviser glanced at a portrait of the martyr dominating one wall of the study. This was the most delicate subject of all.

'What's the matter?' Julio César growled.

'I was just thinking ... Angel's no property expert. D'you think he's the right person to send?'

'I'd go myself but there's too much pressure here. Anyway, the property's incidental.'

'It's just that he's . . . rather impetuous.'

'Enough!' Julio César's fist crashed down on the desk, sending up a miniature snowstorm from the silver dish. 'He's my son! My only son now. He's got to learn every aspect of the business. And if there's one thing he does understand it's how to enforce respect. You can count on it, I won't be the only one who's thought of such a move, and the others will have to be dealt with.'

'That's true. Perhaps you're right.'

'I *am* right. So when he gets back I want you to brief him thoroughly. It's vital he realises how important this is. The way we're being hounded out of here, Spain might well be our next base.'

'Where is he now?' Canafisto asked.

A cruel smile stretched Julio César's lips. 'Teaching one of our gringo friends a lesson.'

At that moment a twin-prop Piper Navajo was flying along Colombia's northern coastline. A thousand feet below it was the blue-green water of the Caribbean, and immediately to its right the Guajira Peninsula stuck out from the landmass like a sore thumb. Semi-desert and flanked on either side by a barren shoreline, only one road, the *Troncal*, penetrated this lawless wilderness, and even that was infested with bandits.

Two men sat in the Piper's cockpit: a middle-aged American pilot, nominally in command, and Angel Mosquera who was flying it from the right-hand seat. Angel loved planes almost as much as fast cars, and his full lips were parted in a smile of child-like gratification. He was a good-looking twenty-year-old, clearly of Spanish rather than Indian descent. His hair was quiffed fifties-style, and he was wearing a pair of Levi 501s and a loose-sleeved sports-shirt – having been largely educated in Tampa Angel was more influenced by American than Colombian culture.

Looking ahead through the windscreen he could see mile after mile of empty coastline. Suddenly Angel spotted a grey line in the sea, close to shore, and several dots on the adjacent beach. As they flew closer the line gradually took shape as an armed *Guardacosta* patrol boat with a smuggler's black-hulled speedboat tied up alongside. A white cloud was spreading around them as grey-uniformed coastguards dumped cocaine into the Caribbean. The dots proved to be four-wheel drive vehicles, most of them police-khaki.

The Piper roared over the scene and the American pilot turned to Angel. 'What now?'

A frightening change had come over the youngster. His face wore a murderous scowl. 'Straight and level.'

'Shouldn't we –?'

'Straight and level!' Angel snarled as he clambered out of his seat.

The pilot nodded and took the controls. He'd been out of work for over two years when these jokers had offered him a hundred thousand dollars a month to fly for them. At times like this it didn't seem nearly enough.

Angel ducked into the passenger compartment. Two seats faced forward and two aft separated by a small aisle. Armed guards were occupying the right-hand pair, while an American Drug Enforcement Administration agent called Dutton sat in the port-side forward-facing seat with his arms handcuffed behind his back. He was about ten years older than Angel, of a similar height but more heavily built. He'd been trapped that morning with the informant who'd tipped off the DEA about the shipment. The informant was already dead.

'See that?' Angel asked the American.

Dutton smiled grimly.

'Was it worth it?' Angel sat down opposite him, looking genuinely puzzled.

The agent shrugged his cuffed arms. 'I'm in no position –'

11

'No, I mean suppose we hadn't caught you. Suppose you were down there right now, dumping it in the sea.' Angel sounded like a child now.

Dutton took it for weakness. 'Sure it was worth it.'

'Why?'

'*Why*? Because we stopped that shit reaching the States. Stopped innocent people poisoning themselves.'

'Come on, man, they're animals. All they'll do is use something else and you know it. The real problem is that your government can't tax the stuff, admit it.'

Dutton shrugged and looked away.

'I don't get it,' Angel said. 'What makes you do a government's dirty work? I mean, you could have made a fortune.'

No response.

'Know what we'd have paid you to look the other way?'

The agent met the Colombian's eyes. He didn't see someone who had him in his power now, just a pretty boy bemoaning his losses. Suddenly Dutton's hatred erupted. 'I wouldn't take your stinking money! People like you are a cancer. We'll cut you out whatever happens to me . . . whatever else your men do, you little scumbag!'

The plane droned steadily onwards but there was a momentary illusion of silence inside the cabin. Angel's eyes flickered towards his guards. They'd clearly understood the insult but were waiting to see what he'd do about it. It was a matter of respect. A terrifying change came over Angel's face again. Almost spitting with fury, he sprang out of his seat and smashed a fist into Dutton's nose. Blood spurted over both of them.

'*Hijo de puta!*' Angel screamed, battering the agent's head.

His guards were shouting encouragement now. Ignoring them, Angel rushed forward and clamped a bloody hand on the pilot's shoulder.

'Turn round and fly over the ships again. I'm going to feed this *maricon* to his boyfriends.'

The American stared at him in astonishment. 'You can't open the door in mid-air.'

'We've done it before.'

'No way.'

'Do it, or I'll throw you out too!'

The pilot blinked. He'd seen Angel like this before and knew he was crazy enough now to carry out his threat. 'Okay,' he said unhappily, and banked the plane sharply round.

As Angel returned to the prisoner, his guards moved to help him. 'No!' he snarled. 'This is my treat.'

Dutton lashed out with his legs. Angel sidestepped them, then battered his face with both fists. He tried to lock an arm round the agent's neck to pull him out of the seat but the blood made him lose grip. Grabbing Dutton's hair instead, Angel dragged him, kicking feebly, towards the rear door.

The lower half supported some folding stairs, the top half had a curtained porthole. Letting go of Dutton's head, Angel grasped the latches of both sections, braced himself, then yanked them open. There was a noise like a thunderclap as the doors flew outwards and a hinge gave way. Instantly the plane yawed violently to the left and a hurricane engulfed the cabin. Angel grabbed the doorframe to stop himself being sucked out.

The pilot didn't need to look round to know what had happened. Frantically he kicked on right rudder and pulled back the throttles. The loose door was hammering against the fuselage. If it came off it would probably smash into the tailplane and that would be that. Hands shaking, he lowered the flaps to lose even more speed. As the ships loomed up ahead, the stall warning buzzer came on and stayed on. He felt a warm sensation in his lap, looked down and realised he was wetting himself.

At the back Dutton had struggled up on to one knee. Angel took a kick at his head which floored him again. Diving on top of him, Angel wrestled the agent towards the gaping doorway until both their heads were sticking out into the tearing slipstream. The ships were almost below them now. Angel could see the coastguards' startled faces looking up at them. He ducked back over his victim, lifted his ankles as high as he could, and then pushed with all his force.

Dutton fell out of the plane with a last terrible scream, arms and legs flailing as he cartwheeled down. He hit the side of the patrol boat's bridge, bounced off it and splashed into the sea in an explosion of white water. The plane flew drunkenly onwards as the agent's broken body bobbed to the surface face-down. And around his head an obscene red halo coloured the slick that had cost him his life.

CHAPTER THREE

Ten days after the accident Jack lay flat on his back in an Oxford hospital room with his left leg encased in a knee-to-toe plastercast. Openings on either side of his ankle showed the purple weeping scars from three operations to his multiple fractures. A green nightshirt hid the bruises on the rest of his fit, lean body. However, his sharp-featured, usually quick-to-smile face, with its deep-set brown eyes and thick mane of light-brown hair, still looked pale and exhausted.

'Basic carpentry,' the surgeon had told him. 'You could practically do it yourself from what I hear.' But when Jack asked how soon he could race again, the doctor had just said he was lucky to be alive.

Looking through the rain-spattered window to the right of his bed Jack saw rooftops and a leaden sky that matched his mood. So much for the English summer. He glanced at the 'Get Well Soon' cards and telegrams covering every horizontal surface. He'd received a stream of visitors too: his girlfriend, Liz, had been every day; Frank Brady had called in just once.

Jack grimaced. He'd be seeking alternative employment when he got out of hospital, that was for sure. The thought reminded him of something, and he picked a plain telegram off his bedside cabinet and read it for the umpteenth time:

AM CREATING AN ALTERNATIVE TO MONACO'S GRAND PRIX. SETTING MARBELLA, SPAIN. WOULD LIKE YOUR INVOLVEMENT. ARE YOU INTERESTED? SAMI NASSAR.

The man was either wildly ambitious or wildly nuts, he decided. All the same Jack was intrigued. Helping replace that particular race seemed like a great idea now, especially since he didn't know when he'd be back at the wheel. It would keep him in touch with the game until then, and who better to promote the idea than himself? It took a really big shunt to make a racing driver Page One news. Just ask Niki Lauda. Having received similar media treatment, Jack was ready to capitalise on it, and he had already telegrammed back to the address in Marbella for more details.

So far the silence had been deafening. Sami Nassar, whoever he was, had probably decided to chase a more active driver: someone like Alain Deneuve, who had walked away from the accident with minor cuts and bruises and was now leading the World Championship.

A knock at the door interrupted Jack's thoughts. He looked up and with astonishment saw his ex-wife walk in – the last person he'd expected to visit him in hospital. Anna was a petite but striking blonde in her late thirties. She was wearing a short suede skirt and matching jacket that showed off her still slender figure, and her straight hair was expensively styled to set off her carefully made-up face. She tried to smile but couldn't disguise the brittle hardness in her grey-blue eyes.

'How are you?' she asked, glancing at the plastercast. When she saw the scars her face lost a little colour.

'Not as bad as it looks,' Jack told her. 'They did a sort of chair-leg repair . . . are you all right?'

'Cover it up, will you?'

He pulled a sheet over his legs, then sank back on to the pillows. 'Why don't you sit down?'

Anna slumped on to the chair by his bed. 'My God . . . I'm not going to say I told you so . . . but I knew you'd end up like this.'

'End up?'

She raised long eyelashes. 'You're not seriously thinking of carrying on?'

'Anna, we've been over this a thousand times.'

'I just don't understand you, that's all.'

Jack closed his eyes. 'It's my job, I get paid to –'

'*Got* paid.'

He looked at her with sudden understanding. 'So that's why you're here.'

She squirmed about on the chair. 'I wanted to see how you were. Although, as it happens, my lawyer did mention the alimony problem.'

'Look, I don't want any sympathy, okay, but obviously this shunt has affected my earning power. I was paid on a race-by-race basis –'

'You agreed to that?'

'Best I could wring out of Brady at the start of the season. Things went so well we were going to renegotiate after Monaco.'

'Quite!'

'Of course I'm insured: you'd be better off if I'd been killed.'

'But as you weren't, our settlement's out the window, right?'

Jack gave an astonished laugh. 'That was meant to be funny.'

'Well forgive me for not falling about! I dreaded just that happening every single day I was married to you.' Anna brushed tears from her eyes with an angry gesture. 'Sorry, but you know I hate hospitals.'

'It wasn't all bad,' he said quietly.

'How would you know? You were only home once in a blue moon. It must have affected Katie.'

Jack's eyes narrowed at the mention of his seventeen-year-old stepdaughter. 'She's all right, isn't she?'

'Actually she's just been expelled.'

Shock registered on his face. Jack felt a turmoil of fear, love and guilt – always guilt about Katie. Images flashed through his mind: the sad little waif he'd first known when she was eight, haunted by a father who'd walked out on her;

the light in her eyes when she'd learnt to trust Jack; the accusation in them when he and Anna separated and sent her to boarding school. 'What did she do?'

'You may well ask! Katie and a girlfriend were allowed into town last Saturday. Only the friend came back to school, but she covered up for her. Their housemistress realised Katie was missing on Sunday, and made the friend tell her where she was. She was found in a bedsit with a twenty-two-year-old man, a known drug addict.'

'God Almighty! What had she taken?'

'Does it make any difference?'

'A lot. I mean, hash, heroin?'

'I told you, I don't know.'

'Well had she . . . did she sleep with him?'

'She says not.'

'That's something anyway.'

'Oh, don't be so bloody naive! Katie's hardly going to admit it, is she? She doesn't tell me anything. I never know what she's been up to or what she'll do next. It's like living with a bloody time bomb.'

Jack sighed. 'So what are you going to do now?'

'What are *we* going to do, you mean. I want some help, and I'll make things damned difficult for you if I don't get it.'

He couldn't help grinning. 'Going to break my other leg?'

'God, you can be infuriating!' Anna bit her lip as though regretting the outburst. 'Look, you're the only one she ever listened to. You two used to get on so well. I remember when –'

'Anna, Anna, just tell me what you want.'

She took a deep breath. 'I want to get married again. Oh I know what you're thinking, but this time I'm determined to make it work. And it's not fair on Courtney and me . . . we don't think it'll work with Katie around.'

Jack stared at her. 'What are you saying? Her father walked out when she was seven; I let her down, and now you don't want her. You're her *mother*, Anna.'

She couldn't look at him. 'When I marry again your alimony problem's automatically solved. You'd only be responsible for her until she's eighteen. That's less than a year, and you can't race now anyway.'

'I don't believe I'm hearing this. I mean, you've been doing your best to *stop* me seeing her since we got divorced.'

'Well, things have changed. And I'm warning you, I'll sue for everything I can get if you turn me down.'

Jack took that calmly. 'Don't you think I should talk to Katie first?'

'She's downstairs,' Anna said. 'I'll send her up.'

While he was waiting, Jack thought about the last time he'd seen his stepdaughter. It was on her birthday a couple of months ago. He never missed it if he could possibly help it. He had juggled his schedule and made a quick visit to her boarding school that Wednesday afternoon, bearing a cake and a silver bracelet. But each time he'd met Katie since the divorce she'd seemed more distant, more troubled, and this visit had been no exception.

Jack almost choked up thinking about her eighth birthday, not long after he'd married her mother. Katie had clung to him all through the party, making it clear that *he* was her best present. How had that wonderful start degenerated into this, Jack asked himself. More to the point, what was he going to do about it? Before he came up with an answer there was another knock on the door.

Katie came into the room and stood at the foot of his bed. She had inherited her mother's petite figure, but her blonde hair hid her forehead and tumbled over her shoulders in tangled curls. Her face was more triangular, with a snub nose and bluer eyes. At the moment they looked deeply troubled, though, and she gazed at Jack with a disturbing indifference.

'Hallo,' she said flatly.

'Is that all I get?'

'What d'you want me to say?'

'Come and sit down, and how about Dad?'

The sheet had slipped from Jack's leg, and Katie grimaced as she walked past the plastercast. 'How long are you in that for?'

'Three months at least.'

'Makes you look like one of Frankenstein's monsters.'

'Thanks a lot!' Jack laughed, and she almost smiled.

'Anyway,' Katie said, sitting on the bedside chair, 'you're not are you. My Dad, I mean.'

'Well stepfather's a bit of a mouthful.'

'Nor that much longer.'

'Oh, I see what you mean. How do you . . . what's this Courtney like?'

She rolled her eyes. 'Awful! Mum really picks them, doesn't she?'

This time Jack roared with laughter. Katie gazed at him in surprise, then realised what she'd said. 'I didn't mean you.'

'Don't apologise.'

'I'm not. Anyway, aren't you meant to be giving me a lecture or something.'

'Your mum did tell me what happened. Want to talk about it?'

'Not particularly.'

'Oh well, that's that, then.'

Katie looked surprised. Jack winked at her, and this time she grinned back. 'All right, what d'you want to know?' she said.

'Well . . . what you took for a start.'

'Speed this time.'

'You mean you've done it before? Why, Katie?'

She shrugged. 'I get down and it helps . . . speed does anyway. I'd seen your crash on television . . .'

Jack frowned. So that had been part of the problem. In a strange way he was relieved because it showed he still meant something to her.

'Anything else?' she asked.

'I was just thinking. I'm going to need a gofer when I get out of here – go for this, go for that. Any plans for the next few months?'

Katie looked suspicious. 'So that's why Mum brought me when she's been trying to keep us apart for years. She wants me off her back now, doesn't she?'

'I don't know,' Jack lied, 'but I do need someone to help me, and I'd rather it was you.'

Something like gratitude brightened her little face, like sun breaking through cloud. 'Honestly? I wouldn't just be in the way? Of you and your girlfriends, I mean.'

'There's only one. She's called Liz, and we're not living together.'

'Well, if you really need me . . .'

'Can't get down on my knees, can I?' Jack said.

The American embassy in Bogotá – Colombia's capital, set nine thousand feet up in the Andes – was downtown on Carrera 13. The east-facing windows on its top floor gave spectacular views of Monserrate, a mountain that rose up from the edge of the city. The embassy was a good place from which to admire it. Sightseeing in Bogotá was almost as dangerous as in Medellín.

That day three men sat in one of the embassy's secure offices. Roy Shepard was a stocky West Virginian in his early forties. The Drug Enforcement Administration agent already had two tours of duty behind him, and spoke good Spanish. Headquarters in Washington had sent him out to investigate Dutton's murder, but Shepard intended to take it further than that.

Hal Argetsinger, a younger American with short fair hair and steel-rimmed glasses, was the C I A's station chief. The third man was a middle-aged Colombian police colonel in a khaki uniform. He kept fiddling with his dark glasses as he told them about Dutton's death.

'Unfortunately we do not know who else was in the

21

aircraft,' the colonel concluded. 'We are very sorry of course.'

Shepard looked straight at him. 'We know Dutton went to meet one of Angel Mosquera's men, so who do you think killed him?'

'Thinking is one thing, proving another. That boy has the luck of the devil.'

'What about the plane?' Argetsinger said.

'Reported stolen from an airfield near Santa Marta. The owners know they are dead if they tell us the truth. It will turn up eventually, burnt out of course.'

'So you're just accepting that Angel Mosquera got away with murder again?' Shepard asked.

The colonel spread his arms in a helpless gesture. 'Here in Colombia we need proof before we arrest someone. I thought that was the American way too.'

'I'll tell you the American way. We don't just say sorry and think that's enough. That son of a bitch killed one of our men, and his family's slaughtered dozens of yours. Now what are we going to do about it?'

The colonel pushed his dark glasses up his nose again. 'What can we do . . . within the law?'

Shepard nodded at Argetsinger.

'We'd like to do some listening, Colonel,' the CIA man said.

'Tap their phones? Not so easy. They have a system: someone moves house, apartment, whatever, and the Mosqueras buy the number for a few days. Just until someone else moves in, understand? Then another number, and another. They have maybe fifty at any one time.'

Argetsinger gave a thin smile. 'We've got a computer to handle that . . . with your permission.'

'I don't know . . .'

Shepard glared at the colonel. 'Let's give the American way a try, shall we?'

The big Yorkshireman put his head round the hospital-room door. 'The name's Roland Priest. Sami Nassar wants me to be his project manager. I gather he sent you a telegram too.'

Jack looked surprised but quickly recovered. 'Yes, come in. Pull up a chair.'

Priest sat down heavily by the bedside. Everything about him was big and solid, from his ruddy face and jutting jaw to his broad shoulders and barrel chest. He wore a tweed jacket, crested tie and cavalry-twill trousers.

'Looks painful,' he said, nodding at the plastercast. 'Anyroad, I've brought you some anaesthetic.' He opened his bulging briefcase and produced a bottle of single malt whisky. 'D'you drink this stuff?'

'I do now! There's another glass on the basin.'

Priest fetched it and poured them both generous measures. He raised his tumbler to Jack. 'Cheers.'

'Cheers.' Jack swallowed appreciatively. Makes a nice change from what they've been giving me! Now tell me something about Mr Nassar. I mean, is he serious about replacing Monaco's Grand Prix?'

'Seems to be, and it's not just the racetrack either. He's found a spectacular setting by the Med. Now he wants to build a rival to Monte Carlo there – harbour, hotels, casino, restaurants, shops, apartments, the lot – from scratch!'

Jack shook his head in amazement. 'Is it possible?'

'Almost anything's possible, given the money.'

'He's *that* rich?'

The Yorkshireman drained his glass before answering. 'His contacts are. He's Lebanese, a Christian Maronite to be precise – the wheeler–dealers of the Arab world. Rumour has it he used to sell arms. Now he's in property, capital P. Anyway, the Saudi royal family invest through him. I was working on an airport out there, and they recommended me to him apparently. Like some more whisky?'

'No thanks. Help yourself though. He sounds an impressive character.'

23

Priest shrugged as he refilled his glass. 'I'm not easily impressed. Pays to be sceptical in my line of work. So the first thing I did after getting that telegram was to have him checked out. Looked a bit foolish when the answers came through: "good for ten million pounds". Impressed my bank manager, mind. He bought me a damned good lunch on the strength of it.'

Jack laughed with him. 'All right, so they've got money coming out of their ears. Why a racetrack though? I mean, isn't creating a city by the sea enough for him?'

'Apparently not. A Grand Prix would make it world-famous overnight; stealing Monaco's, doubly so.'

'I've a personal interest in replacing that particular race too!'

The Yorkshireman put his glass on the bedside cabinet and sat forward. 'I was hoping you'd say that, because I think we can help each other. You see, I've built towns all over the world but never a track. I'll be needing expert advice from someone I can understand, not just blah from some prima donna.'

'Doesn't Mr Nassar see that?'

Priest's jaw jutted out in characteristic fashion. 'Sami's all right but he's apt to talk to funny foreigners.'

'Like who?'

'That French lad for starters, the one who pushed you off at Monaco. I reckoned I'd see him for five minutes after press conferences, if I was lucky.'

'No comment,' Jack said. But adrenalin was pumping through his veins as though he was overtaking Deneuve in the tunnel again. This time he was going to beat him!

'I'll say this though,' Jack added: 'I'd commit myself one hundred per cent to the project.'

'Good. I'd like to demonstrate that to Sami, preferably before he saddles me with a so-called expert, or buys an unsuitable site. How long are you stuck in here for?'

'The end of the week.'

'Could you come to Marbella with me after that?'

The surgeon's advice rang round Jack's head — no pressure on the ankle for at least three months. 'I'd like to,' he heard himself say. 'One problem though: my daughter's coming to stay next week. Would you mind if she came with us?'

Priest frowned. 'Couldn't someone look after her until we get back?'

'I'd rather not. Personal reasons.'

'Bring her along, then. She'll be no trouble.'

Jack wished he shared his confidence.

CHAPTER FOUR

Thirty thousand feet above Spain an Avianca DC10 neared the end of its transatlantic flight from Venezuela. Inside it Angel yawned and stretched in his first-class window seat, then raised the blind and looked out.

The rising sun was burnishing the plane's wings. Far below mountain ranges seemed to point towards Madrid in the centre of the Iberian peninsula. From their base the great plain of La Mancha spread south-eastwards – Don Quixote country. Angel smiled as a story about the foolish knight and his fat servant, Sancho Panza, came to mind. The stories formed part of his childhood, and Angel had been to Spain several times before with his father, who often referred to it as the motherland. Despite his education and personal predilection for the States, Angel almost felt he was coming home now.

His journey had started the previous day. One of the Mosqueras' twin-props had flown him to an airstrip near Carácas, the Venezuelan capital. No customs to clear there. A waiting car had taken him to the Aeropuerto Simón Bolívar, where he'd used his Peruvian passport to board the Iberia flight. In that document his mother's family name – Mallendo – was shown as his surname.

Half an hour later the DC10 thumped down at Madrid's Barajas Airport to a round of relieved applause from its passengers. At passport control a *Policia Nacional* took Angel's passport, thumbed through it, looked him over again . . . then stamped in the entry date and handed it back. He was stopped as he wheeled his suitcases through the green channel and asked to open one of them. Angel calmly complied, knowing there was nothing to find.

Outside the curved International Terminal it was already uncomfortably hot. Angel felt tired and dirty after a night in his clothes, but concentrated as his trolley clattered across the road to the car park. Suddenly he spun it round as though he'd forgotten something, and charged back towards the terminal. Everyone seemed to be staring at him. Fine. He wanted to know if anyone avoided looking at him or turned away for no good reason. Angel toured the building, doubling back on himself several times. When he was sure he wasn't being tailed he went outside again.

In the car park he stopped after the fourth row of cars, according to instructions. Nothing happened for several minutes. He was getting hotter and hotter, and was beginning to wonder whether there'd been a foul-up when a black Mercedes saloon pulled out of a parking space and drove towards him.

The driver was alone in the car. Angel recognised him by the ear-to-mouth scar that marked the left side of his brutal face. The Mercedes pulled up beside him and the driver climbed out. Enrique Estinal was commonly known as El Carnicero – the butcher. He was not much above average height but his weightlifter's body made him look enormous. Born in a Medellín slum forty-two years earlier, he had received only a street education, but that had qualified him to become one of the Mosqueras' best men, with a savage reputation to match. They had sent him to Madrid to be their enforcer there.

'Welcome to Spain,' he said, giving Angel an embrace of loyalty. 'You must be tired. I'll take you to your hotel.'

'I'd rather get started. Have you got something for me?'

El Carnicero nodded. 'Collected it from our embassy contact this morning. It's in the car.'

While the strongman loaded his bags into the trunk, Angel glanced at the Mercedes' badges. A 300E. Not bad, but among his car collection at home was a sixteen-valve

27

190E that would run rings round this one. They climbed into the front seats, where El Carnicero handed Angel a large brown envelope. He waited patiently while Angel opened it and read several sheets of typed paper.

'He's done his homework,' Angel said when he'd finished. 'Know what this is about?'

'Your father said you'd explain everything, and told me to follow your orders.'

'All right. You've been complaining for long enough that you're short of product, right?'

'I'm telling you, Spain is narco-paradise. We could sell ten times as much.'

'I hope you mean that.' Angel waved the papers. 'Details of factories for sale with one thing in common – they already use the chemicals needed for processing.'

El Carnicero's hard face broke into a smile. As it did so the ghastly scar seemed to grin too. 'I get it. But how you going to ship in that much paste?'

'That's our problem. Yours is finding enough distributors: we're talking a tonne a *month* now.'

'Easy. All Colombian expatriates have to register with the embassy. Our contact supplies me with likely names. Finding work's tough, and selling drugs is a piece of cake. There's no shortage of volunteers.'

'And informers?'

'I pick only men with close relations back home. If they step out of line, you blow the family away.'

'I know, but this move will start a war, and it won't just be with the drug squads. When the other *capos* realise what we're up to they'll fight for a share.'

El Carnicero wasn't smiling now. 'I'll deal with them when the time comes.'

'Good. Then let's go see these factories.'

The first one was on a modern industrial estate within sight and sound of the airport.

'Too obvious,' Angel shouted above the roar of an incoming jet.

El Carnicero drove him to a smaller but equally busy estate in the nearby town of San Fernando de Henares. Angel felt the same about that too.

He found what he was looking for outside a shabby village a few kilometres from the main Madrid-to-Valencia road. A potholed track led to a single-storey brick-and-corrugated-iron building that had seen better days. The field around it was strewn with metal drums, most of them empty and rusting. When they climbed out of the car they were hit by the smell of chemicals.

'A paint and glue factory,' Angel said, re-reading the details. 'The owner's a good chemist and a lousy business-man by the sound of it. Been trying to sell this place for years apparently. Nobody in their right minds would buy it though – except us!'

'What now?' the enforcer asked.

'Wait here. I'll see if he's in.'

Angel went through the front door into an untidy reception area and asked to see the owner.

'What are you selling?' the young, bored receptionist said.

'Nothing. I'm buying.'

Vaguely interested now, she relayed the message by internal phone, then put down the receiver. 'Señor Fortinez will see you. Come with me.'

She opened a door and led him into a witch's lair. Foul-smelling potions steamed and bubbled away in battered vats, while stalactites of residue hung from the roof and walls and dripped on to the floor. As Angel squelched through the sticky mess, the half-dozen workers eyed him curiously. He thought he noticed a family resemblance. The receptionist led him over to one corner of the factory which had been partitioned off as a laboratory and office for the owner. She showed him in and then left.

Señor Fortinez was a shrivelled-up man in his sixties,

wearing a shabby white lab coat with holes in the elbows. He stood up from a bench stool and peered at his visitor through thick-lensed spectacles. Fortinez frowned at Angel's youth. 'Well? What can I sell you?'

'Your factory.'

He sat back unsteadily on the stool. 'You can't be . . . are you serious?'

'Perfectly.' Angel sat down too.

'Ah, but for how much?'

'Your asking price, on certain conditions.'

The old man sighed. 'There always are. Well?'

Angel asked for a pad, wrote something on it, and handed it to him. 'Know what that is?'

Fortinez studied it line by line, then nodded.

'Say it.'

'A formula for turning coca-leaf paste into cocaine hydrochloride.'

'*A* formula?'

'There are several ways.'

'Can you do it this way?'

Fortinez looked offended. 'Young man, we used to manufacture complex pharmaceuticals here until they let foreign companies in to steal our business. Franco had the right ideas about them.'

'D'you understand what I'm asking? We'd want you to stay on, just as though the ownership had never changed, and process paste.'

'I'm your man, at a price of course.'

Angel almost smiled. 'Of course. Now, who else works here?'

'Family. Can't afford anyone else, the wages they want nowadays. Don't worry, they'll keep their mouths shut if I tell them to.'

'They'd better, because you realise what'll happen if they don't?'

'I told you,' Fortinez said, 'Franco had the right ideas about trouble-makers.'

30

That evening, from his five-star hotel near the centre of Madrid, Angel phoned one of his contact numbers in Medellín and spoke to his father.

'How's the holiday going?' Julio César asked.

'Great. Wonderful shops, one in particular.'

'You've found it already? Good. Got enough money?'

'They're expecting more stock. Once it's arrived I could spend a thousand a month there.'

'I'll increase your allowance right away. You know where to collect it. Done any sightseeing?'

'Not yet,' Angel told him. 'I'm going down to Marbella tomorrow though.'

'Well enjoy yourself, and keep me informed.' Julio César hung up.

Having dealt with business for the moment, Angel's thoughts turned to pleasure. He picked up a complimentary copy of *What's on in Madrid* from his bedside table, relaxed on the large bed, and began to leaf through it. He soon found numerous advertisements offering 'unforgett-able escorts' and 'discreet masseuses'. Angel studied them carefully for a while, then suddenly threw the magazine aside.

'*Putas!*' he said angrily: he didn't need to pay a prostitute for female company. The truth was, though, he was shy of the opposite sex. Angel found it much easier to kill a man than form a lasting relationship with a woman. That was why he preferred the company of teenage girls: their little games and rejections were easier to take.

Picking up the guide again, Angel turned to the list of discotheques. He found one that sounded chic and ex-clusive. Yes, that was more his style. No problem with acceptance there. Climbing off the bed, Angel went to the wardrobe and began to select his most fashionable clothes.

That night on an industrial estate near Bogotá's El Dorado Airport, box-bodied lorries backed up to a loading bay, just as they did all day, every day, three hundred and sixty-five

31

days a year. The sign-writing on their sides proclaimed: 'Avicomida S.A. Feeding The World's Airlines'.

Cooking smells wafted out of the factory — which was really a huge kitchen — as workers wheeled out insulated carts filled with meal trays and loaded them into the lorries. At the back of the building was a maintenance bay, where mechanics serviced the company's vehicles and dealt with occasional problems on the carts such as bent hinges and electrical faults. There seemed to be a lot of occasional faults tonight.

The maintenance foreman took a final walk round the factory to check that only the usual night-shift personnel were around. Then he went back into the maintenance bay and locked all the doors. At his signal mechanics went to work on the carts.

First they unscrewed the aluminium strips holding the top and side panels in place. Those came away to reveal yellowish slabs of insulation. In their place went identical looking slabs, heavier though, because the polyurethane foam had been cast round a thin plastic-wrapped core of coca-leaf paste. There was no way for a dog to sniff this fill.

Two and a half kilos of paste per trolley, twenty trolleys on a jumbo jet, five flights a day to Madrid.

The mechanics used new screws and made sure they didn't scratch the panels when they replaced them.

CHAPTER FIVE

Roy Shepard spent Friday morning talking to top-level informants in Bogotá. All of them had hair-raising stories to tell about the Mosqueras but none of them had proof. It was uncanny how the *capo* and his son managed to stay one step ahead of the law – what law there was in Colombia.

Depressed by his lack of progress, the DEA agent returned to the American embassy at lunchtime. The note on his desk bucked him up considerably: 'Got something for you, Hal'.

Shepard hurried down the corridor to one of the CIA's offices, knocked and entered. Hal Argetsinger was munching a sandwich at his desk, but when he saw the stocky Virginian he reached over and triumphantly brandished a reel of tape.

'Been waiting for you,' he said through a mouthful of bread. 'Want to know how we managed it? Like the colonel said, people move house or whatever, and when they do they want to stop paying the bills the day they go, right?'

'I suppose so, but –'

'Wrong. Some of them sell their numbers to the Mosqueras, so they cancel everything *except* the phone. Our computer program cross-references cancellations, which shows up –'

'Hal, just play it, will you?'

The Company man gave a frustrated sigh, then wound the tape on to a reel-to-reel machine. He pressed play and they listened to Angel's conversation with his father.

'Where did he call from?' Shepard asked when it finished.

'A hotel in Madrid, but he's checked out already. Where's Marbella by the way?'

'Opposite Morocco, so there's a lot of hashish around. Not much cocaine . . . yet.'

'Think that's what he's up to?'

Roy Shepard frowned. 'I don't know, but I'm going there to find out.'

Marbella municipality in Andalusia is a flat coastal strip fifteen miles long by four at the widest. On one side is the Mediterranean, with the African coast just visible on the southern horizon, and sometimes the Rock of Gibraltar can be seen as a hazy hump in the west. The land-side is walled in by sierras – low mountain ranges – and towering over the town itself is the shell-shaped peak called La Concha.

Before the Second World War this fertile strip produced olives and oranges. Then Prince Max Hohenlohe bought the Finca Santa Margarita, renamed it the Marbella Club, and harvested the rich and famous instead. That was the start of modern Marbella – nothing to do with farming, not much to do with the real Spain any more: a fantasy land for people intent on pleasuring themselves.

Angel was staying in one of the club's white-walled, ochre-roof-tiled bungalows. It was set in its own sub-tropical garden, surrounded by a purple-flowered bougainvillaea hedge. In front of the terrace was a Roman-style swimming pool, and beyond was a line of classical pillars. Exotic plants perfumed the air while in the background the sea swished on the club's private beach. Paradise, Angel thought as he ate a light lunch on the terrace: a pity he didn't have an excuse to spend more time in Marbella.

Glancing at his watch he realised it was time to leave for his site meeting with Sami Nassar. Angel was going alone. He couldn't stand any more of their land agent's gush about the man and his possessions, and wanted to make up his own mind about him.

After that morning's flight from Madrid to Málaga,

Angel had rented a Mercedes 230E at the airport. It was the only car he considered vaguely decent, and he'd gone from desk to desk to find it. Collecting it now from a nearby parking area, Angel turned left out of the Marbella Club's entrance on to the Golden Mile. That led him past a recently built mosque, enormous hillside villas with views of the sea, and a full-size palace belonging to an Arab prince. Next came Puerto Banús, an impressive marina set in a grandiose imitation of an Andalusian *pueblo blanco*. Each kilometre post after that marked a gradual decline in prestige of the surrounding property. The site was on the very outskirts of Marbella municipality.

Suddenly the hotels and pseudo-villages gave way to two hundred acres of open land, sandwiched between the coast road and a strip of sandy beach. Optimistic developers had levelled the site and cross-hatched it with broad black-topped roadways. The weed-infested squares of land in between had never been built on – Marbella's planning committee had seen to that. The original developers had sold on to an ever-changing number of speculators – five at the last count. One of the Mosqueras' offshore companies owned over half the site.

Angel turned off the main road and drove down a ramp towards the sea. It was calm and gun-metal blue under a cloudless sky. A white Bentley Mulsanne Turbo was parked halfway along the extra-wide roadway fronting the beach. That's him, Angel thought. As he drew nearer, the Lebanese climbed out of it. Despite his plumpness he looked cool in expensively casual summer clothes. Angel parked his hired Mercedes behind the Corniche, feeling outgunned but determined not to show it.

'Señor Mallendo?' Nassar asked. 'I'm delighted to meet you. I thought your agent was coming too.'

'No. I've come alone.'

'Fine. We can talk freely then.'

'Possibly. I believe you want to make us an offer.'

'Shall we sit in my car? It's air-conditioned.'

'I'd rather walk,' Angel said, refusing to be placed at a disadvantage by moving to the Arab's territory.

Nassar hid a smile as they fell into step along the roadway. 'What I actually want to do is buy an option on your land.'

'We're not interested in that. I'm here to negotiate an outright sale.'

'Then I'm afraid there's no basis for a deal, and I'll just have to find another site for my project. A pity, because the landowners stand to benefit as much as I do.'

'Oh. How?'

'As you know, the town hall has turned down all planning applications so far because the surrounding zone is overbuilt. It's going to take something of exceptional benefit to the municipality to change their minds. I'm confident I've come up with that.'

'Do tell me,' Angel said sceptically.

'All right. I plan to build a town and harbour as spectacular in its way as Monte Carlo, with all the same facilities, including a modern motor-racing track running right through it.'

The young Colombian stopped and stared at him. 'Here? Can you be . . . are you serious?'

'Perfectly. And I intend to steal Monaco's Grand Prix from them. Imagine the prestige that would bring to Marbella. Enough for the *Ayuntamiento* to change the zoning here, I think.'

'Incredible,' Angel murmured, shaking his head. 'It's a fantastic idea.'

'Just so. And while it's still an idea I'm only interested in options on the land. I say "only", but I'd pay you a million dollars for one.'

They began to walk again. In the sea a couple of speedboats raced towards Puerto Banús, while further out white-sailed yachts progressed more sedately.

'Fair enough,' Angel said, but you mentioned something about the landowners benefitting as much as you.'

'Let me explain. Nobody will pay more than a hundred thousand dollars an acre for this land at present. Planning consent for my project would double that overnight. And if FISA – that's motor-racing's governing body – give us the Spanish Grand Prix, the hotel and casino chains will want in and the sky's the limit. So how do we value the land? The only fair solution is for me to give you a choice.'

Angel frowned, trying to understand the deal.

'I suggest we value the land at two hundred thousand dollars an acre right away,' Nassar continued. 'Before the option expires I'll either pay you the balance or you can claim shares to that value in the company controlling the project.'

'How much of the company would we own?'

'Forty-nine per cent.'

'But we own well over half the site!'

The Lebanese looked at him impatiently. 'You must realise there's more to this scheme than buying land. I've come up with the idea, developed it, and I'll finance the options with my own money. In exchange for that I've allocated myself twenty per cent of the shares. I'm not in this for charity, you know.'

'Of course not.'

'There'll be no further share issues though. That means the stock will have eighty per cent asset backing from the word go.'

'I understand,' Angel said, trying to hide his mounting excitement. Forty-nine per cent of the shares: just two per cent more and he'd effectively control the most exciting scheme he'd ever heard of: prime property, including a racetrack! Foreign currency legitimately pouring in and out of Spain – the perfect laundry for the proceeds from drug-trafficking in Europe ... *if* the project got off the ground.

'Don't give me an answer now,' Nassar said. 'Think about it over the weekend and –'

'Will the other landowners sell?' Angel interrupted.

'If you like the deal, why shouldn't they?'

'True. But even if the *Ayuntamiento* grants planning consent, can you be sure the organisation you mentioned –'

'FISA?'

'– yes, will they give us the race?'

'For that we've recruited a Grand Prix star with contacts and influence – Jack Ryder.'

'The Englishman who crashed at Monaco? I saw that on television. I watch all the Grand Prix on television.'

'Then you'll appreciate why he's especially interested in this. His leg's in plaster, but he's coming here next week. Would you like to meet him?'

'Very much,' Angel said.

For Jack Friday was freedom day. He'd pestered the surgeon to discharge him until finally, with a lot of head-shaking, the surgeon had relented. Jack was told he must use a wheelchair for at least a month, but he had other ideas about that too.

In one corner of the hospital room was a pair of full-arm crutches. Using both hands, he moved his plastercast to the edge of the bed and lowered it to the ground. He put his weight on his good leg and stood up unsteadily. He then tried putting some weight on his left one, but pain stabbed through it the moment he did so. So he hopped to the corner of his other foot, and leant against the wall puffing like an old man. He'd have to do something about that.

By the time his girlfriend came to collect him that afternoon Jack was swinging along, crutches under his arms, as though the balancing act was easy. Elizabeth Muire was a twenty-eight-year-old textile designer who'd established a successful studio in Oxford. She was almost as tall as Jack, with a well-developed figure. Chestnut hair hung to her shoulders, framing an oval face full of character, and she wore well-chosen glasses with a frame the same colour as her hair. The eyes behind them were full of fun, and her mischievous mouth twitched into a smile as readily as Jack's. Liz had also personally made the denim-and-satin appliquéd pullover she was wearing with her jeans.

'I might have known,' she said, watching the performance. 'How am I meant to keep you in bed?'

'Like this,' Jack said, stopping in front of her and kissing her on the lips.

'I'll help you pack,' she said softly.

She was closing his suitcase when Sister came into the room. They knew each other because Liz had visited Jack every day.

'Try and keep him off his feet,' Sister said. 'The surgeon recommended three months without any weight on that leg, but our friend thinks he knows best.'

'I'd noticed.'

Sister took an autograph book out of her pocket and handed it to Jack. 'I hope you don't mind signing one more.'

'For your boy?'

'For me actually.'

The message he wrote in it made her burst out laughing.

Downstairs a group of staff had gathered to wave him off. The waiting photographers were rewarded with corny 'Racing Driver Thanks Nurses Who Saved His Life' shots. Liz stayed well out of the way.

Fifteen minutes later she parked her hatchback in front of Jack's thatched cottage and went round to help him out of the passenger seat. Like most of the houses in the Oxfordshire village, it was built in limestone darkened by time. The garden behind it overlooked a tributary of the Thames. In the garden was Jack's workshop, made of timber.

'I can manage,' he said, hauling himself out of the car.

'Won't you let me do anything for you?' She handed him his crutches as he hopped about on his good leg. Then she met his glinting eyes.

'Well?' Jack asked huskily.

'But how can we . . . won't it hurt you?'

'Not half as much as this thing in my trousers!'

Liz giggled. 'Come on then.' She led the way to the front door and opened it.

The cottage was L-shaped, with a kitchen, dining room and lounge downstairs, and the bedrooms and bathrooms above them. Superb wooden furniture stood out against the plain white walls. Jack had made most of it: some were reproductions – early efforts – but the chairs and tables were his own designs. They elegantly combined form and function with an obvious sympathy for the materials. The armchairs and sofa in the lounge were covered in Liz's textiles, which was how the two had first met.

Jack had taken up carpentry as a hobby when he was ten. Even motor-racing hadn't eclipsed it. In fact the sport had made it more important to him. After the transitory madness of a Grand Prix, it gave Jack intense satisfaction to come home and make something solid and lasting. Anna had hated that hobby too, but his efforts had pleased other people. He was always receiving requests to reproduce his pieces and could satisfy only a fraction of the demand. When he finally retired from the sport, Jack planned to take up carpentry full-time.

He followed Liz up the narrow staircase, grimacing with the effort.

'You all right?' she asked, turning into his bedroom.

'I will be soon!'

She laughed as she took off her glasses, and then her pullover. 'Just lie back on the bed. The doctor'll be with you in a minute.'

For once he did as he was told, and watched her strip. Full firm breasts swung free as she slipped off her bra and when she stepped out of her jeans and panties he thought he was going to burst. Naked, she moved to the bed and began to undress him too. His left trouser leg had been slit to the knee, and she undid the safety pins, easing his trousers over the cast. Then she reached for his underpants.

'My God! Did they give you a transplant in there?'

'Never mind my shirt,' Jack said.

Liz couldn't wait either. She knelt over his belly, then sank back slowly, feeling him part and penetrate her.

'Don't move,' Jack gasped, eyes tightly closed, hands squeezing her breasts.

'Does your leg hurt?'

'Yes, but who cares? I love you, Liz.'

'I love you too, Jack.'

She bent forward to kiss him. The exquisite movement was too much for Jack. Shouting with pleasure and pain, he drove up into Liz, lifting her clear of the bed as he erupted deep inside her. And then she was arching her back too, crying his name and clawing his shoulders as she felt herself fuse into one with him.

Afterwards Liz lay snuggled up to him. 'I've got some good news by the way.'

'Oh?' Jack turned his head to look at her.

'Remember that conference table and chairs you made for my best customer as a favour to me?'

'Solly Grossman, the man with the furniture stores. Of course I remember.'

'I met him this morning, and he asked after you. Apparently there's been so much favourable comment that he'd like twenty more sets. Solly wants to feature them in his contract furniture departments and –'

'Wait a minute, wait a minute.' Jack pushed himself up on one elbow. '*Twenty* more sets? How could I possibly make two hundred chairs?'

'We could easily find a small factory. And all those frustrated craftsmen who've helped you part-time: they'd join you like a shot –'

'Hold it, Liz. I'm not finished with motor-racing yet.'

'You haven't?' The disappointment was clear on her face. 'Well, what if your arms get smashed next time? And I'm sorry if that's brutal, but I can't bear to see your talent wasted.'

He shook his head. 'It's not what you think. An Arab's talking about a Spanish alternative to the Monaco Grand Prix. He wants my advice, and I'm interested in the idea. Okay?'

Liz looked at him sceptically. 'There's more to it than that.'

'All right, it'll keep me in touch with the scene until . . . until . . .'

'Exactly!'

It was Jack's turn to sigh. 'I can't leave the sport like this. It'd be like leaving a piece of furniture unfinished. I just couldn't do that. I'd have to finish it, even if it wasn't turning out how I'd hoped. That's how I am.'

'But how can you advise them when you're stuck here for three months?'

He took a deep breath. 'Actually I'm flying to Spain on Monday.'

'What are you talking about? Katie's coming to stay.'

'She's going with me.'

Liz stared at him. 'When did all this happen?'

'The project manager visited me last week. I didn't say anything in case it all fell through, but he confirmed everything yesterday.'

'What about your leg?'

'No problem.'

'Oh, cut the macho bit!' She looked away in exasperation. 'I suppose there's nothing I can say . . .'

Liz stopped in mid-sentence when she saw his throbbing erection.

Jack followed her gaze. 'I can't help it. You're so sexy when you're angry, especially when you're starkers as well.'

Giggling now, Liz knelt up and straddled him again. 'I give in, Superman. Show me what you're made of.'

CHAPTER SIX

Four days after Angel's arrival in Spain, Roy Shepard set off in pursuit. Ironically he boarded a Bogotá-to-Madrid plane carrying meal carts filled with paste. The agent had no idea what was being wheeled past him during the Atlantic crossing.

Having cleared customs in Barajas Airport, a waiting car drove him straight to the American embassy in Madrid's Calle Serrano. Bob Cullington, the D E A station chief, was waiting to see him. He was about the same age as Shepard but taller and leaner.

'Good to see you again, Roy,' he said, stepping round his desk to shake hands. 'Sorry to hear it didn't work out with your wife.'

'She just couldn't stand the thought of going back to Colombia. Can't say I blame her – half her friends' husbands were murdered last time we were there. I miss her a lot though.'

They sat down facing each other across the desk. 'You must hate the place,' Cullington said.

'Just the sumbitches who've made it a miserable hell. I feel sorry for everyone else. Anyway, what you got for me?'

'We found your boy when he booked a flight to Málaga. Calls himself Angel Mallendo and carries a Peruvian passport. It's valid – we checked. When he got to Málaga he made a big fuss about renting a car, and eventually picked a Hertz Mercedes. He gave his local address as the Marbella Club. Whatever he's doing, he's doing in style.'

'Who've we got down there?'

'Ed Wheeler.'

'*One* man?'

'Three of us cover the entire country, Roy. In fact we've loaned Ed from the Company. He's a wireman, but we can't tap phones until we get permission from the Spaniards.'

Shepard couldn't hide his frustration. 'Sounds like Colombia.'

'Far from it. Spain's a delightful country, just coming out of its Dark Age. Since Franco died there's been a backlash against the old fascist ways. A lot of liberal laws got enacted, like no phone taps without a court order, and to get that you'd better have a damn good reason.'

'As well as decriminalising possession of any drugs for "personal" use?'

Cullington nodded grimly. 'That too I'm afraid. And extraditing this asshole's going to take some doing, especially as he's got dual nationality. You'll have to catch him white-handed.'

'Sounds like the cards are stacked against me,' Shepard said.

'Not all of them. I've talked to the *Brigada Central de Estupefacientes* here in Madrid and they'll help all they can. They've had a word with their boys in Marbella and you can use the facilities down there.'

'That's something. When can I start?'

'We'll fly you down there right away,' Cullington said.

Anna drove her daughter to Heathrow Airport that same Monday morning, but in London it was drizzling. Neither of them said much as the Golf G T I whined along the M4 at eighty miles an hour. Anna was in a hurry because she was meeting her fiancé afterwards. She was dressed to kill, partly for his benefit but also because she liked Jack to know what he was missing. In studied contrast Katie wore faded denim, and there wasn't a trace of make-up on her troubled young face.

'Oh do buck up!' Anna snapped. 'It's not as though you're going back to school.'

But you're still getting rid of me, Katie thought, looking out of her side window.

They left the car on double yellow lines outside Terminal Two, and checked in at an Iberia desk. Then they stood around waiting for Jack. Photographers and gaping passengers announced his arrival. The tabloids had played the crash as a life-or-death drama, and were not into the miracle recovery act. Jack came swinging in on his crutches, with Liz wheeling his luggage on a trolley beside him.

'Who's that with Jack?' Anna sniffed. 'Hasn't she heard of contact lenses?'

Katie said nothing, but noted that Liz was wearing jeans too and felt an instant affinity with her.

Jack spotted them, dealt with the press as quickly as possible, and then came over. He kept the introductions as brief as possible before turning to Liz. 'Thanks for bringing me. Phone you tonight.'

She just smiled back and squeezed his hand, knowing better than to make a scene. Liz smiled at Katie too before leaving.

'I really must be going,' Anna announced. 'Well, be good, Katie.' She pecked her daughter on the cheek, then turned to Jack. 'Well . . .'

'Good luck with the wedding.'

Anna searched his face for irony but didn't find it.

He watched her walk away. 'You could have wished her luck too,' Jack told his stepdaughter.

'She'll muck it up anyway,' Katie said with quiet bitterness.

He glanced at her, wondering what he'd let himself in for. Too late to change his mind now. Just then Roland Priest arrived and they boarded their flight together.

The three of them sat up front in a row of Preference Class seats. For most of the three-hour flight, Katie listlessly read magazines while the two men chatted. Jack's leg was aching already, but he wasn't about to admit that. Instead he ordered a couple of free whiskies to dull the pain.

'Let's not be too impressed by the first-class treatment,' the Yorkshireman said.

'What d'you mean?'

'I'm a cautious man, Jack. Oh, I've checked out Sami, and he's got the means to develop this project all right. But who else is involved? What's this site like? Let's be knowing all the snags before we go overboard.'

'Agreed, but we mustn't be totally negative.'

The Lebanese was waiting for them at Málaga Airport. So was the sun. Nassar greeted Jack warmly and helped him into the front passenger seat of the Bentley, where he could stretch out his leg. Katie and Priest climbed in behind them.

Jack almost forgot the pain as they animatedly discussed the project during the drive to Marbella. The coast road, which was being widened and improved in several places, took them past less fashionable resorts like Torremolinos and Fuengirola. He found it all interesting though: doing something constructive again was proving a real tonic.

When they entered Marbella, Jack noticed that his stepdaughter was taking an interest in things too. The high-rise blocks on the outskirts gave way to a more traditional town centre. Crowding the pavements were Spaniards and other Europeans, of course, but there were also many Arabs, Africans and Americans in a gaudy mix of apparel.

Nassar drove through the town and on to the Golden Mile. Shortly after the Marbella Club he turned into the equally luxurious Hotel Puente Romano. From a reception block dominated by a white tower with a dovecote in it, two lines of white-walled apartments ran down to the private beach. Between them was a manicured jungle filled with exotic trees, plants and brilliant-coloured flowers. A stream ran through the centre, crossed by the Roman bridge which had given the hotel its name.

The Lebanese had booked the Ryders one of the apartments nearest the beach. Its two terraces overlooked an asymmetric, fresh-water pool shaded by palm trees. The marble-floored, expensively furnished suite had two large bedrooms, a kitchenette, and a dining room and sitting area which led on to one of the terraces.

'I hope you'll be comfortable,' Nassar said as porters carried in their baggage and took Roland Priest's to a nearby suite.

'It's fabulous!' Katie said from the terrace.

'Wait till you see Puerto Banús. I've arranged for the daughter of friends to show you round while we visit the site. We can meet up for lunch there if you like.'

'Does it have any shops? I didn't realise how hot it'd be, and I haven't brought the right things.'

'I've heard that before!' Jack said. He was pleased by the change in Katie though. Maybe that's what made him give her such a generous allowance.

Jack's first reaction on seeing the site was disappointment. It was hard to visualise the scheme on a bare strip of land.

'You'll have a better idea once you've seen Puerto Banús,' Nassar said, as if reading his mind. 'But the setting's spectacular, no?'

Jack looked at the sierras to one side and the Mediterranean on the other, and had to agree. He reminded himself how much he wanted the project to succeed, and set about demonstrating that to the others. He'd done his homework. As Nassar drove them round the criss-crossing roadways, Jack explained the requirements of a modern Grand Prix circuit. Shortest track length three-and-a-half kilometres. Minimum width nine metres, increasing to twelve where the cars reached three hundred kilometres an hour. A pit area at least two hundred metres long by forty wide. Guard rails capable of withstanding seven thousand kilograms of thrust. Up to five catch fences, depending on approach speed, outside the corners. Spectator fences, escape roads . . . the list seemed endless.

Nassar listened with interest, then stopped the Bentley

facing the sea. 'All this is feasible. But am I to buy this site?'

Priest looked dubious. 'It's relatively flat, and you'll be selling the best views with the properties. How's anyone else going to see the race?'

'Isn't there going to be a broad boulevard fronting the marina?' Jack asked.

'That's right,' Nassar said. 'The Spanish call it a *rambla*.'

'We'll put the circuit's main overtaking points at either end then, with the pits in the middle. That way anyone in the harbour can see most of the action. And remember what Alan Bond did in Perth for the Americas Cup? Turned an oil rig into a floating grandstand. Couldn't we do something similar here?'

Both of them looked at him in astonishment.

'What about people who've bought berths in the way?' Priest asked.

'We'll move them for the week,' Nassar said. 'Give them special privileges – the best seats, tickets to the pre-race ball, that sort of thing. It's a brilliant idea, Jack. I can see why you were so keen to involve him, Roland. So, to buy or not to buy?'

The Yorkshireman grimaced at the awful pun. 'I'll be wanting a thorough soil survey of course. Dot the Ts and cross the Is, I always say.'

'I know. That's what I've hired you to do. How d'you feel about it, Jack?'

'Looks good to me.'

'Let's go and have lunch with the main landowner then – a young Peruvian who's keen to meet you.'

'Here he comes,' Ed Wheeler said as Angel's rented Mercedes pulled out of the Marbella Club and turned west along the Golden Mile.

The CIA's wireman was in his late twenties, with fair hair and an eager face that had never fully recovered from teenage acne. He too had been to Málaga Airport that morning and collected Roy Shepard. The DEA agent was sitting beside him now in the passenger seat of a plain Ford saloon, parked opposite the club's entrance.

'Tail him,' Shepard said. 'I can't wait to see who he meets.'

Wheeler let several vehicles pass before joining the stream of traffic. The Mercedes led them into Puerto Banús. There, Angel parked and walked through the *pueblo blanco* to a plush restaurant beside the marina. Gold-tasselled awnings protected its terrace from the midday sun. He talked to a waiter, and was shown to a table in the shade. Angel sat down and ordered a drink.

The agents went into a nearby bar from where they could watch him. They ordered drinks too.

'We ought to discuss your remuneration,' Nassar told Jack as they drove away from the site. 'D'you mind doing it in front of Roland?'

'Not at all. I'd rather there were no secrets between us.'

'Good. I propose to pay you twenty thousand dollars a month. How does that sound?'

'Generous.'

'As an additional incentive I'm going to offer you stock in the offshore holding company. I've allocated myself ten million of the fifty million one-dollar shares. The balance is reserved for the landowners, but I'll give you a written option on a million of mine.'

Jack frowned. 'I don't want to sound ungrateful, but doesn't that mean I'd have to find a million dollars to take them up?'

'Or simply sell the option. Once planning consent is announced it'll be worth a small fortune.'

'You'll *give* me that? Why?'

The Lebanese overtook a car before answering. 'You're vital to the success of this project, but it's self-interest as well. Why d'you think the Saudi royal family trust me?

49

Because I always give them a fair share. It's the same with you, Jack. Perhaps I could buy you cheaply, *once*. But I want this to be just the start of our relationship.'

Sami led the way into the Puerto Banús restaurant, and was greeted by the owner like a long-lost friend. He showed them to their table, where Angel was waiting for them. Sami made the introductions. They sat down, leaving two empty chairs for Katie and her new Spanish friend. Jack was opposite Angel and was soon being questioned by him.

'May I ask why Monte Carlo should lose its race?'

'You can see what happened to me there.' A waiter had served drinks, and Jack sipped some more whisky to kill the throbbing pain in his leg.

'I'm sorry.'

'Don't be. I'm here to do something about it. The point is, their circuit's unsafe. And then there's the annual slanging match about television rights.'

'Why?'

'The Automobile Club de Monaco want to keep the rights to themselves. F I S A and F O C A – the powers that be in Grand Prix racing – think differently. They control the rights for all their other events and want Monaco's too. They'd like to replace it, but they need somewhere equally photogenic before they can do that.'

'And you think the replacement could be here, in Marbella?'

'Why not?' Sami Nassar said. 'Jack can design a track that will make Monaco's look silly. As for the *pueblo blanco* and marina around it, look at this place and use your imagination.'

Angel did, hiding the excitement he felt.

Nassar's idea seemed quite feasible, but Jack Ryder was the key to making it a reality.

Katie arrived at that moment with a Spanish girl a bit older and taller than her. But not as pretty, Jack couldn't help noting with fatherly pride. As his stepdaughter came up to the terrace she did a twirl in her new clothes – a light-blue denim mini-skirt and a white cotton top, both with a sequinned rainbow on the front. 'Hope you like it – you paid for them!'

More than her change of clothes, Jack loved Katie's new-found liveliness. Maybe it was the sun which shone in her blonde curls and made her blue eyes sparkle. Maybe she'd just needed to get away from that school or her mother. Whatever the cause, it was a big improvement.

Suddenly Katie was blushing as she noticed Angel at the far end of the table. He was watching her, clearly fascinated and smiling at the performance.

'Sorry . . . hallo,' she said. 'I'm Katie, and this is Carmen.'

He stood up to introduce himself. Katie sat down by her stepfather, and Carmen sat opposite her, next to Angel. But it was obvious whom the young Colombian was interested in.

'Are you something to do with this race thing?' Katie asked him.

'I hope so.'

Jack turned to her. 'Angel's being modest. His family own most of the land we're interested in.'

'Should I call him Mister, then?' Katie teased, and Angel burst out laughing.

They smiled at each other a lot during the meal, Jack noticed, beginning to realise how pretty his stepdaughter could be. He'd have to keep an eye on her, and the other on Angel by the look of it.

Afterwards Nassar suggested returning to the site before meeting the *Alcalde* – the mayor of Marbella – later that afternoon. Jack's leg was hurting badly now, and he asked if they'd mind taking him back to Puente Romano first. The Lebanese was full of apologies, saying he should have realised Jack needed rest, and that he'd take him back immediately.

'Let me do that,' Angel volunteered. 'I'm staying next door in the Marbella Club, and I've got to make some phone calls anyway. And your daughter?'

'Can I stay here with Carmen?' Katie asked Jack. 'We've hardly bought anything yet.'

He laughed and agreed.

'Maybe some other time,' she said to Angel.

As they drove back along the Golden Mile, fast but reasonably safely, Jack fished for information.

'Sami said you were Peruvian.'

'That's right.'

'And you . . . what, own land all over the world?'

'The Spanish-speaking countries, Mr Ryder.'

'Jack, please.' He glanced in his side mirror and spotted the Ford Sierra again – the one that had followed them out of Puerto Banús. In a Grand Prix he somehow always knew when someone was chasing him well before he could actually see anyone, and he had that same feeling now. But this wasn't a race, he reminded himself, turning back to Angel. 'D'you do many deals this big?'

'Usually my father, or my elder brother, handles them. But my brother died in an accident recently . . .'

'I'm sorry.'

Angel gave him a charming smile. 'Now we've both apologised. Maybe we can help each other too.' He looked back at the road and concentrated on overtaking several vehicles. 'You see, I'm crazy about racing, and I believe in this project. I think we should invest much more than just our land. But before I can persuade my family I must understand everything about these options and this holding company.'

'I've got an interest in that too.'

'You have? Then I'd be really grateful for your advice. You can see I'm young, and most of this is new to me.'

'Give me a chance to find out more myself, and I'll be glad to help,' Jack told him, liking the youngster more for being so honest.

52

As they turned into the hotel, he watched the Ford sail past towards Marbella. Must have been his imagination, Jack decided.

From his bungalow in the Marbella Club, Angel phoned another contact number in Medellín. He started to explain the land deal to his father but was soon interrupted.

'I told you,' Julio César said, 'we're not interested in options.'

'So, no sale? On the other hand, a million dollars would pay for the shop and stock it.'

Crackling interference on the line. 'That's a point, I suppose.'

'Of course it is.' Angel told him about the project and his talk with Jack. 'Don't you see, if I can take it over, it's the perfect laundry for us.'

'With this race-driver and God knows who else involved?'

'I'll get rid of them once I've used them.'

'What d'you mean?'

'What d'you think I mean?'

Julio César hissed in consternation. 'I think this has more to do with your passion for cars. I think you're involving us in something we don't need. The idea was to buy prime sites in Madrid or Barcelona, remember?'

'This could be the primest property we've ever had. Why give it away?'

'Something smells wrong to me.'

'Well, I'm the one over here,' Angel said. 'Trust me.'

The meeting between Sami, Jack, Roland Priest and the *Alcalde* improved as it progressed.

To begin with the mayor said *he* couldn't give consent for their project; it would require approval not just by the planning committee but by a majority vote of the councillors. But what was his opinion of it, Sami asked in his reasonable Spanish. That depended on the benefits to the community. So Sami listed them, stressing the out-of-season boost to the local economy. Because of Marbella's excellent weather, the Grand Prix could be held early or late in the season, when tourism was normally slack.

With Sami translating for him, Jack explained the build-up and stopover effects before and after a Grand Prix. They could add weeks to the normal season. The *Alcalde* clearly liked that idea, and became more positive.

After the meeting Sami insisted on taking Jack and Roland to his home. He drove out of town on the Golden Mile, turned uphill just before the mosque, and pulled into the driveway of an ornate villa. It resembled an elaborate wedding cake iced by an exuberant Arab chef – blinding white, with Moorish pillars and arches everywhere.

'My house is your house,' Sami said, ushering them into it.

The interior was best Marbella-impractical, with white walls, white furniture, even white floors. Expensive rugs and gold bits and pieces provided the contrast.

They discussed the project for over an hour, after which Sami wanted to take them to dinner.

Jack cried off, saying he'd promised to eat with his stepdaughter. It was a good excuse to rest his leg again, but he also really did want to spend some more time with Katie.

She wasn't in the apartment when he got back to the hotel at seven o'clock though. Probably still in Puerto Banús, Jack thought. Shops didn't shut until eight or nine o'clock in Spain, and they hadn't set a time for her to be back.

He still wasn't worried at eight, but at nine he asked a receptionist to check round the hotel. And by ten he was thinking the worst – Carmen's bloody moped! Why had he let Katie go on the back of the damned thing? Carmen might have been riding too fast, or Katie could have overbalanced it –

The front door handle squeaked up and down, but the

door didn't open because it was locked. It couldn't be Katie because she'd got a key, Jack thought, grabbing his crutches and going to see who was there.

But it was Katie, leaning against the door frame for support, glazed eyes blinking stupidly. In the background he heard the noise of a departing moped.

'Hi, Jack.' She started to giggle. 'Hijack! S'funny . . . ged-dit?'

He tried to help her inside, but his crutches got in the way. Jack put one down, and supporting her with his free arm managed to guide her to the sofa. 'What the hell was it this time?'

'What was . . . wotwozwotwoz?' She started giggling again.

'Just tell me, Katie! I'm in no mood for fun and games.'

'Met . . . some boys . . . in a disco.'

'What was it?'

She tried to focus, sat forward but flopped back again. 'Joint.'

'Oh God. You don't need that here . . . do you?'

'I think I'm going to be sick,' Katie mumbled.

He just had time to pull the cloth off the coffee table and hold it under her chin. She retched repeatedly, and then started to cry. 'My head's splitting.'

'Good. Maybe you'll think twice before doing it again. Now what am I going to do with you.'

He managed to put her to bed, helping her off with her vomit-splashed top and skirt as though she were a child. Jack covered her up with a sheet, and looked down at her pale little face surrounded by tangled curls. There were tears in her big blue eyes.

'Sorry . . . Dad,' she murmured before shutting them.

Jack just stood there, feeling choked up himself. Then he sat on the bedside, bent forward and kissed her lightly on the forehead. Katie didn't stir. He struggled up again and left the room.

CHAPTER SEVEN

At six o'clock on Tuesday morning, Jack was woken by the doorbell. Must be a mistake, he thought, having squinted at his watch, but the ringing persisted. He hopped about as he pulled on his dressing gown, wondering who it could be at this unholy hour. He swung along to the door on his crutches and looked through the security lens. Outside was a stocky man about his own age.

'Who is it?' Jack asked.

'Roy Shepard, Mr Ryder. I'm with the Drug Enforcement Administration. May I come in and talk to you?'

'You're kidding?'

'No, sir. Put the door on the chain and I'll hand round identification. If you've any doubts, phone the American embassy in Madrid and –'

'Okay, okay.' Jack unlocked the door and opened it. 'I can't believe you people deal with something as petty as this.'

'*Petty?*'

'*Pathetic*'s more like it. But as you're here we may as well sit down.'

On the way to the living room, Jack looked in on Katie. She was fast asleep, and he closed the door so she wouldn't be disturbed. He sat down in an armchair facing the American. He was damned if he was going to offer him a drink.

'Don't you think I can handle this myself?' Jack asked.

'I didn't realise you knew about it.'

'Of course I do – she puked up over me last night.'

'Who are we talking about, Mr Ryder?'

Jack shook his head as if trying to clear it. 'Is it too early or something? Who did you come to see me about?'

'Angel Mallendo, or Mosquera, as he's known in Colombia.'

Jack looked totally bewildered. Then understanding dawned on his face. 'He met her and gave her the joint, right?'

'A *joint*? We're talking about a psychopath who's setting up a cocaine–processing and distribution network over here. And we've reason to believe he wants to use your project to launder the proceeds.'

Jack stared at him. 'What makes you think that?'

'Intelligence.'

'So why don't you arrest him. Why are you telling me?'

Shepard grimaced. 'We don't have proof yet.'

'How do I know it's true, then?'

'This boy's a killer, Mr Ryder. He threw one of our men out of a plane in Colombia. Then he came here on his Peruvian passport, set up a factory somewhere –'

'You've told me that already, but you're not answering my question.'

'Angel Mosquera doesn't leave fingerprints behind, or witnesses. But with your cooperation we might be able to catch him.'

Jack looked incredulous. 'Let me get this straight. You want me to help trap this alleged witness-killer, incidentally collapsing our project because then we can't buy the land, but you haven't got a scrap of evidence . . .'

Shepard didn't appear to be listening. He took a miniature cassette player out of his pocket, turned up the volume control and pressed play. On came Angel's phone conversation with his father, tapped by Argetsinger's men in Medellín and relayed to Shepard in Marbella.

Jack heard Angel's voice saying he'd been offered a million dollars for an option on their land, which would 'pay for the shop and stock it'. He heard Angel's version of their talk on the way back from Puerto Banús.

Angel saying,'if I can take it over, it's the perfect laundry for us.'

'With this race-driver and God knows who else involved?'

'I'll get rid of them once I've used them.'

'What d'you mean?'

'What d'you think I mean?'

Jack sat in stunned silence, listening to the humble boy who'd asked his advice the previous day now threatening to kill him. Shepard switched it off at the end of the recording.

'Shop, stock?' Jack asked.

'They talk in code even when they think they're on a safe line,' Shepard explained. 'The shop's some kind of warehouse. Stock's the cocaine they're sending from South America, and they're talking in tons. When they sell that over here they'll have to launder a flood of cash – through your project.'

Jack tried to take it all in. 'But why me? I mean, can't you find this warehouse?'

'We're trying, but it could be in any building anywhere. And you seem to be getting close to him.'

'So it was you tailing us?'

Shepard nodded. 'You heard him tell his father he wants to take over your deal.'

'The way he put it to me, he said he wanted to invest more than just land. He even asked my advice!'

'So you've a good reason to draw him out. Say you're prepared to help if he'll give you a better deal than Nassar's offering. Say you don't like Arabs – they're into that racist crap. But you want proof that Angel's got the means to back up his mouth. You couldn't care less where the funds come from as long as you're sure he's got them.'

'And the site?'

'Have Sami Nassar pay him the option money as soon as possible. That way we can make sure you get legal title to the land once we arrest him – our side of the bargain by the way.'

58

Jack looked doubtful. 'Shouldn't we be telling Sami all this?'

'I get the impression you need the deal more than he does; that he might just pull out if he knows about this. You don't want that, and we want Angel, right?'

Jack winced.

'Leg hurting?' Shepard asked.

He shook his head. 'Suddenly that seems the least of my problems.'

'He won't go away, Mr Ryder. You want a clean project, you have to deal with the son of a bitch first.'

'It was only a joint,' Katie told Jack as they breakfasted on the terrace overlooking the pool.

'Only! You were completely stoned last night. Suppose you'd h..d an accident coming back? You're meant to be helping me, not getting in the way.'

She couldn't meet his eyes. 'How? How can I help?'

'Now more than ever!'

The desperation in his voice made her look at him.

'What I mean is . . . you could keep this place stocked up for a start. And I've got to start phoning contacts today. You could field their calls when I'm not here. And can you type? Because I can't, but we've got to churn out letters between us.'

'I'll try,' Katie said quietly. 'I promise I'll try.'

After breakfast, Jack rang the Marbella Club. An operator said Angel wasn't in his bungalow, so he left a message for him.

'We're meeting another landowner this morning,' Jack told Katie. 'We'll probably have lunch. When Angel calls back, tell him I'd like to see him late this afternoon or early this evening.'

'Here or at his hotel?'

'Doesn't matter, but you and I are sticking together tonight, understood?'

Avicomida's factory outside Madrid looked very much like the one in Bogotá. A steady stream of lorries arrived there from Barajas Airport, unloaded debris-filled carts, and departed with a fresh batch.

There were three eight-hour shifts, but the clerical workers only came in during the day. In his office above the kitchens, Victor Ribera was busy clearing invoices before they were fed into the computer system. The twenty-eight-year-old accountant was rather small, with a gaunt, ambitious face. Even though it was midsummer he was wearing a long-sleeved shirt and tie.

Five hundred one-kilo tins of pears, five hundred kilos of peaches. Ribera initialled the invoice. A hundred kilos of olives? His right hand went out to the desk-top computer and deftly found the information he wanted – Avicomida's customers really did eat that many *aceitunas*.

The next invoice was for twenty-five sheets of insulation foam, and there was a matching requisition form from the maintenance department. A relatively small sum of money. Ribera was just about to initial it when something made him look at the quantities again. Each sheet was two metres by four, making two hundred square metres in total. As he picked up the phone, his suspicious mind was already thinking of possible illicit uses it could have.

'Maintenance,' the day-shift foreman said at the other end of the line.'

'Ribera here, accounts. What d'you use sheets of poly-urethane foam for?'

'Insulation,' the foreman said.

'I know, but in what?'

'The carts of course. Keeps the food hot. Or cold, depending which side it's on. Anything else?'

'Two hundred square metres of it?' Ribera persisted. 'You don't build them down there do you?'

'As near as makes no difference! The way some of them arrive you'd think they'd been dropped out the planes. Probably have been.'

'But that many? How many in for repair right now, for example?'

An exasperated sigh. 'Hang on a minute.' The foreman shouted to somebody, who shouted something back. 'None,' he told the accountant. 'Night shift must have done them all. Is that it?'

'Yes,' Ribera said, and put down the receiver. He thought about it for a few more seconds. Each damaged cart would need a couple of square metres at most, surely. So they'd ordered enough for one hundred major repairs. Filing that away in the back of his mind, Victor Ribera signed the invoice.

Jack spent a grim morning listening to Sami on the telephone, offering options to sceptical landowners. Apparently they all said they'd think about it, but Sami glowed with optimism. Jack made himself smile too, but inside he was plagued by a horrible sinking feeling. What on earth had he let himself in for?

After lunch he was taken back to Puente Romano. In their suite Katie was two-finger typing on an Olivetti that had been delivered during the morning.

'Any calls?' he asked abruptly.

She watched him cross the room and sink wearily on to the sofa. 'Someone from FISA in Paris – I've written down his name and the message; also Angel rang to say he'd come at five –'

'He hasn't been here already, has he?'

'No, he phoned. Why?'

'Because . . . oh nothing.'

'And Elizabeth called, wondering if we were okay.'

Jack massaged his forehead. What the hell was he going to tell Liz?

'You all right?' Katie asked.

'Get me a whisky, would you?'

She obviously wanted to show him the letters she'd laboriously typed, and once he'd had the drink he made himself look at them. Katie had tried hard, and with the help of the correction tape they didn't look bad at all.

'Good work,' he said, and she smiled gratefully.

The knock on the door came at five o'clock sharp, and Katie went to answer it. From the living room Jack heard her greet Angel, Angel's lowered voice replied, and then young laughter. The little sod was chatting her up! When Katie led him into the room Jack met her eyes.

'Why don't you go for a swim,' he said firmly. 'You've been shut in here all day.'

'Don't you need me?'

'No?'

'I'll fix Angel a drink first.'

Minutes later the two men were alone, a situation Jack had been dreading. The moment they began talking, though, he felt a familiar relief wash over him, just like the start of a race. And having started Jack knew he'd finish the job. The sooner the better.

'You look tired,' Angel said. 'Worried?'

'My leg's playing up a bit, what with meeting all the landowners and trying to get them to sell us those damned options.'

'And will they?'

'What's the alternative?' Jack sipped his whisky.

'To sell their land outright.'

'You know Sami won't buy that.'

'But I might.'

Jack stared at him. 'Are you serious? I mean I'd be much happier that way. All these options smell typically Arab to me. But we're talking about twenty million dollars.'

'No problem. And if you help me, Jack, I'll double anything Nassar's offered you.'

'You've really got that kind of finance? Here, in Spain?'

'Not right now, but we will have soon.'

'Look Angel, before I could even think of going out on a limb with you I'd need proof of that. A bank reference, say.'

'I can't give you that.'

'Then you can't expect me to –'

'I think you know where it's coming from.'

'I don't care where it's coming from, as long as it's there. Now my leg's smashed I need to make money some other way than race-driving. *Any* way, but I need to make it, understand?'

'And you don't care where it comes from?'

'I couldn't give a damn.'

'And you really don't have any idea where it's coming from?'

Jack tried to laugh. Even to him it sounded B movie. The whole thing sounded B movie. 'Well, you know, a young Colombian with that much money . . .'

Angel's eyes widened almost imperceptibly.

Shit, Jack thought, *he told me he was Peruvian.*

'You want proof?' Angel asked.

'I want something.'

'And if I give it, will you help me?'

'Yes, if you keep your end of the bargain.'

Angel seemed to relax. 'All right. Can you make a trip with me tomorrow or the next day? I want to show you something.'

'Sure,' Jack said, feeling decidedly unsure.

'I'll phone you with details later this evening,' Angel said, and left.

Back in his bungalow at the Marbella Club Angel tried to contact El Carnicero in Madrid. It took three calls to reach him.

'Everything's going fine,' the scar-faced enforcer said. 'Imports arriving safely. The shop's on overtime to deal with them.'

'Good, but I've hit a problem. I need a good man and a car down here fast. A car with a big trunk.'

'You in trouble? I'll come down myself.'

'Thanks. Bring some samples while you're at it.' Angel gave him detailed delivery instructions.

63

CHAPTER EIGHT

Jack seemed to be lying to everyone.

He phoned Liz the following morning before she left for work – England was an hour behind Spain. 'Sorry I didn't call you last night.'

'Or the night before,' Liz said. 'Is everything all right?'

'Sure. Why shouldn't it be?'

'I dunno. Just wondered if it was, that's all.'

Jack attempted a chuckle. 'A lot more to do than I'd expected.'

'So you won't be back this weekend?'

'Afraid not. I'm not sure when I'll be home actually.'

Liz gave a disappointed sigh. 'Ah well, let's hope the next reunion's as good as the last one. How's the leg?'

'Itchy.'

'And Katie?'

'Ahhh . . . had a spot of bother actually.'

'Oh hell. Where'd she get it from?'

He blinked at how fast she caught on. 'Some lads in a disco. I think it was a one-off though. She's been good since then.'

'You've only been there two days!'

'Yes, well . . . listen, I've got to go to a meeting.'

'If you can't get back, would you like me to visit you?'

God yes, Jack thought. 'Let me think about it,' was all he said though. He didn't want Liz involved too.

After breakfast he joined Sami and Roland Priest in the Yorkshireman's nearby suite. It looked like an untidy design studio now, a drawing board set up near the French

64

windows and plans strewn about the place. The three of them had coffee on the terrace.

'Excuse the mess,' the Yorkshireman said. 'A year's work to do in a month for our slave-driver here.'

Sami laughed. 'You've never been happier, Roland, admit it.' He turned to Jack. 'How did you get on with young Angel by the way?'

Jack swallowed hard. 'All right. He's keen on the project but having trouble persuading his family. I gather they only sent him to deal with this because his elder brother died in a recent accident.'

'It sounds as though he doesn't have their confidence.'

'Perhaps that's why he wants me to meet their advisers. We're off to Barcelona this evening, and back tomorrow.'

Sami glanced at Jack's plastercast. 'I'm grateful for what you're doing of course, but are you up to another trip?'

'Don't worry about me. Katie's the problem.'

The Lebanese looked embarrassed. 'Ah yes. I had a difficult call from Carmen's father, rather blaming your daughter for that unfortunate incident the other night.'

'Yes, well, the point is I'm not too happy about leaving her, even for one night.'

'I'll take responsibility,' Priest volunteered. 'I've two daughters of my own, a good bit older now, mind, but I reckon I'm qualified to look after her.'

'If you're sure you don't mind.'

'Not at all.'

'I didn't even know you were married.'

Priest guffawed. 'Afraid so! My good lady doesn't like the heat or foreign food though. She tends to stay at home.'

'Good lady?' Sami said. 'What an extraordinary expression. I'd hardly describe the two I've divorced like that.'

Both of them laughed uproariously until they saw Jack's unhappy face.

'Don't worry, there'll be no fooling around while I'm responsible for Katie,' Priest assured him.

Jack had phoned Roy Shepard as soon as he had heard from Angel the previous evening. The DEA agent had listened, then said the arrangements couldn't be better. They'd cover him all the way.

How, Jack asked?

Well, Ed Wheeler could wire him up with a mike-transmitter unit, but if Angel's men searched Jack they were likely to find it and get rough.

Jack said he'd rather stick at one broken leg. So Shepard said they'd tail him with the help of a bug they'd already managed to fit to Angel's rented Mercedes. What if he came in a different car though?

No problem, Shepard assured him. Ed Wheeler would fix that too.

Now, at eight o'clock on Wednesday night, Jack and Ed Wheeler were waiting for the pick-up in the Ryders' hotel suite. Katie had been taken to dinner by Roland Priest, having promised her stepfather she'd be good while he was away. Jack was worrying about that when he heard the knock on the front door. He reached for his crutches.

Wheeler picked up Jack's suitcase and launched into the spiel they'd rehearsed earlier. 'Must have been eighty-five when we saw you race at Detroit.'

'That track makes Monaco's seem wonderful.'

'Right.' The CIA's wireman opened the door with his free hand. 'I remember, because that was my brother's Rookie year at Indy.'

The tubby Spaniard standing outside looked totally uninterested. 'Señor Ryder?' he asked.

'Yes. Who are you?'

He pointed to his Seat taxi. 'Señor Mallendo ask me fetch you.'

'Where to?'

'Marbella Club.'

'But that's practically next door.'

The Spaniard shrugged and turned towards his taxi. The two men followed him.

'It's been great talking to you,' Wheeler said. 'Maybe we can have dinner one night.'

'Good idea.'

Jack made a show of stumbling just as he reached the taxi, and the driver put out both hands to help him. Wheeler kept going to the boot of the taxi with the suitcase. He pressed the button and the lid flipped open. It took him seconds to stow the bag and find a home for the magnet-backed transmitter under a light cluster. Meanwhile Jack was hobbling round the front of the taxi, explaining to its driver that he'd be more comfortable beside him. As Jack settled into the front passenger seat, Wheeler slammed down the boot lid.

'Safe journey,' he called out.

'Thanks,' Jack said.

Wheeler hurried to his own car and got on the radio to Shepard who was calling moves from the incident room in Marbella's *Policia Municipal* station.

'A taxi's taking him to the Marbella Club,' Wheeler reported. 'It's wired.'

'Stand by,' Shepard said, and checked with the Spanish detective who was watching Angel's bungalow and car. The Mercedes hadn't moved. 'Cover the entrance,' the DEA man told Wheeler. 'He must be waiting for him there.'

But Angel wasn't. He had climbed out of a back window and slipped down to the beach an hour earlier. Then he'd strolled along it until he reached a path leading into a neighbouring development. El Carnicero was waiting for him there in a big BMW.

The taxi stopped outside the Marbella Club's reception building, and Jack struggled out of the front seat. A hotel guest wanting to go into town took his place, and the Seat left for Marbella moments later.

By now Ed Wheeler was parked on the main road with a

view of the entrance. His eyes told him the same story as the pinging receiver beside him – the taxi was coming out of the Club with a passenger. He reported to Shepard, who again checked that Angel hadn't moved and then told Wheeler to tail the taxi: he'd send someone to cover the entrance as quickly as possible.

Meanwhile Jack had walked inside the building, where a friendly receptionist phoned Angel's bungalow for him. No reply. While she was trying again, the operator said she had him on the line wanting to speak to Jack.

'Sorry about this,' Angel told him. 'My day's gone mad and I didn't want to keep you waiting. Another taxi's coming for you now.' He hung up.

Seconds later the doorman came in to say it had arrived. Jack sank into the back seat this time, praying Shepard's surveillance was working. This taxi driver didn't speak a word of English. He just kept saying Angel's name as though that explained everything. They drove west on the coast road until they reached Puerto Banús, then turned on to its broad access road and stopped halfway down it.

'Here?' Jack asked.

'Señor Mallendo.'

'Do I pay?'

'Señor Mallendo.' The driver took Jack's suitcase out of the boot and dumped it on the pavement. Then he helped him out too, and drove off.

Even at eight-thirty at night it was hot and humid. Jack felt sweat and pain building up inside his cast. God, he'd be glad to get rid of the thing. He felt something else too – people staring at him. Maybe some of them recognised him. More likely he just seemed odd, standing there on his crutches with a suitcase beside him.

One thing was sure – Angel had picked a perfect drop-off place to check whether Jack was being followed. Jack began to wonder if he had been, if Shepard had actually covered the taxi switch. Maybe he should call the whole thing off.

Just then a large grey car appeared from the *peublo blanco* coming towards him. It was a BMW, and as it drew near Jack recognised Angel in the front passenger seat. The driver pulled into the kerb beside him and Jack noticed the hideous scar on one side of his face.

Angel jumped out babbling apologies. 'So sorry I'm late . . . talking to landowners . . . Spanish time.'

He held the back door open for Jack who hesitated, then climbed in. There was a vague chemical smell in the car which he tried to identify while Angel went round to the other side and got in beside him. Petrol? No, something else. They set off towards the main road where they turned west towards Gibraltar. It was high season now and an endless stream of traffic raced along in both directions. The driver seemed content to stay in the inside lane. Jack was behind him. All he could see was the man's wiry black hair, bull neck and massive shoulders.

'Why meet me back there for heaven's sake?' Jack asked Angel.

'I have to take precautions. You should understand.'

'With me?'

Angel looked sheepish. 'I seem to have offended you. I'm sorry, but you'll understand why all this was necessary soon.'

'I hope so.'

They drove along in silence until Angel pointed through Jack's side window. 'Look, there's the site. It's important you know which is our land.'

The BMW turned down the ramp towards the sea, black now in the fading light. No one else was around. 'See the sixth roadway in from the east boundary?'

Jack focused his eyes and started counting them. He didn't see Angel reach under the seat in front of him and bring out a small plastic bag.

Angel leant closer. 'We own everything from there to –'

He ripped the bag open and clamped the ether-soaked pad inside it over Jack's nose and mouth. His victim turned at the sudden stench, but was sucking in air as the pad hit his face. Jack gulped down ether instead. He tried to jerk back but banged his head on the side window, and felt pain and overwhelming dizziness at the same time. He grabbed Angel's wrists, but the car must have stopped because the driver was fighting him too now. Then Jack was falling away from them into darkness.

Kneeling on the floor Angel laid him out along the back seat. He looked round to see if anyone had noticed the struggle but the traffic was too far away. El Carnicero handed him a syringe and an ampoule from the glove compartment. Angel loaded it, then stabbed the needle into a vein in Jack's wrist and squeezed home the plunger.

'Stick him every couple of hours,' he told the enforcer. 'Put him in the boot when you're in the hills. Know what to do after that?'

El Carnicero nodded.

Angel climbed out just before the next town, and walked in when the BMW had gone. A taxi took him back to Marbella.

CHAPTER NINE

Darkness. Agony.

Jack felt himself floating upwards, towards the dark and the pain, out of eerily bright, sickeningly green depths. He was lying on his left side with his aching legs drawn up in a foetal position. But when he tried to straighten them his feet hit a barrier of some sort. He raised his right hand a few inches and felt a solid lid.

Buried alive! Jack thought, fighting back panic.

Well, if so, there must be an earthquake in progress. The coffin was bouncing about, sliding him around inside it. Not a coffin, a car boot of course – the BMW's boot. That explained the constant movement and the smell of exhaust fumes. Jack felt spasms in his throat and knew he was going to be sick. He threw up violently, then tried to roll away from the mess, but his cast jammed against the boot lid. Jack sank back into his previous position, utterly drained but clearer in the head.

At least he wasn't tied up. At least he was alive! And if Angel had wanted to kill him, wouldn't he have done it straight away? Or had he misjudged the injection? Academic, Jack thought, because I'm going to suffocate in here.

He willed himself to raise a fist and began to hammer on the boot lid. The effort was murder, but he made himself keep it up, the noise reassuring him that he could still do something.

And then the car was stopping. Engine off, a door opening, footsteps . . . the boot lid flipping up and a light coming on at the same time, unbelievable relief as cool air flooded in . . . and a hand coming straight for his face, the stench of ether again, the same sickening giddiness as he tried to struggle.

Just time to think, *not very clever* . . .

When Jack came round again he felt as though he was choking to death. Then he threw up again, and found that he could breathe almost normally.

And as his head cleared he thought, I'm still here . . . so they're not trying to kill me . . . and I'm not going to die, damn it, but if I get out of this they bloody well might.

They? Whoever the hand belonged to – presumably Angel or his scar-faced driver. Well, neither of them was going to help him escape, so he'd just have to work it out for himself.

First thing, don't hammer on the boot lid!

Second, move your left leg about because you can't feel it any more. Five minutes of limited movement – knees up to his chest, stretched out to the side of the boot, back to his chest again – and pain was throbbing through it. That was almost welcome now.

Third point, find something to hit the bastards with. Where did they keep the jack in these cars? Probably in the spare-wheel well, but he was lying on top of that, dammit! Jack tried to slide towards the rear seat and scrabbled round the edge of the carpeting with his hands, but there was no way he could lift the panel underneath. He put a hand up to wipe the sweat out of his eyes and brushed something under the boot lid. A plastic tray of some sort, about the size of a book, with a wing nut recessed into it. He turned the nut and the tray fell towards him, except for one edge which stayed fixed to the lid. Jack felt around inside it – a tool kit!

A screwdriver . . . pliers . . . a plug-spanner: now that would make a wicked knuckleduster! Jack slotted the screwdriver through a hole in the plug spanner, then clenched the cylinder in his fist with the blade sticking out between his fingers. That might do the trick. Now shut up for a while, he told himself.

He didn't have long to wait. The BMW slowed, turned right, and crunched over a different surface. Then it stopped and a door opened. Jack did the dead act he'd been practising – still on his left side facing back, eyes wide open and staring, left hand clawed round his throat as though he'd choked to death, loaded right hand hidden behind his back. He'd smeared his face with vomit to make it look worse.

Footsteps crunching on gravel now . . . a click, the boot lid going up a fraction and the light coming on . . . the lid lifting more. Jack just lying there, not breathing at all now.

'*Mierda!*' someone said. A hand came down to his head, hovered in front of his nose to see if he was breathing. Then the scarred driver's worried face appeared inches away from Jack's.

NOW! Jack thought, swinging his right fist round from behind his back and slamming it into El Carnicero's head with all the force he could muster.

There was a sudden scream as the blade pierced the man's cheek, another yell as he jerked back and cracked his head on the boot lid. The driver ducked forward again and Jack punched his fist into his nose, heard a crunch and felt blood spattering down on him. Then the man had both hands to his own face and was reeling away.

GET OUT! Jack told himself. He put both hands on the sill, but his legs wouldn't support him. *Want to stay here?* he asked them, and something gave him the strength to swing his right leg over the sill and find the ground, then drag the rest of his body after it. Jack tried to see where he was. It was night-time but at least his eyes had adjusted to darkness. Moonlight showed up several stationary lorries and a few cars in a makeshift parking area. Between those shapes was the glare of artificial light from a building about fifty yards behind them. Some sort of transport stop? Could he reach it? Jack was wondering where his crutches were when he realised the driver was coming for him again.

73

He still had one hand up to his gory face but the other was bunched into a fist. Jack put both arms back on the boot sill to steady himself, let him come closer, closer still, then swung his cast up into the man's crutch. Pain exploded in Jack's leg, but his opponent went down moaning and clutching his groin.

Jack glanced at the building between the lorries, decided it was too far, and began to hop and pull himself round the BMW towards the driver's door. *Please let the keys be in the ignition!* he prayed. But they weren't, and he wasn't going back to ask for them. Jack started to hop towards the nearest car, a Renault 18. That was locked too. And now he could hear the driver groaning and cursing somewhere behind him, getting closer. Jack's heart and legs felt as though they were going to burst as he started his ridiculous hopping stumble again, this time towards a battered old Volkswagen Beetle.

Please God, PLEASE! The driver's door opened in his hand, and yes, YES, the keys were inside. Jack collapsed into the seat and dragged his cast in after him with both hands. The man was almost on top of him now, blood-smeared teeth bared in a snarl, murder in his eyes. Jack slammed the door and banged down the lock. A moment later his assailant was hammering on the window, trying to cave it in.

Jack concentrated on starting the Beetle. He couldn't use the clutch because of his leg, so he rammed the gear stick into second, then turned the key so that the battery jerked the old car forward. He squeezed the accelerator, and the engine coughed and banged into life. Never had exhaust fumes smelt sweeter! The man was hanging on to the door handle though, running alongside the car and shouting, but as it picked up speed he was forced to let go.

Where to now? Jack thought. Into a ditch unless he got the lights on! He tried for them, put on the windscreen wipers instead, then the indicators, and finally found what he wanted. Jack was heading away from the building towards an exit to a road. Should he turn back to the building for help? But suppose that was where he was being taken? A moment to make up his mind . . . and he turned on to the road.

With luck there'd be a police station in the next pueblo, or was it the *Guardia Civil* out here? Out here – an undulating two-lane blacktop heading almost straight towards a cleft in a range of hills. Farmland on either side. Not a house in sight. A pair of lights was coming towards him, a lorry judging by their height. Jack flashed his main beam on and off, on and off, and slowed down. He got full beam in the face in return, and the lorry whined past him at undiminished speed. So much for that idea.

Jack whipped the burbling Beetle along with the gear-stick, changing up with just a lift of the accelerator, down by shifting into neutral, blipping the throttle and then finding a lower gear. No problem. The stick was even by his right hand, just like a Formula One car. Somewhat less power though! A smell of burning rubber competed with the leaky exhaust now. Look on the bright side, Jack thought, the tank's a quarter full. And then he glanced in the rear-view mirror.

Powerful headlights ripped through the belly of the night as they raced closer. It might not be the BMW though. Sure, Jack thought, crunching down a gear and flooring the accelerator as he came to a rise.

He reached the cleft in the hills just before whoever it was caught up with him. The road narrowed as it went into the canyon and began to twist and climb along one of its steep walls. That wall was to Jack's left. He was in the right-hand lane, with just a strip of dirt and an occasional barrier protecting him from the drop to a dried-up river bed.

Jack arrived at a hairpin bend with the other car right behind him. Now we'll find out, he thought. As he started to turn, his head was rocked back by a slamming impact – the BMW was trying to ram him off the road. Jack let the

Beetle spin through 180 degrees, effectively taking the bend, then controlled it with opposite lock and set off uphill. The BMW screeched to a halt inches away from the barriers, reversed, and tyre-squeeled after him.

Jack charged on, thrashing the grumble-spit engine as hard as he dared. If that big mother got ahead of him it was all over. Oh for a Porsche engine back there, uprated suspension, a set of slicks ... just like twenty years ago when he'd started out in the sport, racing an old Ford Anglia against the rich types in their works replicas and bloody well beating them. How? Like this.

As the BMW caught up again Jack began to weave from side to side, anticipating its attempts to overtake and frustrating them. They were nearly at the next hairpin – a right-hander this time – but Jack kept going flat out towards it and weaved further right than usual. They should have been braking by now, but the big car leapt at the opening and tried to overtake. Sucker! Jack yanked up the handbrake and spun the Beetle's tail round again as the BMW locked up its tyres and skidded straight into a steel barrier with a tremendous clang.

Let it stay there, Jack prayed.

But the impact had only crumpled a front corner. The BMW backed away from the precipice and chased after him again, just one of its headlights slashing the darkness now.

Only one thing for it, Jack thought – *put him over the edge*.

The road followed the contours of the canyon wall. As his pursuer closed in, Jack began to dart about again. They were coming up to a blind left-hander with an unprotected drop to their right. Jack weaved left, and lifted off the accelerator for an instant. The big car began to overtake round the outside of the corner, centrifugal force pushing it out towards the edge. The moment it drew level, Jack broadsided the Beetle into it, bounced off and swung back for another go.

76

He glimpsed his opponent's shocked face as the BMW skittered towards the edge. Jack pulled away for one final shove, but something made him look back at the road as they rounded the bend. Lights were coming straight at him on his side. Jack saw a lorry looming up and heard the ghastly screech of its brakes. He threw the VW's wheel over towards the rock-face and collided with it. The Beetle tipped up and crash-banged along it in a wall-of-death act, somehow missing the lorry, but then toppled on to its roof and slid along the road upside down in a shower of sparks until it slammed into the rock-face.

Not again! Jack thought in the instant before his head hit the windscreen and he blacked out.

'What the hell was going on?' the lorry driver asked as he helped carry Jack's body to the BMW.

'Some kind of nut,' El Carnicero said.

'He tried to overtake me in that heap and lost control.'

'But how could he drive with a busted leg?' They laid Jack out on the back seat. 'And your face . . .'

'I'll get him to hospital.'

'What about the police?'

'Afterwards. Want to come?'

The lorry driver looked at the road, wondering what speed he'd been doing when he'd jammed on the brakes, what kind of trail he'd left. He turned back to the scarred stranger who was covered in blood. 'Doesn't need two of us, does it?'

CHAPTER TEN

Jack was sure he was dreaming. Someone kept mispronouncing his name, but he couldn't see anyone, just a blood-red glow.

'Can you hear me, Meester Ryder?' The voice seemed to come from behind him.

Jack opened his eyes a fraction, felt burning white light, and screwed them shut again. He tried to put his hands up to his face but couldn't move them.

'Don' fight. We don' wan' to hurt you.'

'Christ . . . that takes some believing!'

'We had to be sure you were alone, that you don' lead anyone here.'

'Where's here? Who the hell are you?'

No answer. 'Open your eyes, slowly.'

Jack did, gradually adjusting to the light from a bare bulb over his head. He was strapped to a high-backed office chair, naked except for his underpants and the plastercast. That looked rather the worse for wear, and he began to feel pain inside it again. Jack could move his head a little, and saw that he was in some kind of windowless room. A wall in front of him that didn't quite reach the ceiling was made of clear plastic bags filled with something white.

'Pure cocaine hydrochloride,' the voice behind him said. 'Worth $300 a gram on the street *before* they cut it with shit. You're looking at over a tonne. We sell a tonne a month. Can you do the sums?'

Jack closed his eyes wearily.

A hand slapped him hard on both cheeks. 'Concentrate, Meester Ryder! We don' bring you here to sleep.'

'Screw you!'

Two more stinging slaps. Jack looked at the man who was in front of him now, but a black balaclava hid his face. Whoever he was, he took what seemed to be an eye-drop bottle out of his pocket and held it up so that Jack could see the label.

'Read it.'

'Cobalt Thio . . . Thiocyanate.'

'Tha's right.' He walked to the wall of bags, pulled one out, returned to Jack and dumped it in his lap. The man drew a flick-knife out of a pocket with his free hand, released the blade and slashed an opening in the plastic. Putting the knife away, he squeezed the teat on the bottle, then unscrewed the eye-dropper and held it over the exposed flakes. Another squeeze, and drops of liquid splashed down, turning the flakes bright blue.

'Terrific,' Jack said. 'What's your next trick?'

'That proves it is cocaine. But maybe you think I choose a special bag? Maybe you like to choose one yourself?'

'No, I believe you. All I want to do is get out of here.'

'You will, you will. But first you try some.'

Jack stared at him. 'You're kidding?'

The balaclavaed wonder shook his head. 'You made a difficult journey to see this. We mus' be sure you know what it is. Jus' snort a little for me.'

'No way!'

He shrugged and nodded at someone behind Jack, who stepped into view for a moment. Jack glimpsed the scar-faced man again, but was more interested in what he was handing over — a hypodermic syringe.

Jack began a futile struggle.

'Goodbye Meester Ryder,' the man in the balaclava said, stabbing the needle into Jack's arm. 'Enjoy the trip.'

He felt nothing except the pain of the jab for some time. Then WHOOSH! A beautiful firework exploded in Jack's heart, sending fiery fingers racing through his veins. Another one blossomed in his head, filling it with dazzling light.

He felt himself blasted off the ground, still strapped in the chair, as though it was an ejector seat. Jack ducked his head into his shoulders for the inevitable collision with the ceiling, but it never came. This was scary but fun, like one of those fairground rides. Jack heard himself laughing. God this was funny . . .

Where had he heard that before?

From Katie! And as he realised the answer he began to fall, faster and faster as though the parachute hadn't opened. He'd be killed when he hit the floor, and then who'd look after his stepdaughter?

Jack passed out, screaming her name.

It was Thursday morning.

In Marbella Angel had already been to the Land Registry to find out who were the owners of the rest of the site: a Brazilian, two Germans, a Spaniard living in Madrid, and another one in Marbella. He decided to start with the local first, a notorious but ageing playboy.

Angel made an appointment to see him that morning, and duly arrived at a luxury villa in Los Monteros on the Málaga side of the town. The playboy was a tall man in his late forties. He'd been through three wives and a large part of his family's fortune, and the effort was beginning to show. He gave Angel a somewhat supercilious greeting, then led him on to a terrace overlooking his sub-tropical garden.

'As I told you on the phone,' Angel began, 'my family owns most of the site. We're interested in buying the rest.'

His host smiled, clearly pleased with himself. 'You're not the only one.'

'I'm aware of that, but we're willing to buy outright.'

'For how much?'

'A hundred and fifty thousand dollars an acre.'

'Young man, the deal I've been offered values it at two hundred thousand dollars.'

'Yes, but if you're referring to a certain Lebanese gentleman, he's only interested in an option to buy.'

'Perhaps, but there must be something in these rumours of a Spanish Monaco or why would this Arab be interested? And I hear the Saudi royal family's backing him. Just who do you represent, by the way?'

Angel left shortly afterwards.

From his bungalow in the Marbella Club he managed to contact the Spaniard in Madrid and one of the Germans. Despite upping his offer, their responses were similarly snotty. So he couldn't take over the project by buying the rest of the land. Anyway, a further change of ownership might alienate the town hall.

What now? Angel could sulk and refuse to sell Nassar his land, but that would only result in his taking the project elsewhere. Far better to let the Arab be the figurehead, and gain control of the holding company later. Did Nassar really own that critical twenty per cent he said he had kept for himself? And what had Jack meant about having an interest in the company? Angel decided to find out.

He phoned the Ryders' apartment at midday and spoke to Katie. 'Your stepfather asked me to send you his love and say he'll be back this evening.'

'Oh, thanks.' She sounded puzzled. 'Why didn't he come back with you, though?'

'I had a meeting here I couldn't cancel. He volunteered to stay and persuade the doubters. He's been fantastic.'

'You'd think he'd have phoned me.'

'Don't worry, he's fine. Just a little concerned about you.'

She sighed. 'Well, I've been here all the time. Mr Priest's seen to that.'

'*All* the time?'

'I get to swim now and then.'

'Hey,' Angel said, 'why don't we . . . what I mean is *may* I take you to lunch? How about that place on your beach. We won't even leave the hotel then.'

'Great,' Katie said, feeling herself blushing.

*

81

Just after one o'clock Angel walked along the beach from the Marbella Club, wearing loose cotton trousers and a tank top. He spotted Katie lying on a sunbed in front of the Puente Romano Beach Club. All she had on was a small turquoise bikini, and he took his time reaching her so that he could admire her exquisite little body. But there was also an innocence about her that touched him, and he felt an unexpected pang of remorse about what he was going to do.

Katie saw him coming towards her, and sat up smiling. 'Hi, Angel.'

'Hallo. Want to stay in the sun a bit longer?'

'No thanks, I'm baked and I'm starving.' She got up from the sunbed and tied a matching wrap round her waist.

They walked side by side to the beach restaurant, an open-sided, terracotta-floor-tiled area with a cane roof. Mouth-watering smells wafted from the barbecue pit at one end, and an old fishing boat in the centre was loaded with sea-food and salads. Angel had booked a table, where they ordered lobster and Cuba Libres, then settled back to wait for them.

'I've been stuck in worse places,' Angel said teasingly, looking at the sun-lovers on the beach and the swimmers splashing about in the sea.

Katie laughed. 'Did I make it sound grim? It's just boring having to stay in one place.'

'Why? I mean why d'you have to?'

She looked embarrassed.

'Don't tell me if you don't want to.'

But she did. Angel was almost her age, and she rather liked him already . . . a little more than that. Their drinks arrived, and they sipped them through long straws.

'I haven't exactly earned this holiday,' Katie said. 'Actually I've just been kicked out of school for . . . well, for doing drugs.'

Angel's head rocked back.

'Shocked?'

'It's just you don't look the type. Why did your stepfather bring you here then?'

'My mother wants to get married again. She and her new man don't want me in the way, and Jack said he'd look after me. The way he put it *he* needed looking after, but I think he was trying to be kind. Isn't this boring?'

'No. I've been thinking about my family too since I came here.' Suddenly he looked sad and lonely.

'Are your parents . . . splitting up too?'

Angel shook his head. 'My brother died in an accident recently. That's why I'm doing this deal instead of him.'

Instinctively she touched his hand on the table. 'I'm sorry, rabbiting on about my stupid problems when you've –'

'But I'm interested, really.' He took her hand and met her eyes. 'You're very pretty, Katie.'

'And you're very nice.'

A waiter arrived with their barbecued lobsters and Angel moved closer to help her extract all the flesh. It provided an excuse for more body contact and laughter.

'Think I'll be allowed to take you out?' he asked.

'I don't know. You see, I took drugs again the night we got here. Carmen, you remember her, took me to Puerto Banús, and we met some boys in a disco who gave us a joint. God, it was awful!'

'I know.'

'You do?'

'Sure. The stuff they sell here tastes like . . . I can't say it in front of you!' They both laughed.

'I didn't think *you* were the type who did dope,' Katie said.

'What's a drug?' Angel was serious now. 'I mean, we're drinking rum. You seen alcoholics? And cigarettes. Ever see someone dying of cancer? Maybe I shouldn't be talking like this –'

'You're right, it's so hypocritical.'

'That's the word. Like where I live, the Indians have

chewed coca leaves for thousands of years. It helps them work high up in the Andes. Our doctors prescribe coca-leaf tea for mountain sickness. But over here it's a dirty word.'

'Coke?'

'Yes. It's not habit-forming, and it's the best thing when you're down.'

'Really?'

Angel looked concerned. 'Maybe I shouldn't be telling you this. I mean if your Dad found out –'

'I won't tell him.'

'Well, if you want to try it . . .'

'You've got some?'

'For when I start thinking about my brother, sad things like that. Or when I just want to be up.'

'Here? I mean with you now?'

'Sure,' Angel said.

Katie let Angel into her apartment, then went to Roland Priest's and knocked on his door.

The Yorkshireman opened it. 'Back already?'

'I want to get on with those letters for my stepfather.'

'Good girl. Have you heard from him?'

She hesitated. 'Yes. He'll be back this evening.'

'Everything all right?'

'Yes, thanks.'

'I'll leave you to it then.'

When she returned to her suite, Angel was leafing through a motoring magazine on the sofa.

'Okay?' he asked.

'Just wish I'd spoken to Dad, that's all.'

'He's fine, don't worry.' Angel flipped the magazine on to the coffee table and took a small silver box out of his trouser pocket. He opened the lid. Inside there were two compartments, one filled with white powder, the other containing a tiny spoon with a pointed bowl.

Katie couldn't keep her eyes off the box, fascinated and afraid at the same time. 'Coke?'

Angel nodded. In fact it was cocaine hydrochloride cut with amphetamine sulphate, a jolting mix designed to impress new users – or stun them. Angel spooned a thin line on to the lid, put a rolled up banknote to one nostril, pinched the other one shut, and then snorted up the powder. He closed his eyes tightly to hide the initial rush from Katie, then opened them and made himself smile at her. 'See? Nothing to it. I feel great, no problems. You try.'

She sat down beside him, not taking her eyes off the box as he spooned out a thicker rail. Angel handed her the tube and held the box up to her face. 'Go on.'

Katie looked nervous but he smiled reassuringly. She put the straw to her nose, bent forward, and sniffed up sharply.

Nothing. Then her whole body began to twitch and jerk as though she was having a fit. Her eyes were wide open and watering, her nose on fire, and she started to gasp for breath.

Angel grabbed her shoulders. 'You're okay, you're okay.'

Suddenly she stopped shaking, and slumped against him. 'Feel . . . better . . . bit sick.'

'Lie down for a while.' He lowered her on to the sofa and lifted her legs up on to it. As he did so the turquoise wrap fell open and he stared down at her almost naked body. Cocaine-fuelled desire welled up inside him, but then another emotion caught him by surprise – a burning tenderness that almost made him cry. He wanted her badly, but it had to be beautiful for both of them. It would ruin it if he took her now, like this.

Angel covered up her legs again and stroked the hair out of her face. Katie had her eyes closed, as though in a trance-like sleep. He reminded himself what he'd really come for, and tiptoed away.

There were two bedrooms in the apartment. He guessed Jack's was the bigger one with the double bed and French windows leading out to another terrace. He found what he was looking for in a small desk set against the wall – papers to do with the project. Tucked inside a bound proposal were some handwritten notes, and a typed contract of employment signed by Sami Nassar. He read it with mounting excitement. Jack had been offered twenty thousand dollars a month, and an option on one million shares – two per cent of the holding company. Added to the Mosqueras' forty-nine per cent option, that would give them control. Perfect!

Taking a list of numbers out of his pocket, Angel picked up the phone and dialled Madrid. His second call found El Carnicero. 'How's the tourist?'

'Had problems getting him here, but he's seen the sights. Needs a doctor though.'

'Christ, what happened?'

'He got into a fight.'

Angel wiped sweat from his forehead. 'Can you get him back here?'

'Yes, but he won't appreciate the scenery.'

They arranged a rendezvous not far from Marbella, and Angel put down the phone. He went back to Katie who was still sprawled on the sofa.

Her eyes fluttered open. 'Where've you been?'

'Had to call someone.' He knelt down beside her and stroked her cheek. 'How you feeling?'

'Good, now you're back. Don't leave me again.'

'Don't worry,' Angel told her, 'I won't.'

CHAPTER ELEVEN

When Jack came round in the dark hours of Friday morning, he was strapped into the front passenger seat of a Mercedes. Angel was driving.

Closing his eyes again, Jack moved his limbs just enough to discover whether they were still tied up. Only a seat belt restrained him now, but his left leg hurt abominably. He decided to throttle Angel with his bare hands and was slowly turning towards him when the Colombian noticed the movement.

'Hallo, Jack. Glad you're –'

He grabbed Angel's neck with both hands and tried to choke him. Angel jammed on the brakes, throwing his attacker forward and sending the Mercedes into a screeching skid. It stopped sideways on the road.

'What are you doing?' Angel yelled, fighting him off.

'Trying to kill you!'

'But we're partners now.'

Jack stopped struggling, dumbfounded. 'You can't be serious? You have me kidnapped, roughened up, injected with God knows what –'

'We're not playing games. You wanted to know our business. Other people do too. I had to be sure which side you were on, and now I am. You were clean, you weren't followed – you're one of us.'

'Great,' Jack said ironically. 'What are the other benefits?'

'I help you take up your option, and you help me take over the company.'

'How the hell d'you know about that? Anyway, why should I help you?'

'Because when we succeed, I'll give you two million shares.'

Jack groaned. 'I'd trade the lot for a doctor right now: I think my leg's broken again.'

'I'm taking you to the Marbella Clinic, if you let me! Stick to the story I told them – you fell down some stairs.'

'Just get me there. Where are we, by the way?'

Angel reversed and then set off again. 'Not far from Marbella.'

'Katie! Does she know –'

'Relax. I told her the same story, and said I was going to fetch you. She wanted to come but –'

'You've seen her?'

Angel glanced at Jack's angry face. 'No, I phoned.'

'Good. Keep it that way.'

The Marbella Clinic was a small but modern hospital on the eastern outskirts of the town. The coast road to Málaga passed right in front of it, while behind was a fishing port.

While Jack was being X-rayed, Angel repeated and embellished the story to a sceptical doctor. No bones were broken, but the battered cast was cut away to reveal severe bruising. Jack would have to stay there for observation, the doctor insisted, and he needed rest.

When Angel had gone, the doctor did some extra tests. Jack fell into an exhausted sleep before they were finished.

Almost twelve hours later he woke up in one of the clinic's private rooms. Roy Shepard was waiting at his bedside, and Jack heard him breathe a heartfelt sigh of relief.

'Thank God you're okay,' the DEA agent said. 'I thought we'd lost you.'

Jack blinked sleep out of his eyes. 'How . . . d'you know I was here?'

'Your doctor was suspicious of Angel's story and ran some tests. There were traces of cocaine in your blood, so he rang the *Brigada de Estupefacientes*. They tipped me off. You up to telling me what happened?'

'Once I've spoken to my daughter.' Jack phoned Katie at the hotel. She was clearly distressed but calmed down when he repeatedly assured her he was all right. He told her to come and see him in half an hour's time, and to take a taxi.

Then Jack gave Roy Shepard all the information he could: the pick-up in Puerto Banús and the knock-out; escape and recapture in a canyon he could describe pretty well; the proof Jack had demanded – a roomful of dope; no idea where that was though; no idea how he'd got back to Marbella either.

'You did an incredible job,' Shepard said when he'd finished, 'but we really blew it. Thank God he decided you were on your own, or you'd probably be dead. Better to get you and your daughter back to England as soon as possible, though.'

Jack forced himself up on an elbow. 'Let Angel sell that stuff and take over our project? Sod that!'

'You've done all you can. Leave it to us now.'

'Have I hell! You know he trusts me, or I wouldn't be here. So let me finish what I started. That bastard owes me, and I'm going to collect.'

'Collect what?'

'His land for a start. You said if he sells us that option you'd arrange legal title, whatever happened to him, right?'

'Right, but –'

'Put that in writing?'

'Yes but –'

'Put it in writing!'

Shepard sighed and shook his head. 'I admire you, Jack, but d'you really understand what they're capable of?'

'What more can they do to me, for God's sake?'

'Or your daughter?' he said quietly.

'All right, I'll get her out of here, but I'm not running away. I won't let Sami and Roland down, and frankly I need the money.'

The American met his eyes. 'You'd have to go on working undercover. Pretend you're friends with the creep while trying to find out who *his* friends are. And a lot of the time we won't be able to cover you in case he gets suspicious. Are you prepared for all that?'

Jack nodded. 'If it helps catch the bastard.'

When Jack told Katie he was sending her home, she burst into tears.

'Look at me,' he said. 'One fall and I'm flat on my back in hospital again. I'm in no fit state to look after you.'

'But I'm meant to be looking after *you*.'

'Well, it hasn't worked out that way.'

Katie stopped crying and stared at him. 'Is this something to do with Angel?'

'No, but I don't want you seeing him.'

'Why?'

'Because . . . I've told you, it's nothing to do with him.'

'Then it's still that joint.'

Jack nodded.

'Come on, Dad, it was no worse than getting tipsy; and don't tell me you never did that when you were seventeen.'

'Things are different –'

'You just want to get rid of me like everyone else.' She started sobbing again.

'Look Katie, I can't really explain –'

'You don't have to! Anyway, where's home?'

Good question. When Katie had left him, Jack phoned his ex-wife. He told her the lie about why he was in hospital again, and asked if she would have her daughter back for a while.

'You made a promise,' Anna said coldly.

'But I didn't know this would happen.'

'Something always happens, Jack. I had to look after her on my own for years, in sickness and in health. Remember that phrase? Anyway, Courtney and I are getting married next week, and then we're off on honeymoon.'

'Couldn't you delay it?'

'No. You'll just have to manage.'

'But Anna –'

'Do I really have to threaten you with alimony proceedings again?'

'You just did,' Jack said angrily, and slammed down the phone.

He thought about his family, but his widowed mother was too old for this sort of thing now, and his only brother lived in Canada. Finally he called Liz, told her the hospital story too, then asked her advice on what to do with Katie.

'Stop treating her like a criminal,' Liz said.

'Oh come on! She's . . . well she's in the way here, that's all.'

'She's in everyone's way apparently. Someone better start loving that girl or she'll go right off the rails.'

Jack didn't know what to say. If he opened his mouth he'd only be telling more lies.

Liz filled the silence. 'Listen, why don't I join you next week for a few days? Let's see how Katie and I get on. If we do, she can come home and stay with me for a while.'

It was typically generous of her, but Jack hesitated. He didn't want Liz involved, but what was the alternative?

'Thanks,' he said finally. 'You're terrific.'

'Keep her busy until I get there,' Liz said.

Keep Katie busy! Easier said than done from a hospital bed. Jack had been ordered to rest but his mind wouldn't let him. He kept going over the problems and trying to come up with solutions. Seeking some respite he turned on the television set in the corner of his room.

The mid-afternoon news: Gorbachev shaking hands with Reagan . . . politicians making speeches . . . Ballesteros playing golf somewhere . . . a Formula One car crashing heavily and bursting into flames – one of Frank Brady's cars! Of course: the French Grand Prix was on Sunday and the first qualifying session was today. Jack tried to understand what was being said about the driver but the picture changed to a weather chart.

Katie had brought in some of his things including his address book. Jack grabbed it, reached for the phone on the bedside table and started dialling. It took some doing, but eventually he managed to get through to the Circuit Paul Ricard near Marseilles.

'Jack Ryder here. I'd like to speak to someone in Frank Brady's team.'

'Wait please,' a Frenchwoman trilled. 'I try for you.'

Jack gripped the silent receiver for several minutes. Suddenly he heard racing engines in the background, and then a familiar no-nonsense voice.

'Brady speaking.'

'It's Jack Ryder here, calling from Spain. I just saw the shunt on television. What happened?'

'What happened is I put some arsehole with more sponsorship than talent in your car.'

'But is he all right?'

'Unfortunately yes, which means he'll probably wreck the spare tomorrow!'

Jack burst out laughing. Same old Frank.

'Glad you're amused. We're missing you, Jackie boy, I'll tell you that.'

This was new. The team-owner had visited him once since the accident. 'Missing me?' Jack asked. 'How come?'

'Don't be so modest. I'm just keeping the seat warm until you're fit again. In the meantime I'd like to talk to you about this project you're involved in.'

So that was it. Frank Brady was an entrepreneur who had turned his hobby into a business. He was always on the look-out for opportunities, and twisting Jack's phone call round like this was just his style.

'How d'you know about it?' Jack asked.

'Because you've contacted practically everyone except me.'

'Just the authorities, Frank. It's still at the planning stage.'

'Never mind the bureaucrats: I make things happen in this sport, and don't you forget it.'

Jack chuckled.

'I'm serious,' Brady said. 'Get yourself here and we'll see the people who matter.'

'You mean this weekend?'

'Where are you now?'

'In Marbella.'

'Right. My plane'll collect you from Málaga Airport at fourteen hundred hours tomorrow. Don't keep it waiting.'

'But Frank . . . my stepdaughter's with me.'

'Bring her too.'

Jack was about to argue when he remembered Liz's advice about Katie. 'We'll be there,' he told Brady.

That evening in Avicomida's factory outside Madrid, Victor Ribera was working late on the month-end accounts. The gaunt-faced accountant often stayed on well into the night, sacrificing family and social life to his obsessive ambition. Being the clever son of desperately poor parents had made him that way.

Ribera was scanning a row of figures on his computer screen before jotting down the total, when one of them caught his eye. A relatively small amount but somehow familiar. He looked left for the corresponding item – twenty-five sheets of insulation foam.

Twenty-five *more* sheets. Already? This time he was going to check it out for himself. Ribera phoned his wife and told her he'd be very late tonight. The night shift clocked on at ten o'clock, and shortly afterwards he started his supper of stale bread, cold tortilla and lukewarm coffee. He thought about his boss: the finance director had left at six as always, after asking him to have the accounts ready by Monday morning. The fat pig was probably stuffing his face in one of Madrid's top restaurants by now, along with his even fatter sow of a wife. Each bitter mouthful of Ribera's meal made him more determined that his sacrifices would pay off one day.

His thoughts were disturbed when his office door opened. He turned to see a man in his twenties in maintenance department overalls.

'Saw your light,' the mechanic said. 'Thought it'd been left on by mistake.'

An employee concerned about wasting the firm's electricity? Ribera was instantly suspicious. 'I'm doing month-end accounts,' he said evenly.

'Will it take long?'

'I hope not. My wife's expecting me.'

'Need anything from downstairs? I'll switch the stair lights on if you do.'

'No thanks. I'll stay here until I've finished. Then I'll go straight home.'

'All right. Good night then.'

'Good night,' Ribera said, and watched him leave.

He waited another half hour before leaving his office and groped his way down the stairs to the ground floor without turning the lights on. Then he crept along the corridor that led past the noisy kitchens, breathing in greasy cooking smells, until he reached the back part of the factory. It was partitioned off from the rest, and an internal door led into the maintenance department. Ribera grasped the handle, then pushed it down and shoved the door. It wouldn't open.

Was it his imagination or had all noise ceased on the other side?

'Who is it?' a voice demanded.

'Ribera, the accountant.'

'What d'you want?'

'I need to check stock for the month-end accounts.'

Whispering; then, 'Can't it wait?'

'It'll only take a minute.'

'The door's jammed.'

'Well unjam it or I'll come round to the back entrance. And if that's jammed too, I'll call my director!'

More muttering. Finally the door handle was jerked up and down a few times and the door opened.

'That's fixed it,' the night-shift foreman said unconvincingly. He was about thirty, with an unshaven face and rat-like eyes.

In front of Ribera was a line of service bays with lorries and vans in some of them. He began to walk along the line with the foreman keeping pace.

'What you looking for?'

Ignoring him, the accountant stopped in a bay full of empty meal carts. The panels had been stripped off some of them. Ribera looked at the docket stuck on one of the carts, then at a second and a third. They'd come off a flight from Bogotá. 'What's wrong with them?'

'Damaged.'

'They don't look it.'

The mechanics had stopped working and were staring at them now. The foreman tried to laugh away the silence. 'You're sharp. It's the insulation actually. Just seems to wear out. You know, hot food goes cold, cold food melts.'

Ribera examined a cart that was missing its outer panels. He looked at the cavity where insulation had been, then at a replacement sheet on the ground. He picked it up. 'That explains all the foam you're using.'

'Aaah. Satisfied now?'

'Frankly I thought you were pinching it to use at home.'

An explosion of mirth. 'Hear that, lads?' the foreman asked, turning to share the joke with the mechanics. They seemed to think it was hilarious too.

'I'd just like to see the old stuff,' Ribera said.

Tense silence again. 'What?'

'You know, the foam you're throwing away. Just to make sure that's what you *are* doing with it.'

They were eye to eye now. 'Come on,' the foreman said quietly. He led the way along the back wall to a pile of slabs.

They did look old, Ribera decided; a faded beige instead of the bright yellow replacement material. Just my nasty mind he thought, picking up one of the slabs . . . and finding he needed both hands to do so. It weighed much more than the new insulation, as though there were something inside it . . . something from Colombia! He turned round clutching the panel. 'I'm taking this with me.'

'Oh no you're not!' The foreman grabbed him by the shoulders and slammed him against the wall. 'If you've any sense you'll get out of here and keep your mouth shut!' The mechanics were right behind him now.

Ribera was shaking. 'If . . . if I don't?'

'We'll shut it for you. Permanently!'

'And the computer? It's waiting for an answer. Whether I'm there or not it's going to ask the same question. Know how to shut that up too?'

Gradually the foreman released his grip. 'What do you want?'

'A meeting with whoever's behind this.'

CHAPTER TWELVE

Angel was woken on Saturday morning by a phone call from Madrid.

'Now *I've* got a problem,' El Carnicero told him. 'An accountant's tumbled the imports. He wants a meeting.'

'An *accountant*? Surely you can deal with him?'

'He says he's programmed his firm's computers to ask questions, whatever we do to him. That's beyond me.'

Angel muttered an obscenity. Just when he wanted to get his and Jack's options settled. 'I'd better come right away,' he said.

'Be careful, someone knows you're over here. They've been asking questions in the embassies.'

'Who! No, don't tell me on the phone. Let's meet at the shop at seven tonight.'

He disconnected, then dialled room service and ordered breakfast. Angel had shaved and dressed by the time it arrived, and had the tray carried out to the bungalow's terrace. He was pouring coffee when Katie walked into the bungalow's garden. She was wearing the denim mini-skirt she'd bought in Puerto Banús, and the sight of her sent a thrill of desire shooting through him. But she looked as though she'd been crying. He stood up to greet her.

'Hi, Katie. What you doing here?'

'I came to say goodbye,' she said miserably.

'Goodbye. What's happened?' Taking her hand, he led her to the cane sofa on the terrace and sat down beside her.

'My stepfather called from the clinic. We're leaving today, and I don't know if I'll come back.'

Angel looked astonished. 'But how's that possible? His leg wasn't fixed when I saw him last night.'

'All I know is he told me to pack right away. We're going to see the French Grand Prix apparently. Something about promoting the project.'

'That makes sense, but surely you'll come back afterwards?'

'Jack will, but he wants to get rid of me.' She wiped away tears with the back of her hand.

'But why?'

'I think it's something to do with you and me.'

'Christ, does he know about yesterday?'

'I don't think so, but he's definitely got something against you. Me seeing you anyway.'

Angel put an arm round her shoulder and drew her to him. She didn't resist. 'Maybe he's just not used to you. I mean, your not being a little girl any more. He doesn't know how to handle it, so he's playing the heavy father.'

'Whatever it is, he won't let me see you and he's trying to send me back to England.'

'Trying?'

'No one wants me there either. Perhaps I will come back to Marbella. I just don't know.'

Angel took her hand. 'Sure he'll bring you back, if you use a little psychology. I mean, when he mentions me, say you can't stand me.'

Katie looked into his eyes. 'But I do like you, Angel.'

'I like you too, Katie, very much.' He kissed her lightly on the lips. Suddenly they were clinging to each other, hearts racing, bodies trembling. 'I'm going away too for a few days,' Angel said. 'I'm going to miss you, little one.'

'I don't want to leave you.'

He kissed her again, and this time she parted her lips, then returned the pressure.

'D'you have to go right now?'

'No,' Katie murmured.

*

A new cast had been set round Jack's lower left leg early that morning. When the doctor arrived to check it, his patient was swinging round the room on a new pair of full-arm crutches.

'What are you doing?' the doctor demanded.

'Getting my balance back – I'm leaving this morning.'

'*What*?' He stood in front of Jack, forcing him to stop. 'Now you listen to me, Mr Ryder: I don't know what really happened last week, and perhaps it's none of my business, but this is! I can't make you stay here, but your leg needs resting or –'

A knock on the door interrupted him. Both of them turned as Sami Nassar came into the room and greeted them each by name.

'You two know each other?' Jack asked.

'I came last night to see how you were,' Sami explained. 'You were asleep, so he put me in the picture.'

'Well, now he is awake, perhaps you can talk some sense into him,' the doctor said. 'If you'll excuse me, I have saner patients to attend to.' He went out and shut the door behind him.

'What was all that about?' Sami asked.

Jack sat on the edge of the bed. 'Frank Brady's invited me to the French Grand Prix. He's sending his Learjet to collect Katie and me from Málaga at noon. He's interested in promoting our project.'

Sami sat down on a chair. 'From what you've told me he's in a good position to do that. But aren't you pushing yourself too hard?'

'Don't you start! This isn't my first accident, you know. One thing I've learnt is my own rate of recovery.'

The Lebanese gave him a quizzical look. 'You seem angry. Is it something I've done?'

'Of course not.'

'Angel, then?'

Jack brazened it out. 'What's bugging me are the delays. He keeps telling me he's seriously interested in the project, but he hasn't committed his land yet.'

99

'You *are* in a hurry! I only started negotiating with the landowners last week, remember. But as a matter of fact I'm giving them an ultimatum this weekend – sell me options within seven days, or we'll find another site.'

'Good. Start with Angel. Now will you help me pack and give me a lift back to the hotel?'

'Well, if you've made up your mind –'

'I have, so save your breath.'

'Don't jump down my throat,' Sami said good-naturedly. 'I was going to suggest we dropped in on Angel and put the ultimatum to him together.'

'Good idea.'

Hand in hand, Angel and Katie walked into the bungalow. He left her to fetch something from his bedroom, then joined her in the living room with its flowery curtains and matching upholstery. They sank into the soft-cushioned sofa, and Angel showed her the little silver box. Katie watched nervously as he spooned a line on to its mirror-like lid, rolled a banknote, then offered them both to her.

'You first,' she said.

'All right.' Angel snorted the powder. He closed his eyes, lay back, and let the drug take its effect. 'It's wonderful up here! Join me.'

Biting his lower lip to steady himself, he laid a rail for Katie; much finer than her first one because he wanted her to be aware of everything this time.

She took the banknote, hesitated, then positioned it over the lid. Her hand was shaking as she snorted up the mix. Nothing at first, but soon a rush that made her gasp. Then she was floating away from all her worries, losing her balance.

'Hold me,' she said.

Angel took her in his arms and kissed her again. He slid a hand down her body, on to her thigh, and then upwards. Katie stopped him.

'I want to love you,' he murmured.

'I want you to but . . . it's the first time.'

'Just relax,' Angel said. He began to undress her, gently removing her top and mini-skirt. All she had on underneath was her tiny white panties.

Katie was trembling now, eyes closed, lips slightly parted. Angel kissed them, then her sweet breasts. As he licked her nipples she began to moan softly. Filled with the taste of her, he knew he couldn't stop now. He went on kissing her wonderful body, but had to stand to remove his trousers. He glanced at himself, and knelt down quickly so as not to frighten her. Laying her down on the sofa, Angel slid off her panties and tossed them aside. He stared at the triangle of glistening blonde curls, then parted her legs and climbed between them.

At that moment the phone rang.

Angel tried to ignore it, but the ringing filled the room, and then his head. He glared at the phone, willing the sound to stop, but it went on and on. Livid, he rushed to the desk and snatched up the receiver.

'Who is it?'

'Sami Nassar here, in reception with Jack. We'd like a word with you.'

Angel fought for words, as though he'd been struck dumb. 'I'm . . . I've . . . only just got up.'

'That's all right, unless you're with someone.'

'Of course not, but –'

'We'll be with you in a minute, then.'

'W . . . wait,' Angel stuttered, but the line had gone dead. For a few moments he just stood there, stark naked, staring at the receiver. Then he dropped it and started shouting. 'Christ, your father's coming! Get some clothes on!'

Katie tried to sit up, but collapsed back on the sofa.

'Come on, come on!' Angel lifted her up in his arms, and stumbled towards his bedroom. He kicked the door open and screamed as he split his big-toe nail. Somehow he managed to carry her to the bed. 'For God's sake, keep quiet!' he told her, before hopping out again, slamming the door shut behind him.

Clothes seemed to be strewn about everywhere in the living room. Angel snatched up his shirt, put it on and frantically tried to button it up. He had one leg in his trousers when the door bell rang. No time for his socks and shoes. Angel kicked them and the rest of the clothing under the sofa, ran his hands through his hair, then went to the door.

'Hello Mr Nassar,' he said as calmly as he could. 'Great to see you out of hospital, Jack.'

'Is it?' Jack asked.

'Of course. Come in.' Angel was leading them into the living room when he noticed Katie's panties on the sheepskin rug. He bent down quickly and stuffed them into his trouser pocket, hoping they hadn't been noticed. When he turned to face his visitors, though, Sami was wearing a knowing smile.

'I hope we haven't disturbed you.'

'Ummm . . . not at all.'

'Good. Because Jack's off to the French Grand Prix to promote the project, and we need to know where we stand on the site.'

'I . . . understand.'

'Do you? Forgive me, Angel, but you seem rather distracted. I'm asking whether you'll sell us an option on your land next week?'

The Colombian tried to clear his mind. 'I need more details . . . of this holiday company . . . how many shares you're going to issue –'

'I've told you already, and that there'll be no dilution of stock. It will all be in the prospectus which forms part of our contract. Satisfied?'

Angel glanced at Jack, who gave him a curt nod. 'In principle, yes,' he told Sami.

'Fine. Then if you'll excuse us, Jack's in a hurry.'

Once they'd left, Angel hurried back to the bedroom. Katie was clutching the bedspread round her with one hand and holding her head in the other.

'Oh God, what do we do now?'

Angel sat down beside her and held her shoulders. 'Don't panic, little one. Go back straight away, and say you were walking on the beach.'

She sighed with frustration. 'What a let down.'

'I'll be waiting for you,' Angel said, bringing her close to him. 'Just remember what I said, about pretending not to like me.'

'I'll try,' Katie said, 'but I won't mean it.'

CHAPTER THIRTEEN

When Katie returned to the apartment in Puente Romano, Jack, Sami and Roland Priest were holding a hurried conference. Plans and drawings were spread out around them in the sitting area.

'Where've you been?' Jack asked when she let herself in. 'I was getting really worried and –'

'For heaven's sake, Dad, I just took a walk. I'll finish packing.' She avoided his eyes and hurried into her room.

Jack frowned, then looked down at some perspectives of the proposed harbour-front and main straight area. 'They're excellent, Roland. You must have had the architects working all hours. I'd like to take a set with me if possible.'

'Go ahead,' Priest told him. 'These copies are for you.'

Sami insisted on driving Jack and Katie to Málaga Airport, and they arrived there minutes before Brady's Learjet.

Less than two hours later they landed at Marseille Marignane in the South of France. Typically the team-owner had bent the rules and driven his Ferrari 412 on to the apron. Jack and Katie only had to climb out of the plane and step straight into the sleek red coupé before leaving the airport.

Brady glanced at Jack in the front passenger seat. 'So tell me what you've been up to.'

'You seem to know most of it already.'

'But when did you join Nassar?' They reached the autoroute to Marseille and the team-owner blasted into the fast lane.

'He approached me just before the race at Monaco.'

'And several other drivers. How did you land the deal?'

'By smashing your car and my leg to pieces. He's paying for my PR value.'

Brady gave him a curious glance, then concentrated on bullying a slower car out of his way. 'Good contract?'

'Better than I ever screwed out of you.'

'How good? D'you mind discussing this in front of your girl by the way?'

Jack twisted round to look at Katie in the back seat. She still had a slightly dazed look about her, as though she was half asleep. If she was taking any interest in what they were saying, she certainly didn't show it. He turned back to Brady. 'I'm getting a salary which is none of your business, and an option which might be – a million one-dollar shares at par in the holding company.'

The team-owner gave him another appraising look. 'You've changed, Jack.'

'Meaning?'

'I think you've found the hard edge you were missing. You'd have won a World Championship with it, because you'd have negotiated yourself into the right team at the right time. Might still do, when we get together again.'

'Why are you buttering me up, Frank?'

Brady roared with laughter. 'See what I mean? You'd have swallowed that bullshit not so long ago. Seriously, though, you're on to the right idea at the right time now. We're all browned off with Monaco after what happened this year, and determined to replace it. I think you're on to the answer, and I want part of it. I'll need to know all about this holding company of course, but providing it's sound I'll lend you the money for half the option, and buy the other half million shares myself.'

Jack was frowning. Angel thought he'd been promised the option, but that would give him control of the company. God knows what the little maniac would do before he was finally arrested. Brady's offer would enable him to head off that threat. He'd just have to think up a way of explaining it to the Colombian when he got back.

'Agreed,' Jack said finally, 'provided the loan's interest-free.'

'You have changed! But all right. And I'd like to know what other shares are available. We're having dinner in Bandol tonight with the F I S A and F O C A brigade, by the way. That should get things moving.'

The Ferrari was rapidly closing on a Porsche 911 in the fast lane. A collision seemed inevitable, and Jack grabbed the dash. 'If we get there.'

The Porsche chickened out and moved over. Brady blasted past as close to it as possible, then gave Jack a pitying look. 'Lost your nerve too?'

'Too?'

'Your replacement's a complete disaster.'

'Release him then, before he kills himself or someone else.'

Brady sighed. 'You knows who really pays for this game – rich businessmen who like motor-racing. One of them coughed up for his favourite to drive my car.'

'Give him back the money.'

'You know me better than that. Anyway, it's earmarked for your option now. Do me a favour, though, talk to the lad before the race.'

'I'll see what I can do,' Jack promised.

Angel reached the old paint factory outside Madrid later that evening. Heeding El Carnicero's warning, he'd left the Mercedes at the Marbella Club, slipped out of the back of the bungalow and taken a taxi into Marbella. There he'd hired an Avis car and driven it to Madrid.

El Carnicero was waiting for him outside the factory and joined him in the hired Ford. 'Anyone tail you?'

'No. Who else knows I'm here though?'

'The Ministry of the Interior. They asked the Colombian and Peruvian embassies for reports on you. Our contacts dealt with that.'

'But who put the ministry up to it?'

The enforcer shrugged his massive shoulders. 'Local narco agents, DEA, who knows?'

'Tell me about the accountant.'

'Name's Victor Ribera. Works at Avicomida. He found them stripping out carts, and says he'll blow us unless we talk to him.'

'We'll talk to him all right,' Angel hissed. He looked through the windscreen at the factory. 'How's Fortinez getting on?'

'He's a different man since you said you needed him. We're getting regular deliveries. The first lot was shit, but it's better each time.'

'Saleable?'

This isn't the States – no one here knows the difference, especially the way we're cutting it.'

'What about distribution? If we flood the market, prices are going to drop.'

'They're dropping already.'

'Then we've got to take out the opposition. When can you get your men together?'

'You'll meet them tonight. Like to look round here first?'

The factory's former owner had indeed found a new lease of life. Fortinez gleefully showed off the processing plant, as though he was getting his own back on the economy that had almost put him on its scrap heap. He had hidden the equipment at the far end of the dingy building behind soap vats and crude partitions. Three members of his family were working a late shift, and they grinned conspiratorially at the visitors. Their morale had obviously leapt too.

Paste slabs from the carts had been placed in large aluminium baking trays and covered with ether to dissolve them. A newly fitted extractor fan in the roof dissipated some of the stench and the risk of explosion.

'How much ether are you using?' Angel asked Fortinez.

'About a litre per kilo of paste. We can process a tonne a month with the chemicals we usually receive.'

'Don't order more than that,' Angel said. 'It's a sure way of attracting unwanted attention.'

Next they came to a line of large glass vessels looking like giant eggs, each with a capped opening at the top and a tap at the base. The solution from the trays had been poured into these vessels and mixed with sulphuric acid. Each 'egg' was then vigorously shaken so that the cocaine-in-ether separated from a slurry of heavier waste products. These were drained away.

Now the problem was to evaporate the ether without blowing everything to bits. Two-foot-tall reaction flasks rested over electric cooking rings. El Carnicero watched the cakes of cocaine forming in the bulbs of the flasks with fascination, but Angel kept his distance.

Finally diluted hydrochloric acid was added, giving off a strong smell of chlorine. The resultant solution was poured into baking trays and carried outside. Even at seven-thirty in the evening the sun was strong enough to evaporate the liquid, leaving behind the finished product – flakes of cocaine hydrochloride. It would be ground into powder, adulterated with a variety of cuts, and finally sold for several hundred dollars a gram.

The three men stood at the back of the factory admiring their handiwork.

'It certainly beats making soap,' Fortinez said with a wry smile.

Roy Shepard discovered his bird had flown by mid-afternoon. Frustrated and angry he called the DEA station head at his Madrid apartment.

'It's ridiculous,' Shepard said in his West Virginian drawl. 'The son of a bitch nearly killed Ryder, showed him a stack of cocaine, and all the time we had one man on full-time surveillance. You've got to get permission to do it properly before Jack comes back from France. I daren't involve him again otherwise.'

'I'm doing what I can,' Bob Cullington told him,

'but the embassies insist that Angel's a blameless citizen.'

'What does that tell you?'

'Nothing new – the Colombians even use diplomatic pouches to bring in the product! Anyway, now both Ryder and Mosquera have left Marbella I need you and Ed back here.'

'Why? What's happened?'

'Unprecedented quantities of cocaine have hit the streets in the last few days. Care to guess where they came from?'

'We're on our way,' Shepard told him.

El Carnicero had an apartment in Carabanchell, a workers' district in the south of Madrid notorious for its grim prison. His wife had prepared a Colombian-style *cazuela de mariscos*, and their simple dining-cum-living room was filled with the smell of stewed seafood.

Six enforcers sat round the table with Angel and their host. Five were Colombian expatriates, hard men in their thirties and forties. All of them had worked for Julio César before coming to Spain and owed him total allegiance. Whatever they might have thought about his son's youthfulness, they treated Angel with deference.

The sixth enforcer, José Garravillo, wasn't in fact much older than Angel. He had been born in Spain to Colombian parents. That and his quick, vicious nature qualified him to join the group. Garravillo was better dressed and groomed than his colleagues, and clearly aware of his dark good looks. He was greatly influenced by television's *Miami Vice* and was dressed accordingly in a loose cotton suit and sports-shirt. Every now and then he threw Angel an amused glance.

Señora Estinal ladled seafood into each man's soup plate, opened more beer bottles, then returned to the kitchen and closed the door behind her. For some minutes there was only the sound of contented slurping and an occasional unashamed belch.

El Carnicero turned to Angel on his right. 'As good as at home?'

'Better. I'm honoured to be here among friends. I spoke to my father a short while ago, and he sends warm regards to each one of you.' Angel looked from face to face to emphasise the message. Everyone seemed impressed, except Garravillo, who just grinned.

'Down to business,' El Carnicero told them. 'You already know we're having a sales drive. That's why Señor Angel's here. What you don't know yet is the final target – the entire market.'

Everyone stopped eating and stared at him.

'You all stand to earn ten times as much *if* we secure it, but that means eliminating the competition.'

One of the enforcers skewered a prawn with his fork, and held it up. 'Like this?'

'Exactly, Godofredo. Tomorrow's a night of knives. I want professional hits, so take a back-up team. And bring me evidence you've done the job – something that'll scare the shit out of anyone left. I'll give you your targets later. There's a million peseta bonus per head by the way.'

'Tax free?' someone asked, and everyone laughed.

'What about this accountant?' Angel said.

José Garravillo gave a mocking snort. 'Don't worry, Angelito, we'll deal with him too.'

The disrespectful nickname brought shocked silence to the room. Everyone waited for Angel's reaction. His face was cold and blank. He turned chilling eyes on Garravillo, then spoke to his host in a calm voice.

'How do you kill nowadays, Enrique?'

'With piano wire. It's easy to hide and very effective.'

'I'd like to borrow some.'

Garravillo's face was losing its colour. 'Look, it was just . . . I didn't mean to be rude.'

Ignoring him El Carnicero took a coil of wire with wooden handles attached to each end from out of his pocket and gave it to Angel.

Still staring at the young enforcer, Angel unwound the wire and stretched it taut. 'This will do fine.'

Garravillo was sweating now. He looked round for support, but nobody moved. 'Come on now . . . oh God, please . . .'

Angel gave a surprised laugh. 'What's the matter, Josélito? It's for the accountant.'

The others roared at Garravillo's shamefaced discomfort.

CHAPTER FOURTEEN

Paul Ricard Circuit was built in the sixties high in the Provençal hills north-east of Marseille. The setting should have made it a classic, but its developer had chosen the only piece of flat land in the area. Now it was dominated by a long concrete-and-glass pits-building which made the place look like a provincial airport.

Frank Brady drove Jack there early on Sunday morning to beat the race-day traffic. The road wound up from Bandol – a small town on the Côte d'Azur – through vineyards and forests which gave sudden, spectacular views to the Mediterranean far below. They had stayed at the Hôtel de l'Île Rousse, and dined there with the power brokers of Grand Prix racing. Katie had eaten at another table with Brady's young designer, who had offered her a lift to the circuit this morning in his Lotus Esprit.

As usual the team-owner was driving like a maniac, overtaking everything and squeeling the big Ferrari through the corners. Jack hung on to the door and looked over his shoulder to see if the Lotus was keeping up.

'Don't look so worried,' Brady said.

'You haven't got a seventeen-year-old daughter!'

'But I've got a designer who's meant to be concentrating on the race.' They both chuckled. 'Seriously, you did a great job last night. You had them eating out of your hand.'

Jack shrugged. He wasn't so sure. The men who ran FISA and FOCA tended to treat drivers like overgrown schoolboys. Last night they'd been almost too respectful to him, though, and raved about his project. Did they really want a replacement for Monaco's race, he wondered, or just a weapon to force its organisers to concede to their demands?

'What's up?' Brady asked, flinging the Ferrari into a hairpin bend and powering out of it with an armful of opposite lock. 'My driving bothering you again?'

'Actually I was wondering whether they're just playing politics.'

'Could be. So what we've got to do is get the media behind it.'

'Hold a press conference?'

'They're ten a penny. No, something with much more impact than that.'

'Like what?'

'I'm working on it. It'll come to me.'

At the circuit's main entrance, Brady shamelessly overtook the line of cars already queuing up and was waved through to the paddock behind the pits-building. It was crammed with transporters, motorhomes and support vehicles. The Lotus followed them in. Katie came over to help Jack out of the Ferrari and retrieved his crutches from the back seat.

'I see you've made another conquest,' he said teasingly.

She met his eyes. 'Who's the other one?'

'You know . . . Angel.'

'Why d'you keep going on about him, Dad? You don't think there's anything between us, do you?'

'I thought you liked him, that's all.'

Katie shook her head. 'He's a pain, full of himself.'

'Really?'

'Yes, *really*. Anyone else you're worried about?'

'Ummm . . . not at the moment.'

'Then can I go off on my own for a while, or do I have to stick with you the whole time?'

'Of course you can. I promised Frank I'd talk to someone anyway, but let's meet up for coffee at eleven?'

'Stop worrying about me, Dad. I'm seventeen years old, you know.'

That's the trouble, he wanted to say, but bit his lip and watched her stroll off through the paddock. He turned towards the pits-building, a long row of drab concrete garages between two floors of viewing galleries and offices.

Frank held open the back door to his team's garage, and Jack hobbled through. Suddenly he was back in his racing world, hearing it, smelling it, *feeling* it in his heart. His ex team-mate came up to have a word with him. Mechanics called out friendly greetings but didn't stop preparing the team's two cars for the morning warm-up session. Engines were fired up, then snarled viciously. Jack breathed in high-octane fumes and felt again that tingling anticipation in his body. But on one face he saw thinly disguised fear.

His replacement was an Englishman called Mark Sandersen, fifteen years younger than himself and quite a bit smaller. Mark had swept up all the prizes in Formula Three racing, backed by the businessman who had now paid Brady to give his protégé a Grand Prix drive. But Formula One cars were a different proposition, with a power-to-weight ratio ten times greater than the team-owner's road-going Ferrari, for example. Fifteen-hundred brake-horsepower-per-ton was great if you had it totally under control. If not, it hit hard, and Mark Sandersen looked punch drunk.

That could be me, Jack thought as he was introduced to him. He wondered how he'd have coped if he was making his comeback today. You never really knew how a shunt had affected you until you climbed back into a racing car. Sometimes it was as if nothing had happened. More often there was that horrible sensation of being off-balance. You braked too soon and too hard, fumbled gear-changes, steered clumsily. And you just didn't know if or when you could put your act back together again. Some drivers never did – Jack decided to try and stop Mark becoming one of them.

With less than an hour to the warm-up session, he swung towards Mark's car on his crutches. He needed something more than words to restore the younger man's confidence. He found what he wanted the moment he looked down into the cockpit.

'Isn't that my old seat?'

'They padded it out to stop me moving around,' Mark told him.

'But you're what, two inches shorter than me? There's no way you can see out of the thing properly, let alone control it.'

Jack called over the burly chief mechanic, Herbie Wright, and quietly told him they had to alter the seat. They began to build it up between them with strips of rubber and foam held in place by yards of silver tank tape. Jack new exactly how to place the materials to the best ergonomic advantage. Sitting on one side-pod directing the operation and helping out, he revelled in doing something useful again. He'd almost forgotten that feeling too.

When Mark climbed back into the car he actually smiled. 'Much better.'

'Let's talk about handling, then,' Jack said.

'It's set up exactly how you tested it here earlier this year,' Herbie Wright told him.

'Which was nervous as hell. Fine for me because I was used to it, but I think Mark'd be happier with a touch of understeer.'

'I tried to tell them that,' Mark said, 'but nobody'd listen.'

'I'm listening now,' Herbie Wright assured him.

Madrid's Plaza Mayor was built in the seventeenth century. Two hundred metres long by a hundred wide, it has a bronze statue of Phillip III on horseback in the centre and is completely surrounded by broad arcades supporting tiers of balconied apartments above. From these the nobility once watched bullfights and pageants in the huge square.

This fine June Sunday it was filled with ordinary *Madrileños* and camera-toting tourists. Many of them sat at tables in the dozens of open air cafés. The din of their chatter reverberated around the enclosed area, forcing everyone to talk even louder to make themselves heard.

At a table in the café nearest the south-eastern corner, a balding man in his forties sat determinedly alone. He told enquirers that the chair opposite him was reserved for someone coming soon. He wore a bright red shirt and was reading a copy of *Holá* magazine, just as he'd been told to in the anonymous letter. The man was unemployed and had no idea why he was there; but the envelope he'd found in his letterbox also contained twenty thousand pesetas, with the promise of the same again if he followed instructions.

Angel was watching him from a nearby table.

Just after one Victor Ribera came into the square through the Arco de Cuchilleros. He spotted his contact – the shirt and magazine had been his idea – but didn't join him right away. Instead, the gaunt accountant strolled round the café, pretending to look at the sights while casting furtive glances at the table. Angel studied the area with a more expert eye to see if Ribera was being tailed. He wasn't.

Eventually the accountant sidled up to his supposed contact and sat down opposite him. A bewildered conversation ensued until Angel went over to join them.

'You can go now,' he told the red-shirted man, slipping him four more five-thousand-peseta notes. Angel took his place at the table.

'Who are you?' Ribera asked nervously. 'I want to meet the man behind those imports. He was meant to come alone.'

'And I need to know you're alone.' Angel took something like a small transistor radio out of his jacket pocket, extended the aerial, and aimed it at the accountant.

Ribera started to get up, thoroughly alarmed. 'If you kill me –'

'Relax, it's just a transmission detector to see if you're

116

wired.' The warning light didn't flash, so Angel folded the aerial and put the device back in his pocket. 'Anyway, I'm here to recruit you, not harm you.'

'Recruit . . .?' Ribera stopped talking as a waiter arrived at their table. He ordered a *café solo* and Angel asked for a beer. The waiter scribbled on a pad, and then left them.

'Look,' Angel said, 'we need someone in your firm to control those imports. The management doesn't even know about them, and it's obvious that stupid foreman's not up to it. You're in a much better position to do the job.'

'That's true, but I didn't expect . . . I mean, what's in it for me?'

'Twenty million pesetas per tonne of import delivered. You've earned that much already by not reporting what you discovered, and we've paid you in cash as a sign of good faith.'

Ribera was speechless, his eyes bulging in astonishment. Then greed gripped his features. 'Where's the money?'

'In your office. I didn't dare bring it with me – there's too much crime in Madrid – so I had it delivered.'

'I want to see it before I believe you.'

'And we need to discuss future shipments. Can we get into the factory now?'

Ribera nodded and scraped back his chair. 'I've got my own keys. Let's go.'

'Aren't we going to wait for our drinks?' Angel asked, as though they were just as important.

'What the bloody hell did you tell him?' Frank Brady shouted as the French Grand Prix reached the halfway point.

'What?' Jack yelled back. They were standing by the pit wall with Formula One cars wailing past right in front of them. Mark Sandersen had just taken twelfth place, having started from the back of the grid.

'What – did – you – tell – Mark?'

There was a lull in the traffic. 'Nothing much. That seat made all the difference.'

'You and your furniture. By the way, remember that set of dining chairs you made me? Someone offered me twice what I paid. Said you were collectable.'

'*Collectable?*'

'That's what he said.'

Jack smiled to himself and turned to look for Mark. He *had* talked to him before the race, and what he'd said had made a profound impression on the youngster. He'd told him to forget what had happened in practice, and to drive his own race at his own pace. Jack pointed out that last year's final point-scorer had finished over two minutes down on the winner, three seconds a lap slower on average. Mark had done better than that in the warm-up, so he could score today as long as he made a sensible start and stuck to the pace they'd calculated. He wouldn't have to change tyres either because Jack had advised him to choose a relatively hard compound.

The tactics were working perfectly as faster cars crashed or broke down. Two more managed to collide under braking for Signes corner, and Mark screamed past in ninth place this time.

'I don't believe it!' Brady said. 'Talk about a comeback . . .' He stared at Jack. 'That's it! *Your* comeback – demonstrating a Grand Prix car on the site in Marbella.'

Jack nodded down at his plastercast. 'Aren't you forgetting something? I won't even fit in the car.'

'Not this year's, but we're collecting the battleship from a department store in Marseille tomorrow.' The battleship was an earlier design, notable for its size rather than track success. Painted in the sponsor's colours, it was now used for static displays. 'We'll make a special seat and rig something up so you can pop the clutch.'

'It's an idea,' Jack said, 'but the roadways'll need some repairs.'

'Phone Nassar and tell him to get on to it fast. Think of the publicity – One-legged Driver Breaks Lap Record.'

'Or his bloody neck,' Jack muttered.

Victor Ribera parked his hatchback in the factory's car park and led Angel round to a side entrance. He unlocked the door, and they climbed the stairs to the first floor, then entered his office.

'All right, where is it?' Ribera asked.

'Try your desk.'

Trembling with excitement, he unlocked the drawers. In the main one was a cardboard shoebox. Ribera put it on the desk and tore off the lid. It was crammed full of five-thousand-peseta notes. A mad gleam came into his eyes as he stared down at them, and he started to giggle.

'Count them,' Angel said.

The accountant did, laying neat piles of notes on the desk-top. 'It's all there,' he said finally. 'What am I going to do with it?'

'That's your business. But you'd better tell me how you want paying for tomorrow's shipment.'

'I don't . . . I'm not sure. Not like this, though.'

'How about a numbered account in Switzerland? They'll send you transaction details in plain envelopes, so you'll know we've paid you.'

'Yes, yes, that's a good idea. And I want it in Swiss francs.'

'All right,' Angel said, 'but first you've got to convince me you've cleared the computer. I don't want a blackmail threat hanging over me.'

'Why would I do that?' Ribera asked. 'We're on the same side now.'

'Prove it.'

'That's easy.' The accountant sat down at his desk and switched on the computer terminal. He pulled the keyboard towards him and typed instructions. A list of creditors appeared on the screen. 'See that item?'

Angel was standing behind him, looking over his shoulder. 'For twenty-five sheets of insulation foam?'

'Yes. It's a repeat order too soon after the previous one, which made me suspicious. That's why there's a question mark against it. The computer will go on asking questions until I give it my personal clearance code.' Ribera typed in letters and numbers, and the question mark disappeared. 'Now I tell it to accept the entire list, like so, and the problem's solved.'

'But how do I know you haven't laid another trap?'

'I'll prove it to you,' Ribera said, eager to please. 'Look, I'm asking if the computer's got any outstanding queries about that creditor, or about our maintenance department. Read the answer for yourself.'

As Angel did so, he took the piano wire out of his trouser pocket. He kept it low behind the accountant's back as he uncoiled it, so he wouldn't see it even if he looked around.

Ribera still had his hands on the keyboard. 'Satisfied?' he asked, turning his head.

That stretched his neck beautifully. Angel looped the wire round it in an instant, crossed his hands and yanked the handles as hard as he could. Ribera tried to scream, but only spittle and a ghastly strangling sound came out. His hands clawed at the wire, but it had cut too deep into his flesh for him to be able to grip it. Ribera's face was turning purple and his eyes were almost popping out of his head. The greed in them had changed to terror. Death began to glaze them as Angel tightened his grip.

He waited until all signs of life had gone, then carefully extracted the bloody wire to avoid leaving stains. Angel picked up the phone and dialled maintenance.

The rat-faced foreman arrived within minutes and stood gloating over the corpse. 'Well done. Serves the *cabrón* right.'

'How will you get rid of the body?'

'There's an incinerator downstairs for all the waste food. We'll carve him up and burn the pieces in there.'

'His car's in the car park.'

'Leave that to us too.'

Angel picked a bundle of notes off the desk and handed it to the foreman, then began to stuff the rest back into the shoebox. 'That's that then. Would someone give me a lift back to town?'

One of the mechanics drove Angel into Madrid and dropped him near the Plaza Mayor. Angel waited until he'd driven away before taking a taxi to Carabanchell. He paid that off some distance from El Carnicero's apartment block and walked the rest of the way. Lookouts identified him well before he got there and a guard let him into the flat.

El Carnicero was sitting at the dining table, awaiting the return of his men. Angel put the shoebox in front of him, took off the lid to show him the money inside, then tossed the bloody coil of wire on to the table.

The enforcer smiled and nodded approval. 'Like father, like son. You'd better leave Madrid for a while though – the heat's going to be on full blast.'

'Suits me. I've business to settle in Marbella.'

'Take one of my men with you.'

'Thanks. Who?'

'Your choice.' El Carnicero began to tell him about the success of the operation. 'Four less wholesalers to worry about so far. Three more, and we'll have the market to ourselves.'

'With enough product to expand it,' Angel said. The front doorbell rang. 'We're not just talking about the smart set now: within a year I want every teenager in Spain to be able to buy our brand –'

A knock on the living room door interrupted them and José Garravillo was shown in. He walked up to the dining room table, where El Carnicero and Angel were sitting side by side, took a bloody handkerchief out of his jacket and unfolded it. Inside was a severed ear.

'This says I'm no coward.'

Angel indicated the gory coil on the table. 'Now we've both made our point,' he said. He stood up and walked round to Garravillo, who gave him a fervent embrace of loyalty. When they parted Angel held him by the shoulders. 'I need some help in Marbella. Will you come with me?'

'I'd be honoured,' Garravillo said.

CHAPTER FIFTEEN

It was one of the largest houses on a fashionable estate in east Madrid, although the hedge round its carefully tended garden was so high that from outside one could only see the red-tiled roofline. By ten o'clock on Monday morning nine police vehicles and three ambulances were blocking the access road and the neighbours were out in force.

Bob Cullington parked his Ford well back. He and Roy Shepard edged through the gawping crowd, walked down the tree-lined driveway, and were only allowed through the front door after identifying themselves. Police and ambulancemen stood around looking abnormally shocked. The cleaning lady who had raised the alarm was weeping and wailing, while a policewoman tried to comfort her. Luis Beniamin – the *Brigada de Estupefacientes* detective who'd called Cullington – stood at the foot of the stairs talking to a murder squad officer.

'Thanks for coming so quickly,' Beniamin told the Americans. 'I wanted you to see this before they move anything.'

'Bad as that?'

As if in reply a young uniformed policeman staggered out of a room to their right vomiting into his hands.

'Oh, for God's sake!' the detective snapped. 'Someone get him outside.'

'In there?' Cullington asked.

He nodded grimly, and led the way.

Everything in the impressive lounge had been carefully coordinated by someone with expensive tastes. The plush upholstery and curtains were pale-blue velvet while the walls and carpets were shades of cream. They would never be the same.

The killers had herded the entire family into this room. The children couldn't have been more than seven or eight. They'd probably been dragged out of bed, because they were in nightclothes, before being shot against one side-wall. The back of the little boy's head had disintegrated and most of its contents were splattered over the paintwork. His sister lay beside him with half of her face missing.

Their parents had been gagged and tied to armchairs, turned towards each other so that they could see their partners suffering. The woman was stripped to the waist, and had cigarette burns on her face and breasts. He'd lost an ear. Both of them had been killed by a single shot through their caved-in foreheads.

'Seen anything like this before?' Beniamin asked.

'Seven days a week in Medellín,' Roy Shepard said.

'Colombians? You're sure?'

'Cocaine cowboys – it's got their psychotic brand all over it. Who was he?'

'A lawyer who specialised in defending known criminals. We've suspected him of trafficking for some time but never been able to prove it.'

'You just got your proof.'

'This isn't all. We've found seven other mutilated bodies in different parts of the city. We think all the victims were involved with drugs.'

The Americans' eyes met. 'Are you thinking what I'm thinking?' Cullington asked.

'The Mosqueras – they're taking over the whole shooting match.'

'How are we going to stop them?'

Shepard turned to the detective. 'Can we work together on this?'

'Please.'

'Then I'd like to know about every homicide investigation from now on. There have to be links and we're going to find them. Bob, have the El Paso intelligence centre fax us everything they've got on the Mosqueras' hit men. Let's see if any of that ties in.'

'Anything else?' Beniamin asked.

'Yes. I'd like your undercover people to buy as much cocaine as your budget can stand.'

Angel and José Garravillo reached Marbella that afternoon. They drove straight to the Avis garage, returned their Ford, then lugged their suitcases to a rival company where they rented a Renault.

'What a piece of shit,' Angel moaned as Garravillo drove it towards the town centre. 'We'll have to swop every couple of days though: don't forget someone's been asking questions about me. Pull in over there.' They stopped at the foot of the Old Town. 'I'm meeting Sami Nassar. You start looking for a safe house, somewhere quiet. Not through an agent – we want to rent directly from the owner so that can't be traced either.'

'I get the picture,' Garravillo said.

'Pick me up here at five then,' Angel told him and climbed out of the car.

Angel walked up into the Old Town, a warren of narrow streets walled in by white houses festooned with flowers tumbling over their wrought-iron balconies. The notary's office was in one of these ancient buildings. Angel was shown into a sparsely furnished waiting room, where Sami stood up to greet him.

'Thanks for your call this morning,' the Lebanese said. 'Where have you been by the way?'

'Why?'

'I've been trying to reach you at the Marbella Club, that's all. I wanted to show you the option agreement in draft, in case you wanted any changes made.'

'If I do, we'll just have to alter it now.'

Sami handed him several of the officially stamped forms

used in Spain for private agreements. Signing them in front of a notary made them legally binding. 'Basically you're selling me a-one year option on your land for one million US dollars. If I call it, you can either demand payment or shares in the holding company.'

Angel had raced ahead. 'Grandprix Holdings Inc.,' he read out in an amused tone.

'Hardly an original name, but a descriptive one. You'll see it's incorporated in the Cayman Islands by reputable bankers. The articles limit the share capital to fifty million dollars and prohibit the issue of further stock.'

He nodded and turned the page.

'There's a list of each potential shareholder's allocation. In your case, $24,500,000 in cash or shares.'

And in your case 10 million shares, Angel thought, looking down the list. Sami had shown his entitlement as a single block. Of course – he wouldn't want them to know how vulnerable the company was to a takeover. A smile flickered across Angel's face as he remembered how he'd found out about Jack's option.

'You're happy with the agreement then?'

'There's the small matter of one million dollars,' Angel said.

'Under Spanish law I should pay you the equivalent in pesetas. You're welcome to those right now. Or I can transfer dollars to any bank in the world, but that will take a week.'

'I'll give you details of a Swiss bank account,' Angel told him.

Roland Priest was waiting for Jack and Katie when they cleared customs at Málaga Airport.

'Good flight?' he asked, taking hold of their luggage trolley and wheeling it out of the terminal.

'Fantastic,' Jack said. 'That machine of Brady's is quite something.'

'Well I hope you approve of the one Sami's lending you.' They stopped by the Bentley Mulsanne Turbo.

Jack stared at it in disbelief. 'His own car? But any automatic would have done: I just need to get my hand back in before the demonstration.'

'Sami insisted. He said it's the least he could do.'

Jack handed his crutches to Katie and lowered himself into the driving seat. He adjusted the seat and the mirrors while Katie and Roland loaded the luggage and then climbed in themselves. He set off towards Marbella, taking it very steady at first but soon driving with increasing confidence.

'Like it?' Priest asked from the front passenger seat.

'A magic carpet, but what's Sami going to use?'

'Don't worry, he's got plenty to choose from. Would you like to hear what we're doing on site?'

'You've started already?'

'After you called us, Sami chased every contractor in the area. He managed to pressure one into starting this morning. They're repairing the straight nearest the sea, the one inland from that, and the roadways that join them. That gives us a rectangular circuit just over a mile long, which should be in fair shape by Wednesday.'

'I'm impressed.'

'*You* are? We can't get over your being willing to do this.'

'Well, I think Dad's flipped,' Katie said from the back, 'and you're not much better encouraging him, Mr Priest. He's got to be crazy racing a Grand Prix car round there.'

'It's not a race, Katie, it's a demonstration. I'll drive just as slow as I can without looking ridiculous.'

'Oh yeah?'

The Yorkshireman half-turned in his seat. 'I reckon Jack knows what he's doing. We heard yesterday – in strict confidence mind – that the town hall's going to approve the project. This demonstration should set the seal on it.'

Since returning to his villa in Marbella, Sami Nassar had received several of the municipality's secondary bankers.

The one he led into the lounge now was a thirty-five-year-old mortgage broker called Bernadino Mendez. Sami poured two glasses of French brandy, handed him a glass and then sat down opposite him in one of the big white armchairs.

'Tell me, Señor Mendez, what d'you know about my project already?'

'Rumour has it you'll be granted permission. A brilliant coup, if I may say so.'

Sami didn't look pleased by the flattery. 'If we're going to do business you'll keep thoughts like that to yourself. It may happen to be true, but I don't want people getting greedy.'

'I understand,' Mendez assured him. 'I'll treat everything you say as confidential. Perhaps you'd tell me how we might help you?'

'You realise this project's going to be hugely profitable. Our problem will be exporting those profits because of Spain's antiquated foreign exchange laws. So it doesn't make sense to import any currency at this stage. That's why I'm considering funding the initial costs by mortgaging the land.'

'We can certainly help you there.'

'Of course, Señor Mendez. I could go to anyone with something of this quality and you know it. The question is, what are you prepared to advance me against the land and at what rate of interest?'

'I think you'll be pleasantly surprised how competitive we are,' the Spaniard said. 'You've come to the right people.'

Jack dropped Katie off at their hotel, then drove on with Priest to Sami's villa. The Lebanese and Bernadino Mendez were just coming down the ornate stairway in front of it as they arrived.

'Is that Señor Ryder?' Mendez asked. 'Could I meet him?'

Sami frowned. 'Perhaps another time.'

But Jack parked the Bentley near the foot of the steps and clambered out in their path. Mendez stepped forward with a silly grin on his face and an outstretched arm. 'How do you do.'

Jack rested on his crutches and shook hands. 'Hallo, I'm –'

'Oh I know. I have seen you race on television. I just wanted to meet you.'

'Well, now you have.'

Mendez pulled a business card out of his jacket. 'Would you mind to sign this for me?'

'Not at all.' Jack did so and handed it back.

The Spaniard pressed another card into his hand. 'Please call me if I can help you in any way, Señor Ryder.'

'Thanks.' Jack tucked it into his shirt pocket. Out of the corner of his eye he saw Sami watching them disapprovingly. Mendez climbed into his car and drove off with a final wave. 'Who's he?' Jack asked.

'Just some mortgage broker,' Sami said dismissively. 'They're always pestering me to do business, but I'm not interested of course. I'm sorry he bothered you.'

'He didn't. I'm used to it.'

Sami searched his eyes. 'That's all right, then. Come in and tell me about your trip.'

On the way into the villa Jack thanked him for the loan of the Bentley. The Lebanese repeated that it was the least he could do and led Jack and Roland into the lounge. He offered them drinks.

Jack asked for whisky – desperately needing a pain-killer again – and began to tell them more about the demonstration. 'A couple of mechanics are bringing the car. It should arrive sometime tomorrow. Frank's chartering a plane to fly the media into Málaga, so we can rely on them being in the right frame of mind when they get there!'

'Why is he doing all this?'

'Yes, well, as I'm sure you've realised it's not just for fun. Frank likes the project and wants part of the action. He's offered to finance my share option in exchange for half of it, and he's interested in any more shares he can lay his hands on.'

'So am I!' Sami said. 'I'll see what I can do because he can obviously help us; but if you knew the pressure I was under from certain V I P s to cut them in on this. As a matter of fact I was going to offer to buy back your option at a healthy profit. I suppose there's no chance of that now?'

'I'm afraid not.'

'Good for you.' Sami raised his brandy glass to Jack. 'There's nobody I'd rather see make a fortune out of the project. You deserve every cent.'

'Thanks. By the way, heard any more from Angel?'

'Actually, I met him at the notary's office this afternoon. He signed that agreement, and so have the other land-owners. Roland's probably told you the good news from the town hall, so we're really on the way now.'

Priest raised his glass too. 'Let's drink to that.'

When Jack returned to the hotel, Katie told him a Mr Shepard had called several times from Madrid and left a number.

Jack went into the bedroom, closed the door and dialled the number. He was put through to the agent in seconds. Shepard explained that Angel had left Marbella on Saturday morning, that he and Ed Wheeler had subsequently been recalled to Madrid and were working flat out to incriminate him.

'Well, he's back here,' Jack said, and told him about Sami's meeting.

'Is he on his own?' Shepard asked, alarmed.

'As far as I know.'

'Call me immediately if you find out he's not. I think we're on to his operation here in Madrid. That's probably part of the reason he's run back to Marbella.'

130

'How can I help catch him?'

'You're doing it already – giving him a reason to stay there.'

'Are you going to put him under surveillance.'

Shepard thought about that. 'Not for the moment. We'd have to use locals, and frankly they'd probably just scare him away – but I'd appreciate it if you could keep me informed on what he's up to.'

'Fine.'

'Don't take risks, and let me know the minute anyone joins him. We can get the police to you in minutes if necessary.'

'I'll yell if I need you,' Jack promised.

CHAPTER SIXTEEN

Jack and Katie spent the first part of Tuesday morning compiling a press kit. Roland Priest had promised them plans, elevations and perspectives – all photocopied down to A4 size – by that afternoon. Jack had to think up the accompanying text.

It was a hellish task with so much else on his mind. He kept wondering how on earth he'd been talked into a one-legged demonstration of a Formula One car on a makeshift track. Priest had already dashed off to supervise the repair gang, but how much could they do in two days? At least Liz was arriving that afternoon. With luck she would get Katie out of Marbella as soon as possible. How was he going to explain the stunt to her, though?

'What's up, Dad?' Katie asked. She was sitting at the desk in the living room, biro and pad in hand, scribbling down Jack's dictation as best she could.

'Sorry, where was I?'

'"– with viewing points concentrated around the harbour. Floating grandstands will provide . . ." That's where you stopped.'

Jack started dictating again. At least Katie was cooperating now. In fact she was making a big effort. She'd insisted on typing and binding the press release herself.

An hour later Katie read it all back to him.

'That'll have to do,' Jack said, glancing at his watch. 'I've got to visit the site and then pick up Liz. Will you be all right till we get back?'

Katie had already turned to the typewriter. 'I've got plenty to do. *You* be careful.'

The site was humming now. Tipper lorries kept arriving with loads of infill, which they dumped at intervals on the roadways nearest the sea. A cement lorry stood with its motor running, poisoning the hot air with diesel fumes, while its drum rumbled round and round. Roland Priest was directing about two dozen Spanish workmen, communicating mainly by mime.

When Jack arrived in the Bentley Sami was already driving round in a Mercedes. The two of them parked side by side and joined the Yorkshireman, who was examining one of the biggest potholes.

'Had to be concrete,' Priest explained. 'Asphalt wouldn't have set in time.'

'All right,' Jack said, 'but please make sure it's absolutely flush with the existing surface or it'll act as a launching pad. Don't make it too smooth, though. Otherwise it'll act like sheet-ice.'

'Don't worry, we'll cross-hatch it before it cures.'

'I think that's all I can do round here – worry,' grimaced Jack. 'Better leave you to it and fetch my girlfriend.'

'Want me to check up on Katie while you're gone.'

'She'll be fine, thanks, Roland. Got plenty to do.'

Sami and Roland walked back to the Bentley with Jack and helped him into it.

'It suits you,' Sami assured him.

'Don't say that too often or I won't give it back!'

Both of them laughed and waved as Jack set off towards the main road. They watched him leave the site and turn towards Marbella.

'I don't see why you had to lend it him,' Priest said.

'To impress on everyone how nice we are. His girlfriend's going to think so anyway.'

'First his stepdaughter and now her. How many more of his bitches is he going to land us with?'

'Remember what he's doing for us. It's a small price to pay.'

The Yorkshireman looked round at the lorries and

workmen. 'Talking of which, who's going to cough up for this little lot?'

'That's easy – the mortgage brokers start paying out this week. The problem's what to do with the rest of the pesetas. We can't just leave them sitting around, earning nothing.'

'So that's why you're off to Gibraltar this morning.'

'Correct, Roland, a tireless worker for the good of the company.'

Between the site and Marbella lay the small town of San Pedro de Alcántara. A minor road climbed from it towards the sierras. As it steepened, the holiday-housing developments gave way to isolated *casas de campo* – simple country houses belonging to local people. José Garravillo drove Angel to one of these.

It stood on its own at the end of an unsurfaced track that curled between two scrubby hillocks. The one-storey house was hidden from the road. It was solidly built from local stone, with heavy doors and small windows protected by ironwork *rejas*. Garravillo had the keys and unlocked the front door. Despite the blazing sun, the inside smelt musty. On either side of a corridor was a dark bedroom, each with a recently added shower and lavatory concealed behind wood partitions. The corridor led straight to a combined cooking, eating and living area. A back door opened on to a south-facing terrace, but only by climbing one of the hillocks was there a view towards San Pedro de Alcántara and the sea.

'Belongs to an old boy in San Pedro,' Garravillo said. 'His wife died, so he doesn't come out here any more. That's why he rents it to tourists, but he's too mean to pay agents' fees.'

'How d'you find it, then?' Angel asked.

'A notice in a café. Will it do?'

'It's perfect. We can block up one of the bedroom windows if we have to, and put heavy bolts on the outside of the door. No one'll break out of that in a hurry.'

'What now, then?'

'Back to San Pedro. You rent this place for a week, and I'll call Jack.'

Katie was typing away when the phone rang. She made a mistake, and swore under her breath as she lifted the receiver.

'It's Angel. How was the trip?'

'Errr . . . fine.'

'I want to hear all about it, but I need to speak to your stepfather.'

'He's not here. He's gone to Málaga to fetch his girlfriend.'

'When's he due back?'

'Sometime this afternoon.'

Angel laughed mischievously. 'Then I'll come and see you right away.'

Katie hesitated. She wanted to see him again . . . wanted something from him anyway, but the press kit had to be finished. 'I'd like that but –'

The line had gone dead.

The road from Marbella to Gibraltar followed the curving coastline but had four lanes for much of the way. As Sami drove along it in the Mercedes he kept catching glimpses of the Rock ahead of him and to his left. Rearing up from the sea, it looked more like an island than the end of a peninsula attached to Spain.

He found himself passing holiday villages and marinas in various stages of construction, all advertising themselves as the best value, the most sought-after, the ultimate in some way or another. They dwarfed the occasional crumbling watch towers left over from the days when Moors battled with Christians for control of the coast. They could never have guessed that eventually a race of developers would take over and populate it with red-skinned tourists.

At San Roque Sami turned off the main road and

headed down towards the ugly port of La Linea. It was built on a flat strip of land, surrounded by sea on either side and with the Rock of Gibraltar towering up to the south. He stopped at the frontier gates, not just to show his passport but also because a Boeing 737 was coming in to land. Gibraltar's runway straddled what had once been the no man's land between the two countries. On the far side of the airfield was the natural fortress which had withstood fifteen determined sieges.

Once the Boeing had landed, its engines screaming in reverse thrust, Sami was allowed across. Now he could see that the sheer rock-face was riddled with galleries. He drove through Grand Casemates Gate, twin arches in white granite ramparts, and parked the Mercedes in Casemates Square. On display there was one of the depression guns with which the Rock's defenders had fired almost vertically *down* from the galleries on to their beseigers.

Sami walked into Main Street which was packed with an extraordinary mix of races and costumes. British forces personnel in uniform rubbed shoulders with Moroccans in jellabas. Many of the buildings were banks, but Sami passed the well-known names and stopped at one sandwiched between a duty-free perfume shop and a Chinese restaurant.

'I have an appointment with the manager,' Sami told the receptionist, handing her his card.

'Please take a seat, Mr Nassar. He won't keep you a moment.'

Shortly afterwards Sami was shown into a small but well-furnished office. The manager was a neat, little, Swiss man in his thirties who spoke perfect English.

'How can I be of service, Mr Nassar?'

'I'm interested in buying one-ounce gold coins – Krugerrands, Canadian Maple Leafs, or Chinese Pandas – for physical delivery in Zurich.'

'In what quantity?'

'Ten to twenty million dollars' worth. I'll be paying in

pesetas though, so I'll buy approximately one million dollars' worth at a time.'

The manager didn't bat an eyelid. 'Certainly, Mr Nassar. When were you thinking of . . . transferring these funds to us?'

'The first delivery will probably be on Thursday. My representative will be bringing them by sea. Does that represent a problem?'

'Not at all. Several million British visit Spain every year. They all need pesetas, and we fly those to the market-makers in London regularly.'

'Good. Then let's get down to details.'

Angel rang the doorbell of the Ryders' apartment but had to wait some time before Katie answered it.

'You don't look too pleased to see me,' he told her.

'I am, Angel. It's just I promised Dad I'd finish something.'

'Well, can I come in?'

She hesitated, then opened the door wider. 'All right, but you can't stay long.'

He closed it behind him, then drew her to him and kissed her on the lips.

Katie tried to push him away at first, but then gave in. She relaxed in his arms and snuggled against his chest. 'Oh Angel, I have missed you. I've been longing to . . . to . . .'

'Make love?'

'That too, but I meant just being with you and, you know, sharing some coke.'

Angel couldn't help smiling, knowing he had her in his power. And yet something about her vulnerability touched him and made him want to be kind to her. He took Katie's hand and led her out on to the terrace. They stood looking down at the sunbathers lounging around the palm-fringed pool and the swimmers splashing about in it. 'How is Jack, by the way?'

'He's . . . fine.'

'Did you tell him what we agreed – about you not liking me?'

'Yes, but he still seems sort of nervous about you.'

'Maybe it's the pressure of this demonstration.'

'You heard about that? He must be off his rocker to even consider doing it.'

'You've got a point. Who put him up to it?'

'His team manager, Frank Brady. He's lending the car.'

'But why? What's his interest in our project?'

Katie turned to face him. 'I can tell you. You see, Mr Nassar gave Dad an opinion on a million shares –'

'You mean an option?'

'Yes, that's it. Anyway, Dad doesn't have that kind of money or my mother would've had it off him! Brady's loaded, though. He's got jets, Ferraris, all that kind of stuff, and he's offered to lend Dad enough to buy those shares in exchange for half of them.'

Angel felt the anger exploding inside his head at the news of this betrayal, but he fought to keep it from showing. 'How d'you know?'

'They talked about it all weekend. Should I be telling you this?'

He forced a smile. 'I'm glad you did, because now I know how I can help your stepfather.'

'You do. How?'

'Why should this Brady take half those shares? After all, Jack's arranging everything and taking all the risk.'

'That's right.'

'I'm sure my family would offer him a better deal.'

'Heh, that's great! Wait till I tell Dad I've earned my keep for a change –'

'*Don't*,' Angel said brusquely. 'I mean, not till I've talked to my family. Promise you'll keep it a secret till then.'

'Okay,' Katie said.

Angel pulled the silver box out of his trouser pocket and showed it to her. 'Then you've earned a reward.'

Jack was waiting for Liz when she came out of the Customs Hall at Málaga Airport. She dropped her suitcase, threaded her arms between the crutches and his body, and hugged him.

'I've missed you, Jack.'

She was wearing a light summer dress, and he could feel her body through the silky material. 'I've missed you too,' he said huskily.

Liz giggled. 'I can feel that. Let's go somewhere less public.' She picked up her case and walked out of the terminal with him. Jack led her to the Bentley and unlocked it. 'Is this yours?' she asked in surprise.

'My company car. It's Sami Nassar's actually, but he insisted I borrow it.'

'Sounds like I was wrong about him. I'm looking forward to meeting him now.'

'They climbed into the front and Jack turned towards her. 'Let's take our time getting back. What would you like to do?'

She reached out and stroked his face. 'Like I said, let's find somewhere less public.'

Just after Fuengirola Jack took a minor road that headed towards the hills. He turned off that, on to a track that crossed a dried-up river bed, passed a golf course under construction, and then climbed into the unspoilt hilly countryside. They drove round a bend which gave them a superb view of coast and sea, although the track had become almost impassable now.

Jack stopped and switched off the engine. He drew Liz to him, took off her glasses and kissed her longingly.

'Here?' she asked breathlessly. 'How?'

They moved into the back of the Bentley Mulsanne. Liz stripped naked, then helped Jack undress. It was a gorgeous torment for them both, gliding fingers and tongues over each other's most sensitive parts, trying to prolong every sensation after waiting so long, knowing the reward would be almost unbearably thrilling. And when orgasm finally tore through their bodies they were locked together in a fierce embrace, shouting their love and their lust as it seared on and on . . .

Afterwards they sat up and put their arms around each other. 'That's a first,' Liz told him.

'It isn't – we did it once in the back of my –'

'In a Bentley, silly.'

Jack grinned at her. 'Wonder what Sami would say? We'd better get back – I've got to make sure Katie's finished a press kit for tomorrow . . .'

'What's happening tomorrow?'

'Ummm . . . I've been meaning to tell you about that.'

Jack did.

By the time he'd finished, Liz had moved away and was looking at him incredulously. 'Tell me you're joking.'

'I'm afraid not.'

'But your leg's broken. I mean, how can you drive that thing anyway?'

'You've seen how. Herbie's rigging up something –'

'It's madness, Jack, and you know it.'

He turned on her. 'All I know is a super guy's cut me in on a super deal. He's given me an option that'll probably make me a millionaire, but I have to do something in return.'

'Well I've got something to tell you. Remember Solly Grossman? He'll place a definite order for those conference tables and –'

'That's peanuts in comparison!'

'Is that what you think of your craft, your talent?'

'My job's still –'

'You're forty years old, Jack! I'm talking about the rest of your life.' There were tears in her eyes now. 'I just want . . . us to have that.'

He took her in his arms again. 'We will. Trust me. I'm not going to do anything stupid tomorrow.'

'Promise?'

Jack silenced her with a kiss.

CHAPTER SEVENTEEN

Just after five Jack let Liz into the hotel apartment at Puente Romano.

'I'm back,' he called out. 'Liz is with me.'

No reply, but they could hear the feeble click-clacking of a typewriter. They went into the living room. Still Katie didn't acknowledge them. Jack walked up to the desk and looked over her shoulder. The page was a mess.

'What's going on, Katie?'

Her shoulders began to shake, and then tears rolled down her pale cheeks. 'Oh Dad ... I've b ... b ... botched it ...'

He moved round so that he could see her face. It was flushed and sweaty, as though she had a fever. The whites of her eyes were bloodshot and the pupils wide and staring.

'You look terrible. Are you ill?'

Katie just shook her head dumbly.

Liz squatted down beside her, so that their heads were on the same level. 'Come and lie down. I'll get you some aspirins.'

'I ... can't. Got to ... finish ...'

She glanced at Katie's notepad, then at the sheet in the typewriter. 'You're typing up notes, aren't you? I can do that.'

'Can you?'

'My handwriting's so bad I type most of my stuff. Now come and lie down; you don't look well at all.' She helped Katie up and took her into her bedroom.

Jack slumped down on the sofa and massaged his forehead. He could hear Liz's muffled voice and an occasional sob from his stepdaughter. A tap was turned on and off. A few minutes later Liz came back into the room.

'What's wrong with her?'

Liz sat down beside him. 'What d'you think?'

'I dunno – flu . . .?'

'Come off it, Jack. She's taken something.'

He stared at her. 'How d'you know?'

'Because I live in town. I see it every day.'

'But who in God's name is she getting it from? I'll kill them if I find out.'

'You'll be murdering a lot of people, then. Anyone can get it, no problem, in discos, pubs, at school even. It takes 'O' level chemistry and a few hundred pounds to make speed, which is what I think she's on.'

A mixture of understanding and fear registered on Jack's face. 'Not . . . something worse. Cocaine, for example?'

'Let's not get too dramatic,' Liz said. 'I mean, coke costs a fortune. You haven't been doling out that much have you?'

'Not since that first day.'

'And there's no one you can think of who'd give it to her?'

'Why would they do that?'

'Sometimes you're very naive Jack. She's really pretty, or can be. There's a lot of rich young men who'd . . .'

His eyes gave him away.

'You've thought of someone?'

'Errr . . . no.'

She studied his face. 'What's going on? There's something you're not telling me.'

'Please, Liz, let me sort this out my way. But the sooner you get Katie out of here the better.'

'Then I think you should tell me why –'

The phone rang and Jack snatched it up.

'It's me, Herbie,' the chief mechanic said. 'I'm in reception, and the transporter's blocking the entrance. Where should I put it?'

'I could tell you!' Jack paused and drew in a deep breath. 'Hang on a minute and I'll be right with you.' He replaced the receiver and turned to Liz. 'The lads have arrived with the car. I've got to go and sort them out.'

Liz took a deep breath. 'All right, you're going to do this demo, and you don't need all this pressure. I can take care of the press kit and Katie, so that's two less things to worry about.'

Jack squeezed her hand. 'Thanks. You're terrific.'

On the far side of the hotel was a large open car park. The management had agreed that the transporter could stand there overnight and had roped off some space for it. Jack led the way there on his crutches, with the articulated vehicle grumbling along behind him in first gear. Steven – the younger mechanic – moved the ropes and Herbie parked in the reserved area. That done, the chief mechanic jumped down from the cab of the tractor unit and joined them.

'You two must be whacked,' Jack said.

Herbie shrugged. 'Par for the course. But I want to make sure you fit in the battleship before we do anything else.'

A side door gave access to the enclosed trailer. The mechanics climbed in first, then pushed out some aluminium steps and helped Jack up them. The interior resembled a long metal-walled garage, with its front half fitted out as a workshop, while the battleship was strapped down at the back.

The obsolete single-seater bore the same colours and sign-writing as that season's model but looked like a scaled-up version. Its designer's theories about bodywork-generated downforce had proved badly wrong but had earned his creation its nickname.

'What's that?' Jack asked, nodding at a lever sticking up on the left of the cockpit. It was ten times as long as the tiny gear-lever on the opposite side.

'My patent de-clutcher,' Herbie told him. 'You can't use your left foot, so I've rigged a rod to the clutch pedal. An arm's not as strong as a leg, so I've built in mechanical advantage – that's why the lever's so long.'

'It'll never fly!' Jack said in a goonish voice.

'Well, get in it anyway will you, just to please me?'

That was the next problem. Whichever way he tried to climb into the cockpit Jack ended up with weight on his bad leg. He turned to Herbie. 'Can you lift me up in your arms –'

'I didn't know you cared!'

' – and swing me over the cockpit? Once I get my hands on the sides I can slide myself down.'

They managed it with a lot of grunting, swearing and laughter. 'Jesus, you weigh more than my old lady,' Herbie moaned.

'Never mind, I'm in. In fact there's too much room. We'll have to make one of our special seats.' Jack moved his legs around. 'And this clutch rod's in the way. Can you run it flush with the sidewall and weld a bar at ninety degrees to the pedal?'

'Anything else, your lordship?'

'That will be all for the moment,' Jack said pompously, and they all laughed.

It took Liz some time to get used to the electric Olivetti. In the process she made an even worse mess of the page Katie had been typing. Liz ripped it out, and threw it into the almost full waste-paper basket. Then she wound in a fresh sheet and tried again.

Much better this time. She checked the notepad, and estimated there were about two and a half more pages to type. She looked at her watch, then pushed back the chair and went to see how Katie was. She was lying on her bed, staring up at the ceiling.

Liz sat down beside her. 'How are you feeling?'

'Better, thanks.'

'Anything I can get you?'

'I don't want to stop you. That press kit's got to be finished by –'

'Relax, it will be.'

But tears had formed in Katie's eyes again. 'I let Dad down again. He'll never forgive me.'

'Of course he will. You couldn't help this . . . could you?'

Katie's eyes narrowed. 'What d'you mean?'

'If you're ill, you're ill.'

'That's not what you meant.'

Liz dabbed the tears with a handkerchief. 'Listen, we've only just met, so I can't expect you to trust me yet. But I want to be a friend and help you.'

'With what?'

'Just think about what I said. I'm here if you want to talk to me. Now I'd better finish that typing.'

In Madrid Luis Beniamin was driving a haggard-looking Roy Shepard towards University City.

'What did you make of the homicide reports?' the Spaniard asked, steering round Franco's grim *Arco de la Victoria*.

'Each hit was handled by a different team, but with the same purpose – murder and intimidation. Everything points to one sick mastermind.'

'But the squad haven't come up with a single suspect yet. These "cocaine cowboys" can't be that clever.'

'Sounds kind of folksy, doesn't it? Well, they're highly trained professional killers, so don't expect them to leave prints or drop wallets.'

'And none of the street dealers we've hauled in has ever seen their supplier. They pay up front, then collect from drop sites.'

'Let's hope this professor's got something for us.'

'I'm *praying* he has,' Beniamin said. 'From the increased availability we calculate we're talking tonnes not kilos anymore. We've been terrified of this happening ever since the law was changed – organised crime moving in.'

'But how the hell are they smuggling so much into Spain?'

'That's what I don't understand.'

The University City had been built on the orders of King Alfonso XIII early this century. Its plain, rectangular buildings were set in formal gardens divided by internal roads. The campus was almost deserted because the summer vacation had already started.

Beniamin parked beside the chemistry faculty and led Shepard inside. A professor and several technicians had been hastily coopted to analyse the cocaine samples obtained by the *Brigada*. The two men walked down a long corridor with laboratories on either side and stopped at the door to one of them. Inside, the laboratory's white-coated occupants were working away at benches covered with glassware and other apparatus, while the stench of chemicals extended even into the corridor.

A tall, bespectacled man in his fifties came up and introduced himself to Beniamin and Shepard.

'You phoned a short while ago to say you had some results,' Beniamin said.

'Yes. Let's go into my office,' the professor suggested, leading them out of the laboratory and into a side-room with windows overlooking the lab. He sat down behind a cluttered metal desk and handed them several typed sheets. 'Common base. Look at the melting point tests on page one. Common base, I'm sure of it.'

'And the processing chemicals?'

'Page two. Variations in *quantities* used, but I feel that indicates poor manufacturing techniques rather than disparate –'

'But some of these chemicals aren't available in Colombia,' Shepard interrupted, staring down at the list.

'But, they are available here. In fact some of them are Spanish brands. We use them in the laboratory.'

'Will you excuse us a minute?' The American led Beniamin back into the corridor and closed the office door behind them. 'Christ, they're obviously processing here in Spain. But it takes two and a half tonnes of paste to make a tonne of cocaine hydrochloride: how's *that* sort of quantity getting in?'

Beniamin shook his head. 'God knows. We'll check every supplier of those chemicals, but they must have tens of thousands of outlets. It could take months.'

'And that little maniac's loose in Marbella. There must be a quicker way.'

'Tell me and I'll do it. Otherwise I'm reduced to prayer.'

'That's not enough!' Shephard clenched his fists. 'Take me back to homicide. I want to check every case, not just the obvious hits.'

'*Every* one? You'll be up all night again.'

'You got a better idea?'

Señora Ribera had phoned the police on Monday morning to report that her husband was missing – he hadn't spent Sunday night with her, to be precise.

The sergeant who'd taken the call had tried to keep the cynicism out of his voice. That wasn't uncommon, he'd explained. Husbands drank more than they'd intended to, especially at weekends, and slept it off at a friend's house.

Not my husband.

Or they – how could he put it tactfully? – *misbehaved*, and then daren't come home.

Not my husband.

The sergeant had scribbled down details and promised to look into it. The truth was he couldn't wait to get her off the line. They had had bigger problems that morning, like families with their brains blown out.

On Tuesday morning, though, Señora Ribera arrived at *Policia Nacional* headquarters in Madrid with her mother and father, Victor's father and a lawyer, all demanding to know what was being done to find him? That was why a young uniformed policeman had arrived at the Avicomida factory near Barajas Airport that afternoon – so that his superiors could say action had been taken. He had been shown up to the overweight finance director's office.

'Can you think of any reason why he might have disappeared?' the large youth asked.

'None at all. It's a total mystery.'

'Would you describe him as stable?'

'Yes. Reliable, hardworking. He often worked late.'

'Why was that?'

'I suppose I . . . he had rather a lot to do.'

'It couldn't have been a cover for some other activity?'

'Such as?'

'Well . . . seeing another woman.'

The director's jowls wobbled as he shook his head. 'Not the type. Rather humourless. And the work was always done.'

'I see.' The policeman closed his notepad and tucked it away. 'If anything does come up, perhaps you'd let us know. What d'you make here, by the way?'

'Airplane meals. You know, the tray you get when you fly.'

'I never have. Well, mustn't take up any more of your valuable time.'

On the way back from Gibraltar Sami stopped at Puerto Banús.

The marina was roughly rectangular, walled in by the *pueblo blanco* on three sides and a breakwater on the fourth. Eight parallel jetties stuck out into the marina from the north side. The space between them was greatest at the western end, where the largest vessels were berthed, and decreased towards the east end where the day boats were kept. The first two jetties were wide enough to drive cars down. Sami parked the Mercedes a third of the way along Jetty Two.

On his left was a black-hulled forty-foot speedboat. It had a flush deck – although portholes showed there were cabins below – and an open bridge with a sharply raked windscreen. A bearded man of about forty in jeans and a T-shirt was working away in the cockpit. His face was weatherbeaten, with red patches where skin had peeled off.

'I'm looking for a Mr Cornell Horgan,' Sami called out.

The man turned and studied him suspiciously. 'Who wants him?'

'I'm Lebanese. A friend told me you chartered your boat .. for day trips.'

Horgan smiled piratically. 'Come aboard, Mr Lebanese.' He led Sami below into the galley, which was spare and functional. They sat down facing each other on bench seats. 'Now, where exactly d'you want to go?'

'Gibraltar, actually.'

'You don't look the seafaring type to me.'

'No. I won't be coming.'

'What will?'

'Pesetas.'

'Good – there's no problem valuing them. Five per cent. That's what I charge for my service.'

'Exactly the figure I had in mind.'

Horgan reached for the cupboard door beside him, opened it and brought out a bottle of whisky. 'Then we have ourselves a deal, my Lebanese friend.'

CHAPTER EIGHTEEN

'Marbella's got all it takes to host this Grand Prix,' Frank Brady told Sami. 'Sun, sea, plenty of hotels, and international airports either side now that the frontier with Gibraltar's open.'

'Useful, that,' the Lebanese said almost to himself.

They were sitting at the front of an air-conditioned coach which was grumbling along the coast road in heavy traffic. Behind them a busty hostess was serving champagne to Priest and the thirty-strong group of motoring journalists, photographers and cameramen. Brady had chartered a plane to jet them all to Málaga and had made sure there was plenty of liquid refreshment aboard that too. Judging by the noise they were making, the party hadn't been abstinent.

'They'll have to do something about this road, though,' the team-owner said as they crawled past Torremolinos.

'You can see it's being improved. The region's director general for tourism assures me they're committed to an *autovia* the length of the Costa del Sol. He's just as keen to have the Grand Prix as the town hall is.'

The hostess reached the front of the coach and tried to tempt them with champagne. Both men declined. 'By the way,' Brady said, 'did Jack mention I was interested in any more shares that came on the market?'

Sami frowned. 'He did. As I told him, though, I'm under considerable pressure to include a certain royal family in this deal.'

'Which means shares *are* available?'

'Well . . . one of the landowners is in financial difficulties. He let me know he's prepared to sell outright.'

'What numbers are we talking?'

'Twenty-eight acres at $200,000 an acre.'

Brady nodded. 'You or I ought to buy that and trade it for stock. I've read the prospectus and the company's horribly vulnerable to a take-over by the majority share-holder – this Peruvian mob. Two per cent more and they'd gain total control. That's totally unacceptable to me.'

The coach swerved to avoid a slowing car. Someone grabbed the hostess as she teetered and there were shrieks of laughter.

'Look,' Sami said, 'this is essentially a land deal. I owned none of the site, yet I've conjured twenty per cent of the shares for myself, less the two per cent I've given Jack an option on. Are you saying you could have done better?'

'Perhaps not, but don't let speculators get their hands on shares now. You, Jack and I need a big enough block to make it clear who's in charge. I don't want to cheat the Peruvians or the others, but once the other landowners see the position they'll be open to offers.'

The Lebanese sighed. 'I have to admit you're right, but I can't finance such a proposal myself at the moment. I'm fully committed.'

'I'm not.'

'But if you start bidding the landowners are bound to get greedy.'

'So I'll give you funds and power of attorney, and you buy it for me.'

Sami stroked his moustache, apparently deep in thought. 'It makes sense,' he finally conceded.

At the site Jack brought the battleship to a halt beside Herbie and Steven. He cut the engine and pulled off the helmet and balaclava they'd provided him with.

'Well?' Herbie asked, leaning over the cockpit.

'The lever works better now, but I'm hammering the dog rings with every gear-change. Don't know how much more they'll take, so we'd better pack it in until the demo.'

'Doesn't look like there's much grip on this surface.'

Jack grimaced. 'I can't get these old slicks up to temperature. It's just about manageable in a straight line, but when I tried to build up cornering force at the far end I damn near lost it.'

'We noticed! We'll fit a bog roll in the cockpit.'

'Very funny. Better drop the tyre pressures, and increase toe-in and negative camber as much as you dare. Now help me out of this thing, will you?'

Herbie and Steven lifted him out between them and gave him his crutches. Jack was wearing a red racesuit with the left leg slashed and safety-pinned over his cast. He turned away from the single-seater and noticed a Renault driving towards them. As it came closer he recognised Angel in the driver's seat. The Colombian was on his own.

'Damn,' Jack muttered. 'Give me a couple of minutes, lads.' He swung along towards the Renault which stopped a few yards away.

Angel climbed out of it, looking distinctly unfriendly.

'Afternoon,' Jack said. 'How are you?'

'Not too happy.'

'Oh? What's the problem?'

'That's what I've come to find out.'

Jack raised his eyes to heaven. 'Is it bad movie time again, or are you going to tell me what's bothering you?'

'Sure, I'll tell you,' Angel said, clenching and unclenching his fists. 'Have you forgotten our agreement?'

Jack nodded round at the battleship. 'I've been busy, or hadn't you heard?'

'Sure. I also heard you made a deal with this Frank Brady behind my back.'

'Who told you that?' Jack asked, taken completely by surprise.

Angel sneered. That triggered something in Jack — a realisation that attack was his only defense now and an eruption of rage at the whole crazy situation. 'I haven't got time for gossip!' he shouted. 'I'm demonstrating that heap behind me any time now and I can do without any goddamn distractions.'

'*Distractions?* You call one million shares a distraction?'

'I'm calling *you* one, Angel, so get off my back!' Jack turned away and swung towards the single-seater.

The Colombian ran after him and grabbed his sleeve. 'I haven't finished!'

Jack looked down at the restraining arm, then at the mechanics. They were watching him, clearly concerned. Herbie raised a menacingly large spanner and Steven brought a hammer out of the toolbox.

'What are you going to do now?' Jack asked Angel. 'Put us all in your car boot? Better do it quickly, because here comes the press.'

The coach was just turning off the main road. Angel saw it, let go of Jack's arm, and backed away towards the Renault. 'We'll settle this later.'

'Aren't you going to wish me luck?'

The Colombian slammed his car door and drove off.

The coach parked near the single-seater and Sami led the party off it. Some of them looked decidedly unsteady as they came down its steps, and there was a good deal of laughter. Several of them called out to Jack, who waved a greeting. Then one of them paused at the top of the steps and looked around.

'Is *this* it?' he asked in a loud voice.

There was a momentary silence.

'Come along, gentlemen,' Priest barked, pushing himself out of the coach. 'Gather round and I'll explain where everything's going to be.'

Brady detached himself from the group and walked towards his mechanics. They had just finished lowering Jack into the cockpit and were not checking tyre pressures.

The team-owner squatted by the cockpit. 'Did you hear that?'

'Yes,' Jack said.

'Don't take any notice. I can imagine how nerve-racking this must be after your shunt.'

'It won't be, if I'm sensible.'

'That's what I mean – I'll understand.'

Jack's eyes narrowed. 'Understand what?'

'You being scared. Okay, there's not much for this lot to see and it'd make a world of difference if you laid on some fireworks, but –'

'You're winding me up again.'

Brady feigned surprise. 'D'you think I've laid all this on in the hope that you've still got what it takes?'

'It hadn't bloody well occurred to me until you put it into my head.'

'Well, forget it. You're too old to have a prang like that and recover.' Brady stood up abruptly and turned away.

'Just a minute, Frank!'

But the media group were milling around them now. A director beckoned at his minicam crew. 'Jack's posing in the car. Shoot it please.'

Posing? Jack tugged on the balaclava to hide his face. He was so wild now he didn't trust himself to speak. Of course Brady was psyching him up, but that was the crazy thing about this project – it always seemed to be in Jack's interest to go along with every outlandish suggestion. Well, screw it! At least it had landed him back in a racer, where he belonged, away from all the shouters and hustlers. Brady wanted a firework display? Well, he was picking up the tab.

'Fire up,' Jack told Herbie and pulled on his helmet.

Steven plugged an outside battery into the socket under the rear wing. Jack flicked the ignition and petrol pump switches on, then pressed the starter button. The engine roared into life. He kept the revs steady until the oil and water temperature had reached sixty degrees centigrade. Then he blipped the throttle, making the car snarl and quiver like a dog with its hackles up. Exhaust fumes began to penetrate his helmet but Jack didn't care. He almost enjoyed the heady stench. He looked around. Herbie and

Dave were trying to herd everyone back. Cars had stopped on the main road and some were nosing on to the site. Time to go. Jack snicked the gear-lever into first and squeezed the accelerator.

The engine note rose from a menacing growl to a hysterical shriek. Ten thousand revs. Everyone was getting the hell out of it now! He yanked the clutch lever backwards and the cool rear slicks disappeared in clouds of bluey-white smoke. But the car hardly moved. Then suddenly the tyres gripped and shot it forward. Jack flicked the steering wheel left, sending it into a violent spin, then floored the throttle. The car whipped round and round like a Catherine wheel, pouring rubber smoke until it was almost hidden. Finally, when Jack could no longer see where he was, he banged in the clutch and hit the brakes.

Gradually the cloud lifted. He glimpsed the crowd whooping and clapping, egging him on. The cameras were locked on to him. Jack built up the revs again, flicked the car round in line with the straight and kept going.

It was like a drag-car ride, a snaky one because the front slicks weren't as hot as the rears. He fought to keep on course, changing gear with just a flick of his right wrist. Second gear . . . eleven thousand revs, change . . . eleven thousand five hundred, change! Doing a hundred and fifty miles an hour now, the roadsides blurring, end of the straight rushing up incredibly fast . . . *brakes*, but gently until they bit, then really hard, racing down through the box with just a fractional pause to rev each time he found neutral.

Jack turned into the first corner gingerly, feeling for grip. Now there was heat in the tyres! The car danced about but raced through the bend and the following one on to the back straight. He charged down that as fast as he could, took two more corners to complete the rectangular circuit and set off on another lap. As he passed the spectators, a wicked idea for a finale came to him.

They were standing outside the last bend, with Brady up

front as usual. How about winding *him* up? Jack reached the back straight again and lined up for the penultimate bend but then turned in terribly late, all the while keeping his eye on the team-owner. The car started to spin. Jack encouraged it with a kick on the throttle and whirled towards the crowd. Everyone was running but Brady seemed rooted to the spot. By carefully timed dabs on the brakes, Jack finally screeched to a halt broadside on to him and just inches away.

Brady's jaw hung open. He closed it, then smiled broadly. 'Some comeback! Just what was needed.'

'You . . .!' Jack tugged off his helmet and sweat-soaked balaclava, intending to say just what he thought of him. Then he spotted Liz and Katie standing by a taxi. As soon as he was out of the cockpit and on his crutches he set off towards them.

Katie had obviously been crying and Liz had an arm round her.

'I thought we'd agreed you wouldn't come.'

'We couldn't just sit in the hotel, not knowing what happened,' Liz said, 'so we took a taxi.'

'I can see that. What's up, Katie?'

'N . . . nothing, Dad.' She flicked hair out of her face and wiped her eyes with the back of one hand.

'She saw your performance and got frightened. *I* was frightened.'

'I didn't know you were watching,' Jack sighed. 'Look, it may have seemed scary but I was just . . . well, showing off a little.'

'A *little*?'

They were looking straight at each other. 'I know what I'm doing, Liz.'

'You sure?'

Sami interrupted them. 'We're taking everyone to Puerto Banús for lunch. I'd be delighted if you ladies would join us. In fact, I insist!'

*

'Ten men,' the chief of police told Shepard and the head of the *Brigada de Estupefacientes*, 'that's all I can spare you.'

They were sitting in his old-fashioned office in the *Jefatura Superior* whose windows overlooked the Puerta del Sol, a square considered not only the centre of Madrid but of Spain as well.

'With respect, Señor Jefe,' the head of the drugs squad said, 'that's not enough. We have to check every customer of every chemical supplier in Spain, and as fast as possible.'

'I understand, but there are other priorities. It's not the end of the world.'

'It's pretty damn close,' Shepard said impulsively.

The chief stood up, looking at Shepard as though he'd made a rude noise. The interview was clearly over. The American struggled to find the right words. 'It's not just the drugs – they come to seem the least of the problem. It's the scale of corruption and violence they bring with them. Ever been to Colombia?'

The policeman shook his head impatiently.

'Then imagine a country taken over by criminal organisations. Multi-nationals with the most enviable cash-flow in the Americas. Billions of dollars to corrupt every politician, civil servant, judge and policeman they need, and if they can't bribe them, they kill them – the Minister of Justice and the Attorney General being just two recent victims. That may not be the end of the world, but it's the end of society.'

There was silence for a while. 'Very well,' the chief of police said finally. 'Twenty men for a month, but you'd better have some results to show me.'

Beniamin was waiting for them in the corridor. 'Well?' he asked when they emerged from the office.

'Twenty men for a month,' his boss told him. 'I stuck my neck out for you two. Now get the job done or my credibility's ruined.'

They watched him stride away. Beniamin put an arm round Shepard's shoulder. 'Good work. I'll round up the recruits and get them started right away. Why don't you get some sleep? Frankly, you look terrible.'

'I'm going back to homicide. We must have missed something.'

'But, Roy, you've read all the reports. You can't check up on bodies they haven't found yet.'

The American stopped in his tracks and stared at him. 'Oh yes I can!'

Sami had booked the entire terrace of the waterfront restaurant in Puerto Banús and laid on a seafood banquet. Tables had been joined together in one long run so that everyone could sit together. Jack, now dressed in casual clothes, was in the middle answering a barrage of questions, though he'd also made sure Katie stayed beside him. Every now and then he squeezed her hand under the table, as if reassuring her he was still there, and she returned the pressure.

There was no doubt that the demonstration had been a success. The documentary director babbled on about prize-winning footage and how he was going to add 'impressions' of Puerto Banús to show what the site would look like. Sami and Priest – seated at the far end of the table with Liz between them – were positively beaming.

After the meal the group dispersed to look round the port, giving Jack a well-earned break. He was chatting to Katie when Brady slid on to the seat beside him.

'I just came to say I'm proud of you, Jack. You've done a fantastic job.'

'Thanks.'

'I've done my bit too.' The team-owner glanced round to make sure no one could overhear. 'One of the site owners is broke apparently and needs to sell outright. I've persuaded Sami to buy the land for me and trade it for shares in the company. You'll get ten per cent of them. How does that sound?'

'Worryingly generous. What do I have to do now?'

Brady chuckled. 'I've got to fly back with this lot, so I want you to check the land for me.'

'Can't Sami do that?'

'He's selling it to me, in effect, and I never trust a salesman, even when he's my partner. All you have to do is visit the Land Registry and check this piece hasn't been mortgaged or anything daft like that. I'll give you all the details.'

'Fine,' Jack said. 'It's not much to ask for ten per cent.'

Slumped at a desk in a dingy police office, Roy Shepard picked up yet another missing persons report, rubbed his bleary eyes, and began reading again.

Male, twenty-eight, married . . . missing since Sunday . . . worked as an accountant at Avicomida . . .

Shepard's head rocked back and he read the last bit again. The name burned into his skull like a branding iron – AVICOMIDA, the Colombian-owned airline catering company . . . hundreds of meal carts crossing the Atlantic every day . . .

He grabbed the phone and dialled Beniamin's number.

CHAPTER NINETEEN

Armed with guns, sniffer dogs and a search warrant, the *Brigada* hit Avicomida's Madrid factory less than two hours later. It was eight o'clock in the evening. The night shift was due on at ten.

While the Alsatians nuzzled debris from the trays, Shepard and Beniamin traced the route the carts took through the building. The only place where the trolleys were stripped down was in maintenance, but there wasn't a single one in the department now. Outside it, though, at the back of the factory, a waste-skip was half-filled with broken-up insulation panels. The American fished out a corner piece and showed his colleague the tell-tale groove.

'So *that's* how it got here.'

'How the hell did we miss it before?'

'A young policeman. He didn't see the connection.'

'It's written all over their lorries, goddammit! They should change their slogan to "Feeding The World's Coke Habit".'

Beniamin sighed. 'What now? A stakeout to see where it goes?'

Shepard suddenly turned round. A mechanic watching them from a doorway met his eyes and ducked back inside. 'I reckon the word's out already and they'll shut down the route. I'll get on to our people in Bogotá and have them check their end. You start questioning the employees here, starting with maintenance.'

As soon as a day-shift friend tipped him off about the raid, the rat-faced foreman contacted El Carnicero. They arranged to meet right away in a bar at Alcalá de Henares, a workers' dormitory town east of the airport.

El Carnicero arrived with Godofredo, a younger but equally vicious-looking countryman. The foreman was waiting for them at the back of the almost deserted bar. He scraped back his chair and stood up shakily.

'We're in deep shit –'

'Calm down, sit down, and tell us what you know,' El Carnicero said.

'The pigs just crashed in. How did *they* know? Guns, dogs . . . Jesus Christ!'

'What did they find?'

'You're not going to like this – the insulation. We stripped some out last night and chucked it in a waste skip. But the lorries don't collect them every day.'

Godofredo ground his teeth, but El Carnicero showed no reaction. 'Why didn't you burn it or something?' he asked evenly.

'I didn't think . . . shit, I'm sorry.'

'Forget it.'

'*Forget* . . .? I can't just go back there as if nothing's happened.'

'That's exactly what you're going to do. If you don't, they'll suspect you immediately. Anyway, they can't prove what it was in the insulation, or when. All you know is the carts didn't work properly when you tested them. You were just doing your job.'

'I suppose –'

'Just stick to the story. Don't add anything or try to be clever and you'll be fine. Tell you what, though, we'll take you to the factory tonight and hang around. If things look bad, we'll be waiting to get you out from there.'

'Thanks, but what if –?'

'Don't worry, we take care of our own. Now get us a beer will you? I'm dying of thirst.'

The foreman stood up, grinned at them sheepishly, and walked to the bar. When he was out of earshot, Godofredo bent close to his boss. 'He's the only one there who can tie it to us.'

'I know. You drive, I'll kill him.'

At the end of a gruelling day Jack was stretched out on his bed in the Puente Romano apartment. Inevitably his bad leg had taken another battering and was throbbing with pain. Liz had poured him a large whisky and told him to rest, then taken Katie for an evening swim.

When the doorbell rang Jack was tempted to ignore it, but whoever it was persisted. Finally he struggled up, groaning and muttering darkly, and went to answer it on his crutches. Angel was pressing the bell again just as he opened the door.

'*You!*'

'I want an answer, Jack!'

He felt an overwhelming urge to slam it in Angel's face. After all he'd been through, all he'd achieved with Sami and Priest, and Angel was still threatening the project. Then he remembered Shepard's words – the Colombian wouldn't just go away, he had to be dealt with.

'All right, come in,' Jack said. He led him into the living room and they both sat down. 'It's been a tough day. Sorry I was rude on the site, but listening to stupid gossip didn't improve my temper. Where did you hear this gossip, anyway?'

Angel looked momentarily fazed. 'Ummm . . . from Sami Nassar. He mentioned something about it when I signed the agreement.'

'Well you got the wrong end of the stick. Brady *does* want to buy my shares, and Sami's, and yours no doubt. But we won't let him.'

'Prove it.'

'How?'

'Easy. I'll give you the million dollars to buy those shares. Ask for bearer certificates and give them to me. Once we control the company, you'll have two million shares in exchange. I'll put that in writing.'

Got you at last, Jack thought. Shepard would know how to trace where the money came from. But he mustn't seem too eager now. 'That assurance wouldn't be worth the paper it's written on.'

'And, equally, you could run off with the million. The point is we both need each other – we need you to front the project and you need us to finance it . . . unless you've changed your mind?'

'I told you, I haven't.'

'Then where d'you want the million paid?'

Jack hesitated – he had to talk to Shepard. 'Let me think about it. I'll tell you in the morning.'

'What's wrong with right now?'

'Maybe it'd be fastest to transfer funds straight to the Cayman Islands. I'll speak to Sami.'

Angel eyed him suspiciously. 'Just Sami?'

'Who else?'

'Never mind. I'll be back in the morning.'

'Not here,' Jack said sharply. 'I've told you I don't want you coming here.'

Angel's lips twitched into a smile, as though he'd just thought of something. 'That's right, you did say that, didn't you? We'll meet in town then.'

As soon as he'd left Jack phoned the Madrid number Shepard had given him. The female operator seemed to be expecting his call and spoke to him in English, asking him to wait, then put him through in less than a minute.

'Great work,' the agent said. 'The Cayman Islands will do fine as long as it's a reputable bank – they cooperate with us nowadays. I'll get one of our boys to fix up an account over there right away, and will ring you back with the details.'

'But Angel says he'll deposit the million right away. That means he'll expect the certificates within, say, a week. God knows what he'll do if I don't deliver them.'

'We should have him locked up by then. We're on to

something big here, Jack. I'm convinced I can tie it to him, given a few more days, or I wouldn't expose you like this.'

'Don't worry about me then – just nail the bastard!'

'Is there anyone else working with him?'

'I don't think so.'

'Well call me if that changes. And has Katie left yet?'

'No, but my girlfriend's here to look after her. They should both be gone by the weekend.'

'I'd make sure of that if I were you,' Shepard warned him.

El Carnicero took no time at all to strangle the foreman with the piano wire. Having made some excuse about taking a back route which passed a stinking, smoking rubbish dump, the enforcers disposed of the body there – no time for a careful burial because the top priority now was to warn Julio César Mosquera.

Afterwards Godofredo drove his boss into Madrid and dropped him in the Puerta del Sol. Out of habit El Carnicero spat in the gutter as he passed police headquarters, then turned off the square and walked into an area of increasingly sleazy side-streets. He ignored the mini-skirted prostitutes but stopped outside a porn-and-violence video club. He pretended to study the lurid posters, while carefully angled mirrors at each side of the window allowed him to check for a tail. When he was sure he hadn't been followed he stepped inside.

The man at the counter barely glanced at him before jerking his head towards a door in the back wall. That led to a narrow corridor, at the end of which was a filthy lavatory and a poky little office. On the desk were an unusual number of phones for a small business. El Carnicero took a list of Medellín numbers out of the wall safe, checked the date on a nude calendar, and called the appropriate number.

'I need to speak to the chief. *Now*.'

The receiver told him to call the nineteenth number on

the list. He did so and spoked briefly to Aurelio Canafisto, who quickly fetched Julio César.

'Pigs have broken into the feed-store,' El Carnicero told him. 'You've got to stop exports until –'

'I know,' Julio César snapped. 'They just busted our end too. We're doing everything possible to limit the damage but . . . there are links to me. What about you?'

'One link – I just cut it. And we've got to have imports fast. We can't hold the market without them.'

'You have to! Listen to me: that monopoly is the key to my plans now. I'm counting on you to enforce it until we establish a new supply, and . . . where's Angel? Why isn't he telling me this?'

El Carnicero cleared his throat. 'He's down south, and I can't contact him.'

'God Almighty! Not still on that motor-racing nonsense, at a time like this?'

'It's not just that. After the takeover we thought it best if –'

'*We?* Have you lost your sense too, man?'

The enforcer said nothing.

'Only one thing for it – I'll have to come over and sort this out myself.'

In the Medellín telephone exchange the CIA-installed computer controlling a bank of miniature tape-recorders stopped one of them. A voice simulator added the exact time of the call and the number it was made to and rewound it. Then it dialled a number in the American embassy in Bogotá, electronically interrogated a sophisti-cated answering machine to make sure the line was secure, and played El Carnicero's call to it.

Sami hadn't returned to Málaga with Frank Brady and the media boys. He'd said his goodbyes in Marbella, pleading pressure of work.

That had given him time to visit Bernadino Mendez's

office before it closed. Mendez's office was located in a modern five-storey block on the Avenida Ricardo Soriano. A sign in the entrance announced in five languages, including Arabic, that the mortgage-broker could be found on the third floor. Sami rode up in the lift and walked into a plush reception area. He was obviously expected and was shown straight into Mendez's office. That too was decorated in a contract version of Marbella, impractical – cream-coloured carpeting, a glass desk on gilded trestles and brassy chairs to match.

The Spaniard looked relieved to see him. Despite Sami's protests he opened a bottle of French champagne to toast the start of their deal. Sami signed the paperwork and in return was given a black security briefcase featuring a dye-bomb and screamer. These were to protect the two hundred million pesetas in ten-thousand-peseta notes concealed within – approximately one and a half million dollars' worth. The second instalment would be ready on Monday, Mendez assured him.

As soon as he decently could Sami left the office and drove straight to Puerto Banús. Cornell Horgan and a deckhand were ready and waiting.

It was 4 p.m. in Colombia when Hal Argetsinger checked the answering machine in his office at the American embassy. That was the equivalent of 10 p.m. in Madrid, so it took some time before he located Ed Wheeler.

They were both Spanish-speakers and Argetsinger had been one of Wheeler's instructors at Langley. He had been following the Mosquera case closely and could not resist teasing the younger man now.

'Bugged any good taxis lately?'

'No. Just about everything else though, and not a worthwhile beep between them.'

'Well, listen to this.' And he played El Carnicero's call to Julio César.

'Jesus!' Wheeler said at the end of it. 'Wait till Roy hears it.'

'That hillbilly sure is smoking them out. Now you've got the time of the call and the number it was made to, so if you go on down to the telephone exchange they might be able to tell you where it came –'

'I'm on my way!' Wheeler almost screamed.

The Rock appeared only as a towering shadow in the almost moonless night as Cornell Horgan eased his burbling speedboat past Gibraltar's main harbour. He turned into Marina Bay – sandwiched between the North Mole and the runway – cut his engines and glided alongside one of the jetties. Horgan had no intention of reporting to the harbour master.

While his deckhand stayed on board, he jumped ashore with the briefcase and walked to a telephone box near the Prince of Wales cinema.

The Swiss banker took delivery five minutes later, and Horgan slipped back into the night.

CHAPTER TWENTY

'I have to see Sami, and sort some things out in town,' Jack told Liz as they breakfasted on their bedroom terrace. A sea breeze rustled the palm trees round the pool below them, and although the rising sun hadn't yet reached them, the air was already pleasantly warm. 'Can you handle Katie?'

'No problem. We're getting on fine.'

Angel had changed the Renault for an Opel first thing that morning and then driven it to Puente Romano. Parked between the other cars outside reception, he watched Jack leave in the Corniche. Then he went inside and used one of the wall-phones to call the Ryders' apartment.

Liz answered it.

'Person-to-person call for Mees Ryder from her mother,' Angel said in heavily accented English.

'Hold on, I'll fetch her.'

Soon Katie was on the line. 'It's me,' Angel said, reverting to his normal voice.

She stifled a giggle. 'Clown! What are you playing at?'

'Can we talk?'

A pause. 'Go ahead. Liz just left the room.'

'I took the morning off to see you, Katie, but they seem to be holding you prisoner.'

'You can say that again. One or other of them stays with me the whole time.'

'Your stepfather just left. We had a chat and he was really friendly, by the way. So can't you get away from that woman, come and have some fun with me?'

'I don't know, Angel . . . maybe I shouldn't –'

'Okay, baby, stay with your sitter if that's what you want.'

'I don't. It's just . . . that stuff seems to get me in trouble.'

'Think about the rush. You like that, don't you?'

Katie sighed. 'Wait for me.'

She knocked on the main bedroom door.

'Come in,' Liz called out. 'Everything all right?'

'Mum was just checking up on me. Gets me down. I think I'll take a walk on the beach.'

'I'll come with you.'

'Don't you start!'

Liz gave her a puzzled look. 'I was only going to –'

'Spy on me? I just want to be on my own. Can't you all leave me alone, just for one hour?'

Katie walked out and closed the door behind her. She stood in the corridor, waiting to see if Liz followed her. When she didn't, Katie hurried into her bedroom, put on her favourite denim mini-skirt and a T-shirt, and checked herself in the mirror.

'I'll be on the beach,' she shouted as she left the apartment.

'Heh, you look great,' Angel told her when they met in reception. 'How long we got?'

'An hour or so. I gave Liz a lecture about spying on me. Where are you staying now, by the way?'

'A great little place not far from here. Like to see it?'

'Okay.'

They climbed into the Opel and set off towards San Pedro de Alcántara. 'That was some show yesterday,' Angel said.

'Dad's crazy. He . . . I didn't see you there.'

'I watched him practise. I think he's crazy too. Why's he taking crazy risks for Brady?'

'I told you – he's giving Dad the money for half those shares. I thought you were going to make him a better offer.'

Angel had tensed almost imperceptibly. 'Didn't his deal with Brady fall through?'

'No way – they were talking about it afterwards, at lunch. You'd better make your move soon.'

He gave her a sly smile. 'I'll do that.'

It took more than ten minutes to reach the *casa de campo*. 'Why on earth are you staying out here?' Katie asked a little warily as they bumped along the unsurfaced track.

'Wait till you see the view. Anyway, I needed more room for my friends.'

'Friends?'

'Our age. We'll join them at Puerto Banús when you've had a look round. You'll like them.' Angel parked the car, led Katie to the *casa*'s front door and unlocked it.

She peered inside. 'It's kind of spooky.'

'Real Spanish style, not those phoney hotels. Just look in here.' He opened the first door on the right. The bedroom was totally dark because he and Garravillo had blocked up the window. Angel switched on the light bulb that hung over the metal-framed double bed. There was no other furniture.

Katie stepped past him. 'What's so great about –?'

Angel flung her on to the bed and rushed out of the room. He slammed and bolted the reinforced door behind him.

Jack had arranged to meet Angel in a large café at the foot of Marbella Old Town, but there was no sign of Angel when he arrived.

He sat alone at a table for some time, looking around and glancing repeatedly at his watch. Finally a modishly dressed man in his mid-twenties left another table and joined him.

'Angel couldn' make it,' José Garravillo said. 'He ask me to get those bank accoun' details for him.'

'Who are you? What's going on?'

Garravillo just grinned and produced a profusely apologetic letter from Angel. 'Jus' write the details on there. You can stick in an envelope – promise I won' look!'

Jack thought about it and then complied.

As soon as the stranger left, Jack limped to the café's payphone.

'That's one evil-looking son of a bitch,' Shepard said to Beniamin.

El Carnicero had just stepped into the video shop after studying its window. A stake-out had been organised within an hour of Argetsinger's tip-off and a *Brigada* team had worked through the night to set it up.

A prostitute accepted a staggering amount of cash from a middle-aged man to rent her business premises for a month. God knows what the filthy pervert had in mind, but who was she to ask questions? The window of her fourth-floor bedroom overlooked the video shop, and it was from there that the agents had observed the Colombian. The shop's phones had also been tapped and listening equipment installed in the bedroom.

'Any idea who he is?'

'A *Sudaca* for sure,' Beniamin said, using the derogatory nickname for South Americans. 'Looks like –'

'Shhh!' The technician with earphones on his head waved at them to shut up. 'Someone talking on one of the lines . . . South American accent . . . same voice that called Mosquera.'

'It's him!' Beniamin hissed. 'We'll tail him when he comes out.' He turned his back on the technician and started giving urgent instructions on his walkie-talkie.

Just then the prostitute's telephone rang. Shepard snatched it up and identified himself.

'Jack here, calling from Marbella. I rang your number and someone gave me this one.'

'Good. What is it?'

'Why are you whispering, Roy?'

'We're on surveillance, but go ahead, tell me what's happened.'

Jack did, and described Garravillo.

'Right, I'll come down tonight. Can you keep clear of them till I reach you?'

'Absolutely.'

'And Jack, we're winning at last!'

Jack had also promised Frank Brady to visit the Land Registry, which was above a bank in the Avenida Ricardo Soriano, Marbella's main commercial street. He rode the lift to the fifth floor and swung up to the enquiry desk on his crutches.

'Does anyone here speak English?' he asked an amiable-looking Spaniard in his twenties.

'A little,' the clerk said.

'Thanks, because my Spanish is practically non-existent. I'm trying to find out if there's a mortgage on this piece of land.' Jack unfolded a plan of the site, with the piece Sami had offered to buy for Brady outlined in red marker.

'Is where they want to make a motor race, no?'

'That's right.'

'Someone ask the same question early this week. You wait please.'

He disappeared through a door but soon came back with an enormous register. The clerk opened it up on the counter, turned it round so that Jack could read it, and showed him a written description of the land. 'You can see the present owner has not mortgaged it. If he had, whoever gave him the mortgage would come here and write so at the side here to protect his investment.'

Something was nagging away at the back of Jack's mind. 'How soon would they do that? I mean enter the mortgage in the register after paying it out?'

The clerk smiled. 'It should be done right away, but you know what they say about Spain – *mañana*.'

'You said someone had already asked you about this land. D'you remember who it was?'

'Sure, Bernadino Mendez. He have an office in this Avenida.'

That was what was bothering him! Jack remembered signing an autograph for the broker outside Sami's villa . . . and the odd look the Lebanese had given them. He couldn't understand it at the time, but now a horrible suspicion was creeping up on him.

'That explains it,' Jack said as casually as he could. 'You've been most helpful.'

When Garravillo reached the *casa de campo*, Katie was still hammering away at the bedroom door and yelling her head off.

'Jack was going to double cross me,' Angel explained above the racket. 'Now you're back I'm going in there before she kills herself. Get a gun.' He moved close to the door. 'Shut up, Katie!'

'Let me out! Let me out!'

'Shut up and I'll open it!'

The noise stopped. He glanced round at Garravillo, who'd come out of their room with a MAC-10 submachine gun.

'Get away from the door!' Angel slid back all three bolts and opened it slowly.

Katie jumped at him with her hands up, trying to claw his face. He grabbed her wrists and wrestled her backwards on to the bed. As she kicked and struggled her skirt rode up round her waist. Garravillo had come in behind them and stood at the end of the bed, staring down at her.

'You lied to me!' Katie screamed.

'Jack lied to *me*! When he gives me what he promised, you go free. Now stop it. Stop it!' He shook her hard and slammed her down on the mattress.

Katie gave up. She caught sight of Garravillo, and watched him fearfully. Angel turned round and saw what

173

he was looking at too. He faced Katie again. 'Behave, and I'll be nice to you. You want some coke? *Do you?* Here.' He tugged a paper twist out of his pocket and tossed it on to the mattress.

She closed her eyes and started to cry silently.

Angel let go of her wrists, stood up and backed out of the bedroom. He slammed the bolts shut.

'You didn't tell me how pretty she was, man!' Garravillo said. 'We could have us some fun with little blondie.'

Angel looked at him coldly. 'I'm going to Puente Romano to see what Jack's up to. While I'm gone, you leave her alone.'

Garravillo grinned. 'Want her to yourself, huh?'

'I said leave her alone! I mean it!'

'Okay, okay.'

Bernadino Mendez looked surprised but delighted to see Jack. He ushered him into his office, sat him down, and told the receptionist to bring in some champagne.

'It's an honour and a pleasure to have you here, Señor Ryder. Would it be too much to ask . . .?'

'Go ahead.'

'A photograph, here in the office, with me.'

'Fine. We'll fix something up next week.'

The receptionist returned and poured Dom Perignon into tall glasses. Mendez raised his glass to Jack. '*Salud!*'

'Cheers.'

'Why don't you come with Señor Nassar on Monday?'

'You mean when he comes to . . . errr . . .?'

'Collect the next payment, that's right.' The broker's expression changed to sudden understanding. 'Now I see. You've come to, how you say, chase me up.'

'Not at all. It obviously takes time to raise that much.'

'Two hundred million in cash, yes.'

'*Cash?*'

Mendez blinked at him. 'You did know – ?'

'Of course,' Jack said quickly. 'I suppose it makes no difference – you've the land as security.'

'We have Señor Nassar's *options* on the land and his guarantee to take them up.'

'On which basis you gave us the mortgages, right?'

'Only at the present land value, I'm afraid, because of the planning difficulties.'

Jack winced, then rubbed his bad leg to disguise his reaction. 'What's the latest you've heard on that, by the way?'

'Some of the *consejales* in the *Ayuntamiento*, the older ones, they don't want a big motor race here. Too much noise and disruption.'

'Don't worry, we're working on them.'

'I'm sure you are,' Mendez said. 'Señor Nassar can be very persuasive.'

Jack's mind was in turmoil as he drove to Sami's villa. Could there be an explanation? Could the Lebanese have decided to raise finance that way after all? If so, why hadn't he said so?

Nassar came to the front door to greet him after he'd mounted the stairway on his crutches. 'Come in, Jack. You look tired. Anything wrong?'

'Just this damn leg.'

'Let me fix you a drink. Roland's here too.'

They went into the living room where the Yorkshireman was relaxing in a big white armchair, whisky tumbler in hand. He joined in the chorus of sympathy. 'Put your feet up, lad. You looked knackered.'

Jack sank into a matching chair.

Sami was behind him at the cocktail cabinet. 'Did you speak to Frank?'

'Yes,' Jack lied. 'I told him you'd said we could have bearer certificates, and gave him the bank account details. The funds should be in the Cayman Islands early next week.'

Sami chuckled. 'The British and their tax fiddles! Did he mention that land he wants me to buy for him?'

'He asked me to check if it was mortgaged, so I went to the Land Registry.'

Priest's glass stopped halfway to his mouth.

Nassar came round from behind Jack and handed him his whisky. 'And?' he asked calmly.

'It's not.'

'That's all right then,' Priest said with obvious relief.

'Unless someone's taken out a mortgage in the last few days.' Jack was looking straight at Sami.

'Well I certainly haven't,' the Lebanese said.

'It's an idea though, isn't it?'

'Far too expensive, Jack. You're doing a wonderful job, but leave the finance to me.'

'He suspects something!' Priest exploded when Jack had left.

Nassar was pacing up and down the living room. 'Not necessarily. Frank asked him to check the Land Registry and he did, that's all.'

'So why all the questions about mortgages? You're too greedy, Sami. You should never have tried to con Brady.'

'He was begging to be taken! I thought Angel would go for Jack's shares – that's why I brought them together. But then Brady came into the picture, even more desperate to buy.'

'And you never could resist a mug punter, big or small. Well, I say we clear out now, as soon as that million's arrived.'

Nassar stopped and faced him. 'Go, if you've lost your nerve, but I'm staying for the big prize. I still think I can take Brady for that other deal, and Mendez makes the second payment on Monday.'

'Aren't you forgetting something? That's when you're due to pay Angel for the option on his land.'

'So? If the scam's intact, we'll pay him and keep it running. If not, *that's* the time to disappear.'

Priest gave a deep sigh. 'All right, all right. I'll stay, but don't say I didn't warn you.'

When Jack reached Puente Romano, he could hardly climb out of the Bentley. Black despair weighed him down as he thought about the nightmarish mess he was in – caught between drug traffickers and con men. What else could possibly go wrong? The answer wasn't long in coming.

'Katie's gone!' Liz told him frantically as he stepped into the apartment.

'Gone? Where?'

'She said to the beach, but that was three hours ago. I've been down there and all round the hotel, but I can't find her anywhere.'

'Oh Liz, you said you'd look after her.'

'She didn't want me spying – that's how she put it – so I –'

The phone interrupted them and Jack snatched up the receiver. 'Jack Ryder here.'

'Sorry I couldn't make the meeting,' Angel told him. He had seen Jack arrive and was calling from a pay-phone in reception. 'I'll arrange to transfer the money on Monday – I'm expecting funds then myself. But I've taken out some insurance already to make sure those certificates end up with the right owner.'

'You bastard! You've got Katie, haven't you?'

'Is she missing? I don't know anything about that, but I wouldn't involve the police if I were you. She might never turn up if you do.'

'I want her back *now*, or no deal.'

'No deal, Jack? Don't say that. And don't worry about Katie either. Something tells me she'll turn up just as soon as I get those certificates. I'll keep in touch.'

'Listen to me, Angel –' but Angel had hung up. Jack turned to Liz, his face grey now.

'I think you'd better tell me everything,' she said.

He did, from beginning to end, without interruption.

When he'd finished Liz came up to him and hugged him. 'What are we going to do now?'

We, Jack thought. No recriminations or wasted time,

just support when he needed it most. That was why he loved her. He'd have kissed Liz if he wasn't so desperate.

'Well, from what I've discovered about Sami and Roland, I don't think we've much chance of getting any bloody share certificates out of them now. I've just got to find out where he's keeping her. There's nothing else we can do.'

'But where should we start looking?'

Jack rubbed his forehead as if trying to squeeze out some ideas. 'He's hired his car – I noticed the sticker on the windscreen. It's a long shot but the rental company might have a local address. At least I'd have a registration number to go on.'

'Like me to phone them.'

'No, you stay here and field any calls. And if Shepard turns up before I get back, stall him. If Angel finds out the DEA are involved, Katie's dead.'

As Luis Beniamin pulled up in front of Madrid Airport's National Terminal, he was still talking into the car radio's microphone. Shepard was in the front passenger seat with Ed Wheeler behind him.

'Did you get all that?' the Spaniard asked the Americans as he switched off the radio. 'My men followed the suspect to an underground car park, where he keeps a Mercedes apparently. They're tailing it now.'

'Then call them off!' Shepard said. 'He'll spot it, believe me. Have them bug the Merc later.'

Beniamin frowned, then picked up the mike and gave the order.

'Better make it a passive bug,' Wheeler added, 'so it only transmits when you want it to. That way, if he sweeps the –'

'We know what we're doing, thank you.'

'Then please, please get it right,' the West Virginian said. 'This guy's the bait for old man Mosquera. Don't scare him off, whatever happens.'

'That goes for you and his son too. Just go to Marbella

and concentrate on putting *him* on the hook. I want them both as badly as you do, you know,' Beniamin replied.

'Not quite,' Shepard almost whispered.

CHAPTER TWENTY-ONE

'I'm a friend of Angel Mallendo's family and they're urgently trying to contact him,' Jack told the car rental company's desk clerk. 'I know he hired a Renault from you and I was hoping he'd left a local address.'

The girl glanced at the Bentley parked on the forecourt, then gave him a charming smile. 'I will check our files.' Minutes later she had the answer. 'Señor Mallendo return it this morning. Here is the form. He was staying at Marbella Club. Call them from here if you like.'

He did. Someone told him Angel had checked out on Monday.

Jack drove on to Hertz and sold them the same story. Angel had brought in a Mercedes on Monday but hadn't hired anything to replace it.

It took three more visits to find what he was looking for. A local company had rented Angel an Opel the previous day. The form gave the Marbella Club as his local address . . . and details of the car. Jack made a mental note of the model, colour and registration number. He asked the clerk to contact him immediately if Angel returned it, slipped him a thousand-peseta note, and left the office.

What now? Jack felt dreadful but a second's thought about Katie's plight fired him up again. He decided to check the hotels and drove east to the five-star Los Monteros first.

No, Angel wasn't staying there, but, yes, they would contact him if he checked in. Jack doled out several more banknotes to make sure of that and then swung outside on his crutches.

He noticed a waiting taxi. That was an idea! The driver spoke a little English and Jack even less Spanish, but somehow he made the driver understand what he was looking for and promised a twenty-thousand-peseta reward to whoever spotted the Opel. That made the Spaniard sit up and he broadcast the details on his radio right away.

In Los Monteros Jack had picked up a *Marbella Times* with a list of hotels inside it. He had a town map in the Bentley and plotted the hotels on to it. The logical thing to do was visit the nearest one and work his way back towards the Golden Mile.

From Málaga Airport Shepard and Wheeler drove straight to Puente Romano.

Liz answered the apartment doorbell and peered through the security eye. 'Who is it?'

'Roy Shepard. May I speak to Jack?'

She opened the door halfway. 'I know who you are, but I'm afraid he's not here at the moment. I'm his girlfriend, Liz Muire.'

'He is all right, isn't he?'

'Perfectly. He's gone into town, that's all.'

'And Katie?'

'She's . . . fine.'

But Shepard had read her eyes. 'When will he be back?'

'I'm not sure. He didn't say.'

'Well, would you tell him I'd like to speak to him as soon as possible? He can reach me at this Marbella number, day or night.' He wrote it down on a piece of paper.

Liz accepted it, then closed the door.

As they walked back to their car, Wheeler studied his colleague's frowning face. 'What's wrong?'

'*Something*, but she's not saying what. Well, we've finally got permission to tap phones, so let's start with theirs.'

Angel could hardly believe what he'd seen.

From a parking space near reception he'd watched Jack

leave in the Bentley. A few minutes ago a Ford Sierra had driven past him and stopped outside the Ryders' apartment. Two gringos had climbed out of it – gringo detectives! He could spot them a mile off. They'd paid a brief visit to the apartment, then returned to their car, and they had just gone past him again, turning off towards Marbella.

Angel felt his heart pounding. What the hell was going on? Were they DEA? Had Jack betrayed him to them too? He had to know fast. Right now – with Jack's woman alone in there – was probably his best chance of finding out the truth. He backed out of the parking space and cruised down to the apartment. He switched off the engine and touched the MAC-10 under his seat, but guests and staff were wandering about everywhere. One of them might notice the bulge, and they'd certainly hear the noise if he had to kill her. Fingering the flick-knife in his trouser pocket Angel climbed out of the Opel.

As he walked to the apartment he thought up something to tell her, a way of getting inside. Fixing a helpful smile on his face he rang the bell.

'Who is it?' Liz called out.

'The management sent me, Señora. The operator has been trying to ring you but something is wrong with your phone. I've come to fix it.'

Liz opened the door. 'Please come in. It's most important you –' He had the blade to her throat in an instant, backed her up to a wall and kicked the door shut behind him. 'Who were those men?'

Liz felt the knife cutting into her. For a moment she thought she was going to faint. What could she possibly say? What lie would save her and Katie? She needed time to think.

'I . . . know who you are,' she gasped. 'Is . . . Katie all right?'

Angel swung his free hand back and hit her across the face, sending her glasses flying. 'I ask the questions! Who were those men?'

The blow knocked the fear out of her. Chilling anger leavened with survival instinct rushed into the vacuum. 'Private eyes.'

'So! You admit it.'

'Well, there's no point denying it when it's in all the papers. The English ones anyway.'

Angel looked puzzled. 'What are you talking about?'

'I thought everyone knew. I'm married to a rich American. He has to be a contender for the World's Most Boring Man, which is why I've run off with Jack. Duane wants a divorce and he needs to prove I'm in the wrong. Get the picture?'

'Maybe, maybe not. If you're lying, Katie dies.'

'Take me hostage too, then. That should convince you I'm telling the truth.'

'Is this some kind of trick?'

'Look, we're worried sick about Katie, and I want to be with her. I know you'll let us go once you get those shares.'

'*If* I get them.'

'You will. Jack told me, and I believe him. Don't you?'

'I'm beginning to,' Angel said, almost to himself. 'Right! You're coming with me.'

'I'll go quietly if you let me take some things.'

He thought about that, then moved the blade away from her throat. 'Okay, but hurry. And don't try anything or I'll rip you wide open.'

'I won't.'

Liz picked up her glasses and led the way into the bedroom. The knife was jabbing into her back now. To her right was a built-in wardrobe. Immediately beyond that was the door to the en-suite bathroom. With Angel peering over her shoulder she opened the wardrobe and began to stuff underwear into a laundry bag.

'My handbag's on the dressing table. Check it if you like.'

As he turned away to do so, Liz stepped into the bathroom and locked the door behind her.

A second later Angel was rattling the handle. 'What you doing in there?'

'Having a pee,' Liz said, desperately trying to think of a way to warn Jack about the potentially fatal lie. Angel was bound to check the bathroom now. Where mightn't he look? *Inside* the lavatory.

'Let me in!' Angel shouted, hammering on the door.

'Are you a pervert or something? I'm in the loo.' Liz snatched an eye-line pencil off the vanity unit, turned to the lavatory and lifted the lid, and scrawled five words.

'Open up *now*, or I'll break it down!'

'Coming.' She flushed it as noisily as she could, lowered the lid then unlocked the door. As she threw toiletries into a washbag, Angel pushed past her and began to snoop around. She stepped out of the bathroom and watched as he checked the chromed tissue holder, then the waste basket under the sink. 'What are you doing?'

'Looking for a message.' Angel lifted the lid of the pedal bin next to the lavatory. It was empty. He glanced at the lavatory pan.

Liz swallowed. 'Maybe I wrote one on toilet paper, and flushed it away. Better check the sewage next.'

'Very funny! Come on, let's get out of here.'

He stayed close, with the blade grazing her side, as they walked to the car. At first Angel let her sit up in the front passenger seat, but as soon as there was a break in the traffic, he told her to kneel in the footwell and tied his handkerchief round her eyes. He changed gear with his fist, the knife clenched in it ready to slash her if necessary.

Liz tried to memorise the bends and the time in seconds between them. After about five minutes they turned right off the main road and began to wind uphill. She began to feel car-sick. Then they were bumping along a track and came to a sudden stop. Moments later she was dragged out of the car and marched forward for a few yards.

Angel banged on the *casa de campo*'s front door. 'It's me. Open up.'

Garravillo did, Beretta automatic in hand, and gaped at Liz in astonishment. 'Who's she?'

'Ryder's woman. Put her in with the girl, and I'll explain.'

Liz was shoved into the bedroom and the door slammed shut behind her. She tore off her blindfold but had to shield her eyes from the burning light of the naked lightbulb. There was a stench of vomit. Squinting, she saw that Katie was lying on the bed and had been sick over herself. She sat down beside her, and stroked the damp curls out of her face.

'Hallo, Katie. Are you all right?'

Katie tried to focus through stoned, slow-blinking eyes. 'What . . . you doing here?'

'I've come to be with you. It's all right now.'

'No . . . I've ruined . . . Dad.'

'That's not true.' She wiped Katie's face with the handkerchief. 'What did Angel give you?'

'Co . . . coke. Feel . . . terrible now.'

Liz glanced at the partitioned-off washroom. 'Listen, I'm going to help you undress and shower. Then I want you to sleep for a while. Okay?'

Katie nodded listlessly.

Liz stood up and inspected the washroom, then went to the door and started battering it. She heard footsteps running down the corridor, and then Angel's voice.

'What d'you want?'

'Soap and towels please, and some lavatory paper.'

'This isn't a bloody hotel!'

'I know, but there's no need to make this harder than necessary . . . unless you're a sadist.'

A pause, then, 'Wait.'

By the time they returned Liz had helped Katie out of her filthy clothes.

'I'm going to open the door,' Angel shouted. 'My friend's out here with a gun. If you try to escape, he'll kill you. Understand?'

'Don't come in yet,' Liz called out, helping Katie towards the washroom.

Angel unlocked the door quickly and flung it back to see what was going on. He glimpsed Katie's naked body as she stepped through the partition. Then Liz blocked his view.

'Here.' He tossed two old towels and the other items on to the bed.'

'Thanks, but if you give her any more drugs I'll claw your eyes out.'

'Don't threaten me!'

Liz gave a derisive laugh. '*I'm* threatening you?'

'She wanted some. I didn't make her do it.'

'But you provided that filth. So, just lay off her.'

Angel looked over her shoulder. Water was hissing down on Katie's body now. 'You like her, huh? Maybe more than that?' There was an edge of jealousy in his voice.

'If you're implying I'm gay, I'm not; but I know the difference between right and wrong. Do you, Angel?'

'We'll see who she likes!' He slammed and bolted the door behind him.

It took Jack over four hours to visit the hotels. By the time he returned to the Puente Romano he was almost passing out with pain and exhaustion.

One look in the bedroom told him something was horribly wrong. Liz's clothes were scattered about at the foot of the wardrobe. Her toiletries were strewn all over the bathroom too.

Suddenly it was all too much for him. Nausea surged up through his body and he sank to his knees in front of the lavatory. He flung up the lid . . . and saw the cryptic message:

DUANE SENT TECS RE DIVORCE.

Jack stared at it dumbfounded. He didn't know any Duanes. Nor did Liz as far as he knew, and she certainly wasn't married to one.

The phone call came minutes later.

'Hallo, Jack. What you been up to?'

'Angel! You've got them both, haven't you? If you harm them in any way –'

'Who are we talking about now? Liz? I heard she went back to Duane.'

Fear pricked Jack's scalp as he tried to make sense of it all. Whatever he said could mean life or death. 'How d'you know about Duane? Anyway, he wants a divorce.' In the ensuing silence Jack prayed he'd got it right.

'Forget it.' Angel sounded almost disappointed. 'But remember this – if you think Liz and Katie have been kidnapped. People who go to the police usually never see the hostages again.'

'I'm getting you those shares! What more d'you want?'

'Nothing. Just hurry them up, that's all.' The line went dead.

CHAPTER TWENTY-TWO

When El Carnicero next collected his Mercedes from the underground car park in Madrid, it had been bugged by one of the *Brigada*'s technicians. A passive transmitter the size of a small coin had been superglued into the rear bumper. Before climbing into the car, El Carnicero swept it thoroughly with a transmission detector. He didn't find the device because it hadn't yet been activated.

But it was activated shortly after the Mercedes drove up into the daylight. Two of Luis Beniamin's men were waiting in a car parked near the end of the one-way street that led on to one of Madrid's main thoroughfares. They let the enforcer pass them, waited a full minute, and then followed him out into Friday morning's rush-hour traffic.

Coded signals to the bumper-bug told them roughly where the Mercedes was heading. Tailing it through Madrid without being spotted was a nerve-wracking process, but once they were out of town it became considerably easier. The trail led them past Barajas Airport, through San Fernando de Henares, and into the countryside. Finally the Mercedes parked outside the old paint factory.

Minutes later the detectives drove past and radioed Beniamin as soon as they were out of sight. 'Chemical drums all over the place,' one of them told him excitedly. 'That's bound to be it. Send reinforcements and we can take him right now.'

'No!' Beniamin told them. 'We're after bigger fish. Wait until he moves, and stay on his tail — but whatever happens, don't let him see you.'

*

Inside the factory Fortinez was moaning to his visitor. 'It's been almost a week since we had any paste. What's gone wrong? You owe me the truth.'

'Nothing's wrong,' El Carnicero tried to assure him. 'We want you to make paint again for a while, to stop people getting suspicious, that's all.'

'For how long? I'm losing out, you know. This wasn't what I agreed with young Angel. Where is he, by the way?'

'None of your business. Just do what I tell you or . . .'

El Carnicero left the threat unfinished. The old chemist's question had got to him because Angel hadn't been in touch since the Avicomida bust. That was going to take some explaining to Julio César when he met him in Valencia that afternoon.

Jack had no idea how long he'd slept for. At first he thought the ringing was part of an endless nightmare about Katie, Liz, and what Angel was doing to them, but gradually he realised it was the apartment doorbell. He struggled up from the sofa on to his crutches. Roy Shepard was waiting outside.

'Could you come back another time, Roy? It isn't convenient right now —'

'I heard Angel's call, Jack. We've tapped your phone.'

A deep sigh. 'You'd better come in then.'

The American shut the door behind him. 'He's kidnapped them to force you to give him those shares, right? But who's this Duane character?'

Jack led him into the bathroom and showed him Liz's message under the lavatory seat.

'So somehow he found out we'd visited her,' Shepard said grimly. 'But he doesn't know *who* we are, thanks to Liz. That probably saved hers and Katie's life.'

'But they're dead if he realises you're DEA. So what now?'

'Get him those certificates fast.'

'Not so easy,' Jack said, and told the astounded American

about Nassar and Priest's land scam. 'For all I know they'll just disappear when they've got the money.'

'I'll have Interpol check them out right away,' Shepard promised. 'Meanwhile, you stay right here. I want Angel to know where you are, so he keeps calling.'

'And when he does?'

'We've had the place staked out since last night, and the exchange is wired up too. One way or another I'm going to nail that son of a bitch . . . and get your girls back.'

'Get away from the door!' Angel shouted.

Neither woman was near it anyway. Katie was still under the single blanket on the bed while Liz was washing out clothes in the shower-room. The door flew open and banged against the wall, chipping off plasterwork. Angel stepped in unarmed, while Garravillo stood guard in the corridor.

Angel walked to the bed and looked down at Katie. 'You must be a bit fed up in here. Want to join us for breakfast?'

Liz appeared in the entrance to the shower-room but didn't speak.

'What about her?' Katie said.

'I'm asking you.'

'But when's she –'

'I'm asking *you*, Katie. Don't you want to get out of here? Eat some hot food?' She wouldn't look at him, so he bent down and raised her chin with his fingertips. 'Snort a little coke too?'

Suddenly she lashed out at him. 'Leave me alone! I hate you, I hate you!'

'No you don't. You only think so, because of that bitch over there.'

'You lied to me, Angel! Everything was lies. You told me you loved me only so I'd spy on Dad, and look where it's got me.'

'If he'd kept his word –'

'Oh, stop lying! Why does everyone lie about loving me?'

She rolled away from him and began weeping into the pillow.

Angel didn't know what to say. He backed towards the door, then glared at Liz. 'You're busy poisoning her against all men, aren't you?'

'You don't need my help with that,' she said quietly.

'I almost hope Jack doesn't bring those shares. It'll be a pleasure dealing with you.' Angel slammed the door behind him and bolted it shut.

Liz sat down on the edge of the bed and stroked Katie's head. 'Well done. You don't need that dreadful stuff.'

'But I do! If you knew how much it hurt me to say no.'

'But you did, that's what counts.'

Katie sat up and wiped her eyes with the back of her hand. 'What did he mean about Dad not getting those shares. He will, won't he?'

'Of course, given time.' Liz tried to smile, but during the night the possibility that Nassar and Priest would simply run off with the money had occurred to her too 'Let's think up something to keep our minds off it.'

'And off our tummies – I'm hungry. We could always plan an escape, I suppose.'

Liz snapped her fingers. 'That's exactly what we'll do.'

'Are you serious?'

'Perfectly. Come on, let's think it through.'

'We'll overpower whoever comes in first,' Katie said. 'One of us stands behind the door, and then we –'

'Put our teeth back in? They always fling it wide open, and anyway, how could we stop the other one getting in? There isn't a lock on this side, and even if we did manage something he'd still be in the corridor with that gun.'

'All right then, I'll play along with Angel. Once I'm out, you start screaming or something. One of them'll come, and you can deal with him while I –'

'No way!' Liz said. 'What if it doesn't work and you're left alone with the two of them, having led Angel on? I came here to keep those maniacs off you.'

Katie sighed. 'We'll just have to dig our way out then.'

'Like Steve McQueen, you mean?'

'Who?'

'Haven't you seen *The Great Escape*? I thought he was the dishiest man ever until I met your stepfather.'

'Dad, *dishy*?'

'Well, I think so.'

Katie looked serious. 'Are you two ... I mean, d'you think you'll get married?'

'It's on the cards.'

'Can I ask you a personal question, Liz? Why aren't you married already? I don't mean to Dad. You know, to anyone?'

'The easy answer is I didn't meet the right man. But it's something to do with what happened when I was a child as well.'

Katie nodded at her to go on.

'You see, my parents split up too when I was ten. My father ran off with someone else. I was closer to him than to my mother, and she ... well, she took it out on me afterwards. I always had the feeling – I mean logically it's nonsense – that it was somehow my fault the marriage failed. It takes someone special to help you get over that.'

Katie squeezed her hand. 'You *do* understand.'

'Come on, let's get on with escaping. We're not going out through the door, and I don't fancy tunnelling, so it's got to be that blocked-up window.'

'Right.' Katie threw back the blanket and climbed off the bed in her panties. She joined Liz by the wall and they picked at the filling with their fingernails. 'Stones and some kind of cement. What could we use to dig it out?'

'Let's start looking,' Liz said.

The main room in the *casa de campo* stank of burning olive oil and the air was full of blue smoke. José Garravillo stood by the bottled-gas stove, scraping the contents of an old frying pan on to two grimy plates. He carried them to the table, put one in front of Angel, and sat down opposite him.

Angel stared at the slimy yellow mound. 'What's this?'

'It's meant to be *tortilla* but it sort of came apart.'

Angel picked at it with a fork and tried a mouthful. He grimaced and drowned the taste with a swig of beer from a bottle. 'God, that's awful!'

'It's the best I can do – my mother always cooks for me. Better stick to cold stuff, or get one of the women to cook for us.'

'Forget it.'

The shower pipes started hammering in the background again. Garravillo jerked his head towards the sound. 'They seem to spend their whole time washing.'

'It's like an oven in there. We didn't think about ventilation.'

'When are you going to let them out?'

Angel ate another mouthful, then pushed the plate aside. 'Monday, Tuesday at the latest. Jack swears I'll have the certificates by then. I've got to get back to Madrid . . .'

'I keep telling you, El Carnicero can handle anything that comes up. He's a tough one.'

'All the same, I'd better phone today. I should have called him before . . . and my father.'

'Relax. You're doing a great job here. Wait till they find out what you've achieved.'

'That's the whole point,' Angel said animatedly. 'This project's *my* idea, not my father's. He doesn't respect me yet, José, just like you didn't –'

'Don't remind me!'

'Well, I won your respect, and I'm going to win his too. I've discovered something as profitable as cocaine, and that takes some doing.'

'Sure does.'

The shower pipes stopped hammering. Angel broke off a piece of stale bread and began to spread butter on it. 'Better think about feeding those two, I suppose.'

Liz was kneeling by the blocked-up window, picking at the mortar with a piece of stiff wire from the bed. She was only wearing her bra and panties but was dripping with sweat. Half an hour's work had produced a tiny pile of dust on the bare concrete floor.

'How's it going?' Katie asked as she stepped from the shower-room, drying herself with a towel.

Liz nodded disconsolately at the dust. 'I can't understand it – in escape films they seem to tunnel about a hundred feet in an hour. Their only problem is what to do with the dirt. Angel won't even notice this lot!'

'Maybe we should try my idea –'

'You're not going out there alone, and that's the end of it.'

Katie wrapped a towel round her waist and knelt beside her. 'You're absolutely soaking.'

Liz wiped her face. 'Must be doing wonders for my weight.'

'You shower, and I'll have a go.'

'All right.' She handed her the metal spring and was just standing up when Angel shouted from the corridor.

'Get away from the door! We've brought you some food.'

Liz snatched back the spring and ran into the shower-room while Katie kicked at the dust before jumping under the blanket.

The door flew open. Angel stood in the doorway, tray in hand, and stared at Katie on the bed. 'Still want to stay in here?'

She wrinkled her nose. 'Well, whatever you had to eat doesn't smell very tempting.'

'Suit yourself.' Angel put the tray on the end of the bed, looked around, then backed out and banged the door shut again.

After leaving the old paint factory, El Carnicero drove straight to Valencia. Spain's third largest city was situated two hundred miles east of the capital, half way up its Mediterranean coast. South-American ships docked in its busy port all the time and its airport was one of the main entry points for millions of tourists on their way to the *Costas*. Julio César came disguised as one of them.

He had flown from Carácas to London on his Peruvian passport, but was armed with a false Swiss one for his arrival in Spain. The *Policía Nacional* at the checkpoint barely glanced at it or him – just another old person in the long queue shuffling towards a holiday in the sun. Julio César stooped under the weight of his bag and walked slowly through the customs hall. He wasn't challenged there either.

El Carnicero was waiting for him in the terminal. 'Welcome to Spain, Don –'

The *capo*'s furious glare silenced him. Not another word was spoken until they reached the Mercedes in the car park. 'Who else knows I'm here?' he demanded, climbing into the front passenger seat.

'Only our contact in the embassy. He gave me your flight details.'

'By phone?'

'Personally, as you'd instructed.'

'Were you followed here?'

'No, and the car's clean – I made sure of that.'

'Where's Angel?'

The enforcer gripped the wheel. 'Err ... I haven't talked to him since Tuesday. He was still in Marbella when we last –'

Julio César's fist crashed down on the dash. 'Enough! I don't want to hear about that motor-racing nonsense! Tell me something important. Tell me what's happening in Madrid.'

El Carnicero hardly dared look at him. 'I've just come from the factory. The manager's cutting up because he's not getting any paste. I told him to start making paint again, but he didn't like that. But the real problem is the other traffickers. We hit their best men and grabbed the market, which was fine as long as we could supply it. Now we can't, all sorts of alliances are being formed.'

'In Colombia too,' Julio César said quietly. 'The knives are out for us everywhere.'

'We've got to have more paste and hit the operation before –'

'I haven't come here for fun! I've already arranged to ship more paste in the insulation of frozen-meat containers. The importers have got a warehouse near the docks. We'll see them now, then get back to Madrid as soon as possible.

He gave the enforcer an address. El Carnicero studied a map for some time before driving out of the car park and heading towards the centre of Valencia.

'They're on the move!' the *Brigada* detective reported on his radio. 'Should be coming past you any time now.'

'Got it,' Luis Beniamin said from his unmarked car parked on the forecourt of an airport hotel. He was perfectly placed to observe the main road without being obvious: and when he saw who was now in the Mercedes he gave a low whistle.

CHAPTER TWENTY-THREE

Roy Shepard returned to the Hotel Puente Romano early on Saturday morning. Angel hadn't called again, and Jack hadn't slept much. He looked terrible. The American agent phoned room service and ordered some breakfast. Then he handed Jack several telefaxed sheets of paper. The first one had a blurred picture of a familiar-looking Arab at the top of it.

'Sami Nassar?' Jack asked.

'Among other names. He *is* Lebanese, and he did dabble in arms deals at one stage. Everything else he told you is complete fiction.'

Jack stared at the likeness and ground his teeth.

'His father was one of the Lebanon's leading import-export merchants. Past tense, because Sami blew a lot of the family fortune on a playboy lifestyle and harebrained business schemes. Eventually his father kicked him out and Sami came to Europe.'

'Here? To Spain?'

'Paris first. He sponged off contacts for years while he tried to set up deals. Then he discovered land scams. The French police want to question him about several. The biggest involves a huge theme park that never was.'

'Don't tell me – he bought options on the proposed site, mortgaged them, and disappeared with the proceeds?'

'You've got it. He laid low for a couple of years, and then surfaced here. Rented a big house but gave the impression he'd bought it; but he did buy a stolen Bentley Mulsanne –'

'*Stolen*? I'm driving around in that thing!'

A waiter arrived with their breakfast tray and carried it into the sitting room. When he'd gone Shepard poured them both some strong black coffee.

'What about Priest?' Jack asked when he'd drunk a cupful.

'Look at the next sheet. He's got a dozen aliases too. Specialised in building-contract scams in the Middle East until now. We still don't know how they got together, or why they picked on you.'

'Because I was the perfect mug,' Jack said almost to himself. 'After my shunt in Monaco I sold myself on an alternative Grand Prix. It was Priest who pretended to doubt everything: I ended up being the positive thinker supporting Nassar. And I don't speak Spanish, so I only heard one side of the planning permission story – the side I wanted to believe. Oh, I was the perfect mug all right.'

'Don't blame yourself too much,' Shepard said, refilling their cups. 'You wouldn't believe who got taken in Paris. There are some red faces right up to government level apparently.'

'How did you find all this out?'

'By asking Interpol in Paris. They were *very* interested to hear what that pair had been up to. In fact the French and Spanish police would love to talk to them about it in person.'

'For God's sake don't let them near those two until we've got Liz and Katie back. If Angel smells a rat, they won't stand a chance.'

'Don't worry, we realise that,' Shepard assured him. 'And he's got other things to worry about now. We've wrecked the Mosqueras' operation in Madrid. His father arrived in Spain yesterday to sort it out and we've been trailing him ever since. At some point Angel's bound to see him, and then we'll put an invisible tail on him too. We think that's our best chance of finding Katie and Liz.'

'Well, I'm going to work on keeping Nassar and Priest here. There must be a way . . .'

Jack stopped in mid-sentence, his eyes lighting up.

'What?'

'Frank Brady. They were counting on taking him in a big way and for really serious money. If only he'd help . . . but what can I tell him now?'

'How about the truth?' Shepard suggested.

Jack reached the team-owner at his office and told him everything. Brady listened to the bitter tale in stony silence. There was a long pause at the end of it.

'Are you still there, Frank?'

'Yes.'

'I'm sorry I didn't tell you about the mortgages straight-away, but when I found out Katie and Liz had been kidnapped –'

'What about planning consent?'

'*Planning* . . .? Fifty-fifty as far as I can make out, but what's that got to do with it now? The point is, will you help me con Nassar and Priest into staying put long enough for me to extract some share certificates out of them.'

'Damn right I will! Nobody makes a fool out of me and gets away with it. Saving your girls is more important than personal considerations, of course, but it's the principle of the thing.'

'Thanks. I don't know what else to say.'

'Save your breath. Just have someone meet me at Málaga Airport at . . . thirteen hundred hours.'

Katie woke up with a start in the prison-bedroom, and squinted in the light from the bare bulb. The temperature was lower in the unventilated room now, but the atmosphere was still almost unbearably heavy. Her head ached and she massaged it with her fists. A scraping sound was coming from her left. Turning towards it, she saw that Liz was still working away at the side wall.

'My turn again,' Katie yawned, getting off the bed.

'Forget it!' Liz jabbed the bedspring into a shallow groove around one of the stones. 'One whole night's work, and that's all we've got to show for it.' She covered her eyes with her other hand.

Katie knelt down beside her and put a comforting arm round her shoulder. 'At least it's kept our mind off things for a day. Two more and we'll be out of here ... unless there's something you're not telling me? There is, isn't there?'

Liz nodded reluctantly. 'That Lebanese and the Yorkshireman – they're not all they seem. And that means Jack may not be able to get out of them what Angel wants, I'm afraid.'

Katie stiffened and then stood up. 'Right, that settles it. I got you into this, and now I'll have a go at getting us out – *my* way.'

'Listen to me –'

'No, Liz! And if you want a row, that's fine by me, because that'll start the ball rolling.'

'Well ... we've got to try something, and if you've made your mind up there's not much I can say.'

'Oh yes, there is. You can scream your head off for the benefit of those two, and think of a way to deal with whoever comes running.'

'I'm ready to scream at someone. But you'd better put some clothes on first, or you'll get raped for sure.'

Katie quickly showered, dried herself as best she could, and dressed in her clean but damp T-shirt and mini-skirt.

'Do I look terrible?' she asked when she'd finished.

'Far from it – that's what worries me. For God's sake, be careful.'

'Careful's not going to get us out of here. Now, what shall we fight about?'

Liz scratched her head. 'Okay, imagine I've caught you doing speed. Make that coke.' She raised her voice several decibels. 'I've told you time and time again to leave that muck alone!'

'Leave me alone you . . . you . . .'

'Bitch?'

'Yes. Why can't you leave me alone?'

'Because when I turn my back for five minutes you're bloody well at it again!'

'Mind your own bloody business!'

As the row progressed they heard footsteps in the corridor, and then Angel banged on the door. 'What's all the shouting about?'

Katie ran to it. 'Let me out, Angel. I *do* want to be with you.'

No response.

'Please, Angel, *please*. She's driving me crazy.'

'Get away from the door, then.' He slid back the bolts, and then kicked it open. Garravillo stood behind him holding the MAC-10. Angel grabbed Katie's arm and pulled her into the corridor. He sneered at Liz, who was hiding the groove in the side wall with her body. 'See what I mean?' He slammed the door shut again.

Katie breathed a sigh of relief. 'Oh, Angel, I didn't mean what I said yesterday, but she'd been going on and on at me.'

'Yes?' Still gripping her arm, he drew her to him.

She rubbed her head against his chest. 'Don't be angry. I want to be friends again. Let me cook you some breakfast – I'm starving.'

He glanced at Garravillo, who merely shrugged. 'All right,' Angel said, releasing her, 'but if this is a trick you'll pay for it.'

Katie walked down the corridor and into the main room. It stank of burnt fat, and unwashed cooking utensils were piled up in the sink. 'Better clean these first. Any washing-up liquid?'

'All we've got is powder for clothes,' Angel said, pointing at the packet on the sideboard.

She ran lukewarm water into the sink, sprinkled in powder and whipped it into suds with her hands. Angel stood guard over her as she started to wash up. Every now and then she looked round and smiled at him coyly. After a while he smiled too, then sat down at the table with Garravillo who was leaning back in his chair with the sub-machine gun across his thighs.

'What d'you want for breakfast?' Katie asked.

'There's not much here,' Angel said, nodding at the battered old fridge beside the cooker.

She opened the door. 'Well, we can have boiled eggs and toast. And coffee, of course. How does that sound?'

'I like mine fried.'

'Me too,' Garravillo said.

Katie found an aluminium pan, filled it with water, and set it on the stove. She was having trouble lighting it and Angel stood up to help her. Instead of moving to her side, though, he pressed up against her back and put his arms round her. She writhed and giggled as he fumbled for matches and eventually lit a ring.

'Let's forget about breakfast,' he murmured in her ear.

'I told you, I'm starving.'

He spun her round to face him. 'This, then, to prove you like me.' He kissed her hard on the lips. Katie parted hers and clung to him as his tongue explored her mouth.

'That's better,' Angel said, letting her go. Garravillo was grinning at them lasciviously.

She laid three places at the table, found a chipped tray and began to lay that too.

'Who's that for?' Angel asked.

'She's the bitch, not me. I'm not going to see her starve.' Katie put two eggs in the boiling water, lit another ring and put on a frying pan with some butter in it. But she made sure the food on the tray was ready before she started on the fried eggs.

'Would one of you take it to her please,' Katie said, cracking eggs into the frying pan at the same time.

'You take it,' Angel told her.

'Then your eggs'll be ruined.' She busied herself with a spatula.

He nodded at Garravillo, who gave him the gun, then picked up the tray. The two of them moved down the corridor, but Angel kept glancing back at Katie. She pretended to concentrate on the smoking, spitting pan.

'Breakfas'!' Garravillo yelled through the bedroom door.

'Wait!' Liz yelled back. 'I've got nothing on. I'll get in the bed.'

He didn't understand what she'd said and looked to Angel for enlightenment.

'*Desnudo*,' Angel said and they both laughed. He leant past the enforcer to slide back the bolts, then shoved it open.

Garravillo stepped forward with the tray in his hands. The bed was empty. He was just registering surprise when the door flew towards him, knocking the tray into his face. Next moment Liz came round the door, kneed him in the groin and then tried to push him aside.

Angel blocked the doorway, pointing the gun and shouting at her. 'Stop it or I'll kill you!' He sensed rather than saw Katie rushing down the corridor with the pan of boiling water. Angel turned towards her and flung up his hands just before she threw it at him. Some of the scalding liquid splashed through his fingers and on to his cheeks, and he screamed in pain and fury.

Katie slammed the pan on to his skull and he sank to the ground. Garravillo was doubled up in pain but had locked his arms round Liz's waist. She was pummelling his back but he wouldn't let go.

'Run, Katie, *run*!' Liz yelled.

But she lifted the pan over her head again, intending to crack Garravillo's head this time. Suddenly she was toppling forwards as Angel, still on the floor, grabbed her ankles. Katie landed on top of the other two as he staggered to his feet, gun in one hand, and swung it at her head as she tried to get up.

The barrel hit her smack on the forehead, knocking her out and cutting a bloody groove. Angel whipped the barrel across the back of Liz's head and she too stopped struggling.

Groaning and clutching his genitals, Garravillo extricated himself from the tangle of bodies. '*Hija de puta!*' he moaned, then gave Liz's prone body a vicious kick.

'We'll rope them up this time,' Angel said, blowing on his hands. 'They can rot in there for all I care now.'

Between them they dragged both women into the room and dumped them face down on the bed. Garravillo fetched the cord they'd bought earlier, and trussed their arms and ankles together behind their backs.

When they'd finished, Angel rolled Katie over and examined the deep gash across her forehead. 'Better do something about that.'

'Why? She won't bleed to death.'

'Jack's going to see her when we do the exchange. I don't want him going crazy or anything.'

Angel bandaged the wound with a clean handkerchief. When he'd finished, they went back to the main room where he held his hands under the cold water tap.

'We can't leave those bitches now,' he said through clenched teeth. 'I'd better phone El Carnicero, though, and get some stuff for these burns while I'm at it. You stay here.'

Instead of going down to San Pedro de Alcántara, Angel drove the Opel uphill to Ronda. Instinct made him supercautious now, and he decided to switch the Opel when he got there.

The famous Andalusian town of about thirty thousand inhabitants was split in two by a sheer ravine. On the south side was Ronda's ancient fortified *Ciudad*, while across the bridge was the newer *Mercadillo* area. Angel parked the Opel down one of the latter's side streets, and then went to find a chemist. He bought a tube of burn lotion and smoothed it into his hands and cheeks as he looked for a phone box. There was one near the *Plaza de Toros* – one of the oldest bullrings in Spain.

From it he dialled El Carnicero's contact number in Madrid. Unknown to Angel, he was calling one of the tapped lines to the video shop.

'He's not here,' an anonymous male voice told him, 'but there's someone else who wants to talk to you urgently.'

'Who?'

'Call back in exactly one hour, and you'll find out.'

Angel left the booth and walked slowly back towards the bridge. He was puzzled by the message but was soon thinking about Katie again. He couldn't get her out of his mind . . . her lithe, naked body that day he'd nearly taken her virginity. He wished he'd done that now. His groin burned almost as much as his hands as he thought about it, and he didn't know whether he'd be able to resist raping her before letting her go – she deserved it, the way she'd led him on . . .

For God's sake, Angel told himself, she's just a stupid schoolgirl! Once he'd sorted this mess out he'd find himself a real woman and fuck her silly . . . except that he'd wanted to *love* Katie. For sure she would never let him now.

He stopped in the middle of the bridge and stared down into the deep gorge. It was the shadowless hour. The high, hot sun illuminated everything, but inside his heart there was a darkness. He felt an urge to lean over the parapet. The chasm seemed to beckon him . . .

Angel straightened up suddenly and backed away from the edge. This was ridiculous. He'd forget her if he did something useful instead of just killing time – like changing hire-cars.

An hour later he dialled the Madrid number again from a different booth.

The same voice as before answered the phone, and then handed him over to Julio César. 'So you've decided to honour us with a call at last!'

'F . . . Father? What are you doing in Spain?'

'What you think *you're* up to is more to the point. I can't believe what I've been hearing.'

'If you'll let me explain –'

'Just listen! You don't even know what's happened here, do you? They've cut our supply route and I've had to fly over to deal with it. That's why I'm here, and I want you to join me right away.'

Angel swallowed hard. 'Father, I'm on the point of taking over this entire project –'

'I don't want to hear about that damned –'

'Listen to me! *You* listen for a change. I know how important Spain is for us. That's why I'm doing this. It's the perfect way to launder billions of pesetas, and it's going to be as profitable as our main business.'

'D'you seriously believe that?'

'You heard what I said.'

'What I think you're saying is you won't come back to Madrid.'

'I can't. Not for a few days.'

Julio César fought to control himself. 'Then I'm coming down there, Angel, tomorrow. I want to see this miracle money-machine for myself, and meet this Jack Ryder. He'd better convince me the deal's all you say it is.'

'But Father –'

'But nothing! Now where are we going to meet?'

Roy Shepard collected Frank Brady from Málaga Airport and put him fully in the picture on the way back to Marbella. Jack came to the apartment door on his crutches and let them in.

'Heard anything from Angel?' the American asked immediately.

Jack shook his head before turning to Brady. 'Thanks for coming, Frank. I'm sorry I dragged you into all this.'

'Don't be. I might be able to salvage something . . . but that's incidental now. When did you last speak to Nassar and Priest?'

Jack tried to remember as they trooped into the sitting room. The last forty-eight hours were a nightmarish blur.

'Thursday afternoon,' he said, sinking down on to the sofa. 'Priest seems to have moved in with him, by the way.'

'Then I'd better contact them right away and sell them the Big Lie.'

Jack looked at him quizzically.

'Well, that's how he caught you – all that guff about the Saudi royal family. I'm going to go one better and –'

The phone rang, and Jack snatched it up. 'Ryder speaking.'

'It's me, Angel.'

He threw up his hand for silence and the others immediately realised whom he was speaking to. 'How are Liz and Katie?'

'They're . . . fine.'

'You don't sound certain.'

'Of course I'm certain! Why shouldn't I be?'

'Calm down, Angel. What's the matter?'

'Nothing . . . but someone very important's coming to Marbella tomorrow. Someone very important to the project, and I want you to . . . convince him about it.'

Jack's head jerked back in astonishment. 'You're joking, of course?'

'I'm going to show him the site. Then I want you to explain –'

'God Almighty! You kidnap my stepdaughter and my girlfriend, and now you want me to chat to some investor? You've got to be out of your mind!'

'It's my father,' Angel blurted out. 'You must do this, Jack.'

'Must I, hell!'

Shepard was frantically signalling him to cool it, but Jack winked back to show he was putting on an act.

'That is, unless . . .'

'What, Jack? What?'

'You let Liz and Katie go first.'

'No! Not before I get those share certificates.'

'You'll get them, but now you're asking for something

207

extra. I want something in exchange. The least I'll accept is seeing them before I speak to your father.'

Tense silence followed. Nobody moved. Jack started a prayer.

'All right,' Angel conceded. 'One o'clock tomorrow. Be at the same spot we picked you up before in Puerto Banús. But come on your own, or you'll *never* see them again.' He hung up.

Jack slowly put down the receiver and looked at the DEA agent. 'Did you get all that?'

He nodded. 'We'll have taped it and be tracing the call now. You realise if we can incriminate them both in the kidnapping we can arrest them then and there?'

'Not before I've seen my girls; and he threatened to kill them if I'm not on my own. How are we going to play that?'

Frank Brady rubbed his jaw. 'I can't help you there. You can leave that pair of con artists to me, though, while you figure it out.'

'There *has* to be a way to rescue them,' Shepard murmured.

'Then let's do it,' Jack said. 'Because once I've found Liz and Katie I'm not letting them go again, that's for very bloody sure!'

Back at the *casa de campo*, Angel explained the trade-off to an astounded Garravillo.

'Those bitches have to be nearby, so Jack can see them before talking to my father; but I've got to be able to get them and us out of there if Jack doublecrosses us.'

'I'll blow him away, if he does.'

'For Christ's sake, think before you talk, José! How does that help anyone?'

Garravillo shrugged an apology.

Angel frowned with concentration. Suddenly he snapped his fingers. 'A boat! Of course, that's it!'

The enforcer's face fell.

'What's wrong?'

'I hate the things. Went on a Russian cruise ship with a girl, and we were both sick the whole time.'

'This isn't a cruise! With any luck we won't even have to put out to sea. But I need you to find a boat.'

'How?'

'Go down to Puerto Banús later. It's Saturday night, and the boat-owners will be packing the bars and clubs. Take plenty of coke and pesetas, and see if you can make any friends. Understand?'

Garravillo nodded.

CHAPTER TWENTY-FOUR

It was late June now, and the sun disappeared down into the Straits of Gibraltar only at around ten o'clock. However, that seemed to be the signal for almost everyone in Marbella to get going again after dinner.

By midnight Puerto Banús was overflowing with a tide of humanity. The wealthiest partied noisily on their over-sized yachts, garishly lit from stem to stern. Ferraris, Porsches and Rolls-Royces strewn about on the jetties added to the ostentation. In the *pueblo blanco*, music blared from a dozen open-air bars, with customers all shouting to make themselves heard. A slow moving flock of lesser beings jammed the pavements and roadways, gawping at this fantasy world so near yet so far from them. If they were allowed to sit at some table and wait hours to be served, their faces showed a kind of pathetic gratitude.

Garravillo spent several frustrating hours trying to wheedle his way in among the haves, but those boat-owners he did manage to strike up some sort of conversation with seemed mainly interested in putting him firmly in his place. Finally a snooty-looking Channel Islander propping up a waterfront bar gave him an unintentional break.

'Of course I won't rent you my yacht! Who d'you think I am?' He looked the enforcer up and down with obvious distaste. 'Horgan's the man you want. He deals with people like you.'

'Where can I find this . . .?'

'Horgan, Cornell Horgan. Black-hulled job by Jetty Two, but he'll be pissed out of his brains by now.'

Undeterred Garravillo pushed his way out of the bar and

along the quayside. He walked slowly up the right-hand side of the second jetty but reached the end without finding what he was looking for. Two-thirds of the way back on the other side he spotted the shadowy hull.

'Meester 'Organ,' he called out.

No reply.

'Meester 'Organ. Are you in there Meester –?'

'All right, all right!' A hatch slammed back and a drunk-looking bearded man staggered up into the cockpit. 'Who wants him?'

'We like to rent your boat.'

'Do you now.' He too sized up Garravillo but found something to smile about. Horgan looked around before speaking again. 'South American, are we?'

'How you know?'

'Come aboard.' He led him down into the galley, thumped down on one of the bench seats and poured himself more whisky. 'What d'you want it for?'

'Two women like to spend a day on it.'

'Where d'you want me to take them?'

'Nowhere . . . unless something goes wrong.'

'They're just going to sit around here?'

'No, lie down. They will be very tired.'

Horgan drained his tumbler and frowned at him. 'I see. I've had . . . tired people on board before but I've usually had to deliver them some place. It'll cost you the same, though, maybe even more. The first thing is, how are you going to pay me?'

Garravillo patted the body-bag strapped under his shirt. 'Pesetas . . . or coke.'

'Now you're talking, man! Show me.'

'How do I know I can trust you?'

Horgan roared with laughter. 'Think I'm DEA or something? That would be *really* deep cover! I tell you what I'll do: you show me the goods, my Colombian friend, and I'll snort some to prove which side I'm on. How about that?'

In the early hours of Sunday morning, Liz was woken from fitful sleep by Katie's stifled sobs. They were lying on their sides facing each other, with their wrists and ankles still tied together behind their backs.

'What's the matter?' Liz asked gently, unable to see her in the pitch darkness.

'I've . . . started to wet the bed.'

'Well if you've got to, you've got to. I'll have to soon.'

Katie tried to stop crying. 'If only . . . I'd run when you said. I might've got help.'

'It was a long shot, let's face it. But I'm proud of you anyway.'

'*Proud*? After what I've done to Dad?'

'Wait till I tell him how you fought those two.'

'That's if we ever see him again.'

'Of course we will, silly.'

'Then why've they left us like this? Why aren't they feeding us any more?'

'Because they're having a temper tantrum, that's all. They'll get over it and –'

Liz stopped talking at the sound of knocking on the front door. There were footsteps in the corridor, and then it creaked open and shut again. A muffled discussion began and went on for some time.

Then the bolts of their bedroom door were drawn back, the door flew open and the bare light bulb flared on. Both of them screwed their eyes shut against it. The next instant, Katie was screaming and struggling as Angel tried to gag her with a strip of cloth while Garravillo held her down.

'Let her go!' Liz yelled furiously. 'What the hell are you doing?'

'Taking you both to see your friend Jack, if you'll let us!'

'Like this? I don't know what you're trying to achieve, but one thing's for certain. Jack will go mad if he sees his stepdaughter's face in that condition.'

Angel released Katie's head and looked at Liz suspiciously. 'So what d'you suggest?'

'We've tried to escape and we know it's not on. Now we'll play it your way, I promise you, *if* you'll let us clean up first.'

He searched her eyes as he thought about it. 'All right, but any more trouble and I'll break your arms, I promise *you* that. You've got five minutes.' Angel untied them while Garravillo covered him with the submachine gun. Then they both left the bedroom.

Katie stumbled and crawled to the lavatory, her cramped legs barely able to support her. Liz followed her into the shower-room and began to clean up the girl's nasty head wound.

'What are we going to try now?' Katie whispered.

'Nothing,' Liz hissed back. 'For the moment anyway.'

Even after half a bottle of whisky and the free sample of cocaine, Horgan could judge Puerto Banús's rhythms. By five o'clock on Sunday morning it was a dark and silent place and there was almost no one around.

Angel drove the Ford Sierra he'd hired in Ronda on to Jetty Two and parked with the tailgate towards Horgan's boat. Liz and Katie had passively submitted to being tied up and gagged again and were now rolled up in grey blankets in the back of the car.

With a good deal of muffled swearing, the three men carried the bundles down into the galley and then forward into the bow cabin. There were two bunks arranged in a V, and the women were dumped unceremoniously on to them. There was no question of untying them now.

Frank Brady had organised a Sunday morning breakfast meeting at Nasar's villa near the mosque. Jack drove him there in the stolen Bentley and they presented themselves at the front door just after ten o'clock.

The Lebanese eyed them through the spy-hole before opening up. Despite a welcoming smile he couldn't quite hide the tension in his face.

'Come in both of you, come in. We were worried about you, Jack.'

'Quite a mystery,' Brady said cheerfully, 'but all will be explained.'

Priest looked nervous too despite a hearty front. As they walked into the dining room he was bringing in coffee and croissants from the kitchen, and made a big song and dance about it. 'It's the maid's day off, so Sami recruited me instead. Think I'll hold the job down?'

'I was just saying we'd been worried about Jack.'

'That's right.' The Yorkshireman poured the coffee into white china cups as they sat round the table.

'So you really don't know what I've been up to?' Brady said.

They shook their heads.

'Well, I asked Jack to keep it a secret, and he obviously has.'

'What . . . secret?' Nassar asked.

'My meeting with the Spanish Prime Minister.'

The con men stared at each other, and then at Brady.

'As soon as I got back after Jack's brilliant demonstration, I contacted the Spanish representative of our sport's governing body. He's a personal friend of the Prime Minister, who is really keen for Spain to host top-level international events again. My contact was over the moon about our plans and put me in touch with the P M. We met in Madrid yesterday.'

Nassar's coffee cup clattered on to his saucer. 'This is extraordinary news, Frank. What did he have to say?'

'Just a few words, all of them to the point. He strongly supported our proposal, especially as it was sited in Andalusia: I don't have to remind you where the Prime Minister comes from! He promised that planning obstacles wouldn't be allowed to stand in our way.'

'But they aren't,' Priest said.

'Perhaps not at the moment, Roland, but it's reassuring to know we've got support at this level.'

'I'd put it a lot more strongly than that,' Nassar said, visibly regaining confidence by the second. 'But how does this development affect us in the short term, though?'

Brady buttered a piece of hot croissant. 'All the team-owners want to replace the Monaco Grand Prix next season. I immediately phoned round with this news, and that clinched it. They've empowered me to make you the following offer: we'll complete on that twenty-eight acres next week *and* we'd like to negotiate to buy your options on the rest of the land.'

Something like ecstasy flashed across Nassar's face, to be quickly replaced by a deliberate coolness. 'It sounds like a take-over to me.'

'But you hold all the cards. We know we'll have to make you an offer you can't refuse, and we're prepared to pay that in cash next week too.'

'Why the rush, Frank?'

'Because unless we settle this now, there's no way we can be ready for next season. It's verging on the impossible anyway, but we think we can make it happen.'

'That's why we need those certificates as soon as possible,' Jack added.

'No problem there,' Sami assured him. 'I'll have a courier deliver those on Monday, Tuesday at the latest.'

'Then you're not averse to the idea of a buy-out?' Brady asked.

'That depends on the price of course.'

'Of course.' Brady sipped coffee. 'I'll stay in Marbella until the deal's done then. That'll give me a chance to check all the details as well – mortgages, things like that.'

'M . . . mortgages?' Priest spluttered.

'Yes. Jack checked that twenty-eight-acre plot, but I'll need to look at the rest. No problem, is there?'

'Of course not,' Nassar said, kicking Priest under the table.

'What the hell do we do now?' the Yorkshireman asked as soon as Frank Brady and Jack had left.

Nassar put a finger to his lips and watched through the spy-hole until they'd reached the foot of the stairway in front of the villa. Then he spun round and hurried towards the study. 'We play the game, of course. Brady's intent on dumping millions in our laps and I'm just as keen on taking them.'

'But what about the mortgages?' Priest asked as he followed him. 'Once he starts checking –'

'There'll be nothing to find. Because I'm going to revoke the ones we haven't yet drawn and return that first payment to Bernadino Mendez.' He picked up his address book from the desk, found the Swiss banker's number in Gibraltar and sat down to dial it.

'But what if it's some kind of trap?'

Nassar paused to look at him. 'What it is, Roland, is the finest opportunity you or I are ever, *ever* going to have. And whether you're going to take it or not, I most certainly am!' He started to dial and was soon engaged in an urgent conversation with the banker.

At Marbella's telephone exchange one of Ed Wheeler's automatic recorders caught every word of it.

From the villa Jack and Brady drove straight to the *Policia Nacional* station near the centre of town. Roy Shepard, Ed Wheeler and two senior Spanish police officers were waiting for them in an austere interview room.

'How'd it go?' Shepard asked.

'Greed won the day!' the team-owner reported gleefully. 'They'll stick around now – I'll keep feeding them titbits to make sure of that – and they'll deliver those certificates to Jack if we still need them tomorrow.'

'Let's hope this afternoon's operation means we don't. Then we can arrest those con men too.'

'What are your plans?' Jack asked.

Shepard pointed to a large-scale map of Marbella tacked to the wall. 'The one thing we know is that Angel or his men are picking you up from Puerto Banús, just like the time you disappeared. We aim to prevent that happening again, and instead, have you lead us to Liz and Katie. Ed here'll explain how he's going to wire you and the Bentley.'

The CIA wireman held up two disc-like devices joined by a length of wire. 'This is a voice transmitter which we'll bury in the front of your plastercast, just under the surface. The other disc's a pressure pad which we'll fit in the heel. It'll only transmit conversation when you put weight on it. That way they won't find it if they sweep you with a transmission detector, as long as you're on your crutches or sitting down.'

'Better show me what those detectors look like, so I know if they use one.'

'I'm coming to that. We're also going to put a passive bug in the Bentley, which will only send signals which we tell it to. Once we get those signals we can put direction finders on them and follow you even it we can't see you.'

'Who's we?' Jack asked.

'Four teams in unmarked, specially equipped cars covering all the exits from Puerto Banús. Ed and I will be watching the pick-up from a top-floor apartment there. We've got a car at the ready down below too.'

'Assuming it works and I lead you to my two, what then?'

'That's the hard part,' Shepard said quietly.

Setting out from Madrid in the early hours of the morning, El Carnicero drove Julio César down to Marbella in his Mercedes. Unknown to them two *Brigada* teams tailed them all the way by intermittently activating the bug in the Mercedes' rear bumper. The agents stayed well out of sight, though, especially when it became obvious where their quarry was heading.

The Colombians reached the site at midday. Angel and Garravillo's rented Ford was already parked on the broad roadway nearest to the beach and El Carnicero pulled up beside it. He joined his young colleague while father and son walked away from the cars. From what the enforcer had heard on the way down, he didn't want any part in the family reunion.

'What happened to your face?' Julio César asked.

'Someone . . . too much sun.'

His father gave a snort and looked round at the bare site. 'And this is what you've achieved in all the time you've been working?'

'What did you expect in three weeks?'

'A lot more, Angel, a lot more. All I see is the land we bought. You've got a lot of explaining to do about this famous project.'

'If you'd use a little imagination –'

'That's all you seem to have done!' Julio César stopped and faced him. 'I still can't believe the things you've dreamt up.'

'What d'you mean?'

'Kidnapping Ryder for a start. And he's meant to be a friend?'

'He demanded to see our operation before he'd help me. How did I know he wasn't DEA? How else could I prove to him –?'

'Not like that.'

'Well *how* then?' Angel shouted. 'Negative, all negative . . . everything I say and do is wrong . . . if it'd been my brother you'd have trusted him.'

'Yes! With anything.'

'Now it's out in the open! You never bothered about me before he died and you've never given me a chance since.'

'Spain was your chance!' Julio César sighed and shook his head. 'So you're still jealous of your brother. Well, you're right to be – he had his head screwed on his shoulders.'

'And I don't? Is that what you're saying, that I'm crazy or something?'

'I don't know *what* you are, Angel. I only found out recently that you personally threw that DEA agent out of the plane. You've no idea what trouble that's caused us. And what possessed you to kill that accountant –?'

'You hypocrite! You've slaughtered whole families –'

'*I* haven't. Other people do that for me. Sometimes they get caught, and when they do they go to gaol for years, but there's no way their crimes can be tied to me. Don't you understand the principle, Angel . . . or is it that you like killing?'

'Shut up, shut up!' He was shaking with rage now, clenching his fists in an effort to control himself. 'I think we'd better go now. I'll take you to Puerto Banús and you'll see what this place could be like. You'll meet Jack Ryder too. Perhaps you'll listen to what he's got to say.'

'I'll be glad to, though why he's still talking to you I can't imagine.'

Angel couldn't bring himself to enlighten him.

CHAPTER TWENTY-FIVE

Horgan checked up on his prisoners at least once every half hour. Just before one o'clock he put on a black woollen balaclava and went forward to the tiny triangular cabin again.

They were still lying on the bunks, gagged heads in the bows, wrists and ankles trussed together behind their backs. They didn't appear to have moved since he'd last seen them.

'Good girls,' Horgan said, as though he was talking to children. 'No use getting worked up, is there? You'll find out what's in store for you soon enough.' He left the cabin and shut the door behind him.

Liz listened carefully but there was no sound of it being locked or bolted. There was no need when they were so helpless . . . except that she thought she'd worked out a way of pulling her gag off, or rather up. The wooden side rail on her bunk, which stopped the thin mattress sliding off it, didn't quite meet the fibreglass hull at the bow, and if she could just get the gag to catch over the end of it . . .

The problem was flattening her face against the hull – really squashing it! She'd tried several times already but stopped when her nose felt as though it was going to break. She steeled herself for another try: they *had* to be ready if the slightest chance of escape presented itself.

Her head bent further and further back as she forced her face against the fibreglass and pressed downwards. A muscle tore in her neck and she thought she was going to pass out, but then the gag snagged on the rail. Liz gave one last agonising push and the strip of material rode up over her lips. She spat out the cotton wadding in her mouth and gasped for breath.

Katie was staring at her from the other bunk.

'Can you roll on to your other side?' Liz whispered urgently.

She nodded and writhed around until she'd done so.

'Now stick out your bottom as far as you can so I can get my teeth at your knots; but don't fall off the bunk!'

Jack arrived early at Puerto Banús to make sure he found a parking space on the wide approach avenue. A human tide and its transport had washed back into the area by now and he had to manoeuvre for some time before finding what he was looking for. He finally managed to park the long Mulsanne, then glanced at the clock in its veneered dash: one o'clock. No sign of them yet.

Roy Shepard was watching the scene through binoculars from a top-floor studio at the back of the *pueblo blanco*.

Ed Wheeler was sitting near him, wearing a headset and hunched over a battery of radios and recording machines. He lifted one of the earphones and turned to speak to the DEA agent.

'The Mercedes is on the site but there's no one in it. There's no one at the site either, apparently.'

'Well, what did they leave in, goddammit?'

'The *Brigada* boys don't know: they didn't want to show themselves and missed the switch.'

'Great start!' Shepard exploded.

Driven by Garravillo the Ford Sierra cruised past the Bentley, took the roundabout at the end of the avenue, and returned back up the road.

El Carnicero was in the front passenger seat, eyes darting about. The back was empty. 'Okay,' he said, 'we'll pick them up.'

'What was all the shouting about back there?'

'None of your business. Just do your job.'

The Mosqueras were waiting in a café on the far side of the main road. Once they had joined the enforcers in the car again, Garravillo drove back to the avenue and double-parked behind Jack, facing the *pueblo blanco*.

Angel climbed out, stepped on to the pavement and walked to the driver's door of the Mulsanne. Jack pressed a switch and the window whirred down.

'Sorry we're late, Jack. Come and meet my father.'

'Forget it!'

'Wh . . . what? We agreed –'

'I told you, I'm not doing anything until I've seen Liz and Katie.'

'But –'

'But nothing, Angel! That was the agreement and I'm sticking to it.'

Angel glared at him, then walked back to the Ford. 'He says he's not playing until . . . I think he's afraid we'll kidnap him again.'

'Let me talk to him,' Julio César said.

'Maybe that's not such a good –'

'Check there's no transmission when I'm with him, only don't let him see you,' he said to El Carnicero before getting out of the car.

Julio César went to the roadside of the Bentley, and knocked on the front passenger window. It slid down. 'I'm Angel's father. May I speak to you on my own?'

Jack leaned over and opened the door. When he sat up again he pressed the heel of his plastercast down on the floor-board.

The *capo* slid in beside him. 'I've heard a lot about you, Mister Ryder. I'm pleased to meet you at last . . . and surprised.'

'Surprised?'

'After the way my son's treated you.'

'You people amaze me. That's the least of my worries now.'

Julio César looked puzzled. 'Then you do have doubts about the project?'

'None at all. We look set to replace Monaco's Grand Prix next season.'

'So what is bothering you?'

'What the hell d'you think? It'd be nice to know my daughter and girlfriend are alive before we start gloating about how stinking rich we're all going to get.'

'But . . . what have they got to do with this?'

Jack did a doubletake. 'You don't know? You really don't know? Angel's taken them hostage.'

As they stared at one another, neither of them noticed El Carnicero creeping up in the blind spot behind the Mulsanne. Passers-by glanced at the big, scarred man fiddling with something like a small radio but none of them felt like asking him what he was doing.

In the Bentley Julio César was recovering from the shock. 'I had no idea, please believe me, no idea at all. I've already talked to my son about the way he's handled things here. I'd have handled them very differently.'

'Well, what are you going to do about it now?'

'Wait here please, Mister Ryder. I'll be back shortly.'

El Carnicero was already back in the Ford by the time the *capo* put his head through the back passenger window.

'I don't know what to say to you right now, Angel, but for the moment –'

'Listen to El Carnicero!' his son interrupted.

'There was a transmission while you were talking to him,' the enforcer said.

'Are you sure?'

'Dead sure.'

Julio César met his son's eyes. 'So . . . this changes everything. Where are those girls?'

'On a speedboat in the *puerto*, ready for a quick getaway.'

'At least you thought that through. I'll go back to our friend and say I've ordered their release. You lead us to that boat. Once we've got him on it, we'll make him tell us what's really going on!'

'He was holding a detector all right,' Wheeler said, handing the binoculars back to Shepard, 'and Jack was transmitting while that creep was behind his car.'

'Christ, they know then!' The agent was studying the avenue again. 'Julio César's getting back in the Bentley . . . the Ford's driving past them . . . Jack's pulling out and following it . . . past the roundabout . . . *into* the port!'

'Calling all units!' Wheeler barked into his mouthpiece.

Shepard grabbed a walkie-talkie and ran towards the door. 'I'm going in after them. Cover me as fast as you can!'

Liz felt as though her front teeth were about to come out. She had gnawed and tugged at the knots behind Katie's back, seemingly without any effect, when finally one of them began to loosen. She worried away at it, ignoring her dizziness and pain. Meanwhile Katie was making her hands as small as possible and trying to squeeze them through the fractionally larger loops. Suddenly one hand came free.

At that moment they heard footsteps coming down the steps into the galley and then towards their cabin.

'Pull my gag down!' Liz hissed at Katie, who managed to comply. 'Now roll over!'

She had just done so when the door opened and the man in the balaclava came in again . . . and then Liz noticed the wad of cotton she'd spat on to the cabin floor. She looked up from it instantly, met his eyes and made herself stare him out.

Horgan laughed. 'Don't be angry at me, darling. This wasn't my idea, you know.'

He backed out and shut the door behind him. Shortly afterwards there was a muffled roar and the boat vibrated as its turbocharged engines were started.

Katie rolled round and pulled down Liz's gag again.

'Quick!' Liz said, not bothering to whisper anymore. 'Turn your back to me and we'll finish untying you first.'

The Ford led the Bentley slowly along the crowded quay-side and turned right on to Jetty Two. The jetty was about two hundred yards long by six wide, with berthed yachts and motor boats lining either side. A variety of vehicles were already parked on it, but there was a space by Horgan's boat. Garravillo took it and Jack pulled into a space three cars further back.

'I'll tell Horgan we're leaving right away,' Angel told El Carnicero. 'You fetch my father, and, José, you bring that *hijo de puta*!' He stepped on to the back of the rumbling boat and joined its owner in the open cockpit.

Hands on the MAC-10s under their jackets, eyeing everyone warily, the enforcers marched towards the Mulsanne. Julio César had already climbed out of it but Jack was taking longer to extract his crutches and mount them.

El Carnicero put a protective arm round his *capo* and started to lead him back.

'Come on,' Garravillo growled at Jack.

Just then Shepard reached the head of the jetty. Seconds before, he had broadcast his position on the walkie-talkie and then thrown it into the water. Now he stopped running and tried to breathe normally as he approached Jack. He came up behind him and tapped him on the shoulder.

'I thought I recognised you,' the American said cheer-fully.

Jack turned his head and stared at him.

'I helped at Detroit when your car had a transmission problem, get what I'm saying?' As he was talking the agent had moved round to face Jack, so that he was now between him and the younger enforcer.

Garravillo glanced round. El Carnicero and Julio César had almost reached the boat. 'Let's go,' Garravillo said curtly to Jack.

'I'm talking to the guy,' Shepard said.

'Step away from him.'

'Now wait a min –'

'Step away, or I'll blow you away!'

Shepard slowly turned towards him, so that they were face to face, inches apart. 'I've got a gun too,' he said calmly.

Garravillo snorted. 'Mine's a MAC-10, asshole. My friend's got one too. Going to take us both out?'

'Us? Your friend's leaving you behind, and my Smith and Wesson's good enough for you.'

The enforcer began to look round, then checked himself and faced the American again.

'It's one-on-one now, both of us armed,' Shepard said. 'You're not used to that, right? Well, I've been here before, and that gives me an edge.'

Garravillo's confidence was draining fast. He began to shake. 'Shut up, you –'

A shout from the boat interrupted him. As Julio César stepped on to it Liz came charging up the steps from the galley. Horgan moved to block her but she head-butted him in the groin. He pulled her down with him in a kicking, clawing mêlée. Angel tried to separate them. Then Katie scrambled up into the cockpit, glimpsed her father and started screaming too.

'Dad! Help us, Dad!'

'Shoot them,' Julio César bellowed at El Carnicero, who was still standing on the jetty.

The enforcer had whipped out his submachine gun but couldn't get a clear shot. 'Out the way, out the way!' he yelled at the Mosqueras.

As Garravillo turned his head to look at the bedlam, Shepard drew from his shoulder-holster and shot him twice in the heart at point-blank range. The young thug was blasted on to his back as El Carnicero swung towards them. Shepard fired a fraction of a second before him but both men hit their target.

The DEA agent flew backwards, blood spurting from

his chest and left arm, and knocked Jack down too. Sprawled on top of him, Shepard aimed carefully at the collapsing enforcer and squeezed off another round. El Carnicero took that in the neck, fired a final wild burst that ricocheted off the jetty, then managed to toss the MAC-10 into the cockpit before crashing face-down on the back of the boat.

Angel caught the gun and put the barrel to Katie's head. She was on the floor trying to protect Liz, who was lying there unconscious now. He started to squeeze the trigger, then hesitated.

Having helped to beat Liz senseless, Horgan was staggering back to release the single rope still holding them to the jetty.

'Well, go on, kill her!' Julio César snarled at his son. 'Do *something* right!'

Angel glanced at him and contempt crossed his face. Then he looked down at Katie and smiled sadly.

A shot rang out from the jetty and his expression changed to disbelief. Angel put a hand to the side of his shattered head and touched his brains. The last thing he heard was Katie's terrified screams as he fell on top of her, trapping the gun between them.

The police marksmen sprinting along the jetty tried to hit Julio César and Horgan too, but the owner was back at the controls and rammed both throttles forward. His boat took off as twelve hundred horsepower bit the water, tossing the *capo* to the back of the cockpit and his enforcer's lifeless body into the water. Horgan swung sharp right into the channel between Jetties Two and Three and kept going. One more right turn at the end of it and he'd be heading for the open sea. The marksmen's rifles arced after him as panic-stricken men, women and children on the berthed yachts in the way tried to find cover.

'Cease fire! Cease fire!' a police officer yelled at his men, realising the innocent were most likely to get shot.

Jack heard the order. He had struggled out from under

227

Shepard's unconscious body in time to see the boat roar away. Liz and Katie were still on it! Images of their likely fate flashed through his mind. Well, he wasn't just going to lie down and accept that.

Forcing himself up on his good leg, Jack hopped frantically towards the Bentley. He scrambled into the driver's seat and fired up the turbocharged engine in a second. The boat was halfway down the channel now. At the end of it another channel, at right angles, led to the mouth of the marina and escape . . .

Unless he could block the exit.

Jack flicked the automatic gear-lever into first and floored the accelerator. The big car's tyres screeched in protest, then catapulted it forward. All sorts of obstacles were in the way, but there wasn't time to manoeuvre round them. Jack scraped between two cars parked either side of the jetty, tearing off door handles and side-mirrors. He clipped a motorbike, sending it crashing on to the back of someone's immaculate yacht. The Bentley's engine sounded as though it was about to explode and Jack whipped it into second gear, his right foot still flat to the floor. He glimpsed the boat ahead of him and to his left through a forest of masts, but he was catching up with it, drawing level as they both reached the end of the jetty.

Horgan flung the boat's wheel hard to starboard.

Jack steered straight ahead and braced himself. The Bentley shot off its launching pad into thin air, arced through the air nose-down, then did an almighty belly-flop into the water sending spray twenty feet into the air. The impact slammed his head against the windscreen. Worse than the pain was the fear that he'd landed short, but a moment later Horgan's bows crashed into the Bentley's front left wing. Glass exploded over Jack and water poured into the car as the boat forced it down. Then the propellers hit the Bentley's massive engine block and were torn off, while all that could be heard was the hysterical shriek of metal gouging metal to death. The powerless boat's momentum carried it clear for a short way, then it began to sink as water poured into its shattered hull. Its concussed occupants lay groaning in the cockpit, none of them able even to stand up.

Jack too was almost helpless. Badly winded by the steering column, he was barely able to breathe let alone clamber out of the sinking Bentley. Any second it would go to the bottom of the harbour, taking him with it. At least he'd stopped the boat, he thought, praying the police would get to it before anyone on board started shooting.

Then he heard the sound of an outboard motor – several in fact! A fleet of small boats was putting out from the jetties, hurrying towards them. With a final desperate effort he dragged himself into the front passenger seat, then tried to climb through what was left of the windscreen on to the engine. But it proved just too much for him and he blacked out.

Jack didn't even feel the boathook that locked on to his shirt and finally pulled him clear. Nor did he see the police marksmen scrambling on to what was left of Horgan's boat. He was tumbling down a big black hole again, spinning round and round, and thinking: *Please God, let me have won this time.*

CHAPTER TWENTY-SIX

'Can I come in?' Jack asked, putting his bandaged head round the door of Liz and Katie's room in the Marbella Clinic. It was a larger version of his own next door and also had a view of the old fishing port.

'Of course you can,' Liz told him from her bed. 'We're battered but decent. Well fairly, anyway.' She had suffered four fractured ribs, one more than Katie, whose chest was strapped up as well. They were both sitting up after a good night's sedated sleep.

'You look like the invisible man now,' Katie said as her stepfather hobbled in on his crutches, his left leg sheathed in yet another plastercast. The latest crash had added a broken nose and badly gashed face to his list of injuries. These had been covered up too – hence Katie's comment.

Jack sat on her bedside and took her hand. 'Well, you two don't look so good either. Or rather, you do! There's no one I could be happier to see in any condition . . . I'm so relieved . . .'

He couldn't finish the sentence and Katie squeezed his hand. 'How's Mr Shepard?'

'One lung's punctured, but he'll make it, thank God.'

'And An . . . I mean . . . the Mosqueras?'

Jack glanced at Liz, who gave him a slight nod. He turned back to his stepdaughter. 'You know he's dead, don't you?' he said gently.

'Yes,' she whispered.

'The police thought . . . I think he was trying to save you in the end.'

'Yes.'

'They've arrested his father. If there's any justice he'll spend the rest of his life in jail.'

Katie started to cry and dabbed her eyes. 'Please, Dad, tell me something cheerful.'

'All right. When we get out of here we're all going to –'

A knock at the door interrupted him and Frank Brady barged in, carrying two huge bouquets of red roses.

Jack couldn't help smiling. 'For me?'

'No, for your brave girls of course!' He handed the flowers to Liz and Katie, who tried to look grateful but couldn't hide their instinctive wariness either. 'Glad to see they're looking so well,' Brady told Jack. 'Glad to see your sense of humour hasn't deserted you either. The same can't be said for Sami Nassar.'

Jack's head rocked back. 'D'you know, I'd almost forgotten the blighter. Where's he now?'

'In the police station crying his eyes out. They staked out his villa and arrested him this morning, *after* he'd called all the brokers and bankers he'd dealt with. The line was tapped, of course, so they'll recover most of the money. Priest got clean away, though.'

'He did? How?'

'No-one seems to know, not even Sami. Something made that canny Yorkshireman scarper without even telling his partner. Wonder where he'll turn up next?'

Jack tried to shrug, but pain turned the movement into a series of twitches instead. 'Well, that's that, then.'

'Ummm . . . not necessarily.'

All three of them looked at him.

'I happened to meet the Mayor just now, and he's still keen on the project. Your heroic efforts should offset any bad publicity about what's happened, and with you to provide continuity there's no reason why we shouldn't –'

'Wait a minute, Frank. I've a family to think about now. As soon as they're well enough we're flying home.'

Katie almost crushed her stepfather's fingers. She and Liz smiled at each other.

Brady was trying not to let his frustration show. 'Fair enough, Jack, you need a good rest; but what are you going to do after that?'

'Make furniture, while I've still got two hands.'

'What, full time? Be serious.'

'I'm perfectly serious.'

The team-owner glowered at him. 'Maybe we should discuss this some other time?'

'Now's fine.'

'All right, then, I'll spell it out for you. Don't throw this opportunity away. It's a once-in-a-lifetime thing. You'll always regret it if you do. Don't end up being a loser, Jack.'

He shook his head. 'You don't understand, Frank. I finally won something really worth winning.'

Guy N. Smith

While the forces of nature create a white hell outside, a satanic force from beyond the grave is at work inside . . .

Into this world step three unwitting travellers, driven by the blizzard to seek refuge at a country house hotel. A 'hotel' where the 'guests' live in a diabolical world of lunacy and madness, where demented creatures prowl the corridors, where putrefying flesh lies in the cellar and blood-curdling screams echo from the bedrooms . . .

And, amidst the horrors, the monstrous spawn of a subnormal girl awaits a virgin sacrifice to bring the Prince of Evil to life . . .

Also by Guy N. Smith in Sphere Books:
FIEND

0 7474 0057 1   HORROR   £2.99

the WYRM
STEPHEN LAWS

Everyone in the Border village of Shillingham knows
Frank Warwick is crazy, but shooting at the workmen
moving the old gibbet from the crossroads to the local
museum is going too far . . .

But is Frank as mad as they think? Why does Michael
Lambton feel a sudden shiver of terror as he gazes across
the harsh Northumbrian landscape, and why are children
drawn repeatedly to play around the gibbet, as if called
by a silent voice?

And as the bulldozers roll on unchecked, a dark and
terrible evil imprisoned beneath the gibbet for centuries
slowly awakes – burning with revenge against
mankind . . .

'Fast and clever' *CITY LIMITS*

'A fresh chilling voice'
UNITED PRESS INTERNATIONAL

Also by Stephen Laws in Sphere paperback
GHOST TRAIN
SPECTRE

0 7474 0268 X   HORROR   £3.50

A selection of bestsellers from SPHERE

FICTION

WILDTRACK	Bernard Cornwell	£3.50 ☐
THE FIREBRAND	Marion Zimmer Bradley	£3.99 ☐
STARK	Ben Elton	£3.50 ☐
LORDS OF THE AIR	Graham Masterton	£3.99 ☐
THE PALACE	Paul Erdman	£3.50 ☐

FILM AND TV TIE-IN

WILLOW	Wayland Drew	£2.99 ☐
BUSTER	Colin Shindler	£2.99 ☐
COMING TOGETHER	Alexandra Hine	£2.99 ☐
RUN FOR YOUR LIFE	Stuart Collins	£2.99 ☐
BLACK FOREST CLINIC	Peter Heim	£2.99 ☐

NON-FICTION

CHAOS	James Gleick	£5.99 ☐
THE SAFE TAN BOOK	Dr Anthony Harris	£2.99 ☐
IN FOR A PENNY	Jonathan Mantle	£3.50 ☐
DETOUR	Cheryl Crane	£3.99 ☐
MARLON BRANDO	David Shipman	£3.50 ☐

All Sphere books are available at your local bookshop or newsagent, or can be ordered direct from the publisher. Just tick the titles you want and fill in the form below.

Name _____

Address _____

_____

Write to Sphere Books, Cash Sales Department, P.O. Box 11, Falmouth, Cornwall TR10 9EN

Please enclose a cheque or postal order to the value of the cover price plus:

UK: 60p for the first book, 25p for the second book and 15p for each additional book ordered to a maximum charge of £1.90.

OVERSEAS & EIRE: £1.25 for the first book, 75p for the second book and 28p for each subsequent title ordered.

BFPO: 60p for the first book, 25p for the second book plus 15p per copy for the next 7 books, thereafter 9p per book.

Sphere Books reserve the right to show new retail prices on covers which may differ from those previously advertised in the text elsewhere, and to increase postal rates in accordance with the P.O.